BLACK
LABEL

BLACK LABEL

A Novel

James L'Etoile

LEVEL
BEST BOOKS

First published by Level Best Books 2021

This novel is entirely a work of fiction. The names, characters and incidents portrayed in it are the work of the author's imagination. Any resemblance to actual persons, living or dead, events or localities is entirely coincidental.

James L'Etoile asserts the moral right to be identified as the author of this work.

Library of Congress Control Number: 2021940971

First edition

ISBN: 978-1-953789-14-3

This book was professionally typeset on Reedsy.
Find out more at reedsy.com

"There is no such thing as paranoia. Your worst fears can come true at any moment."

—HUNTER S. THOMPSON

Praise for BLACK LABEL

"Tight, terrific, terrifying. *Black Label* delves into the murky world of pharmaceuticals where profit is prioritized above all else. L'Etoile creates a strong female lead in Jillian Cooper, a woman who faces obstacle after obstacle, but still charges into the abyss. More unnerving than a fistful of amphetamines. Unputdownable." —K.J. Howe, international bestselling author of *Skyjack*

"James L'Etoile's *Black Label* is a delightfully complex and twisty thriller with a ripped-from-the-headlines plot that will make you think long and hard before you swallow your next dose of medication. Add in an intrepid heroine willing to do whatever it takes to uncover the truth no matter the cost, and L'Etoile's newest offering is a winner!" —Karen Dionne, author of the #1 international bestseller *The Marsh King's Daughter* and *The Wicked Sister*

"If this book had a tag, it would say 'proceed with caution' because nothing is what it seems. Told with a vivid and visceral style, this is le Carré's *Constant Gardener* meets *The Fugitive*. As the title suggests, *Black Label* is a top of the line thriller." —Gabriel Valjan, Agatha- & Anthony Award-nominated author.

"Relentlessly fast-paced and compellingly twisty! The talented James L'Etoile sets up an irresistibly high-stakes situation: a woman is certain to be charged with murder and doesn't remember a thing. Can she prove her innocence before she's silenced forever ? A dark journey through the world of big Pharma and big money—you will turn the pages as fast as you can." — Hank

Phillippi Ryan *USA Today* Bestselling author of *The First to Lie*

Chapter One

It was bad this time. Jillian shielded her eyes from the sharp edge of morning light and dug her fingers into the pillow clutched over her face. Deep in her temples, her pulse hammered a fast, painful staccato rhythm. She'd gone months since her last migraine, and this one tightened a vise around her skull. Even with her eyes closed, her vision clouded with a kaleidoscope of bright dots. The rustle of bedcovers sounded like the world fell in around her. Jillian Cooper's world had crumbled down and threatened to suffocate her, only she didn't know it–yet.

She reached for the phone she kept on her bedside table. There was no way she was going to make it to her Saturday morning spin class. Her hand probed for the phone, her head still tucked under the pillow. First one way, then she groped in another direction, knocking over a small brass table lamp. Jillian recoiled from the clatter as the metal lamp rung as loudly as the bells at Saints' Peter and Paul Church over in North Beach. She peeled off her protective pillow and reached for the phone. Her phone wasn't on the bedside table, and neither was the stack of paperback books she habitually kept at hand. Blinding pinpricks of light danced in her vision, making it impossible to focus through the swirling aura.

Fighting against the pounding in her head, Jillian crept to the edge of the bed, dangled her legs off the side, and brushed her toes gently on the polished hardwood floor. Jillian shuddered, a wave of nausea poured over her. The feeling wasn't from a migraine. It came from the realization she wasn't in her apartment. Her place didn't have hardwood floors. Jillian didn't know where she was, or worse, how she got here.

Instead of her phone, a half-empty Gran Patrón Platinum tequila bottle and a wrinkled condom wrapper lay on the nightstand. She spotted her clothes on the other side of the room, in a heap on a leather chair. Jillian pulled the sheet away from herself and peered downward.

"Shit."

She was naked under the bed covers. Jillian couldn't remember the slightest detail leading up to her ending the night disrobed, nor could she feel the lingering warmth of being with someone, in spite of the condom wrapper left on the nightstand. She'd never experienced a blackout from alcohol before. Jillian stayed away from tequila as a rule because of a few bad hangovers back when she attended San Francisco State University. If it weren't for the half-empty bottle of pricy booze, she'd have sworn she hadn't touched the stuff in ten years.

Yet, here she was—tequila, nakedness, and all. She hoped a tall, dark, handsome, athletic man was going to burst through the bedroom door with a tray of cappuccinos and warm croissants. At this point, a short, round, gnomish man with instant coffee and a day-old pop tart would be welcome. It wasn't her habit to "sleep around," as her mother used to call it. However, Jillian Cooper was a woman who enjoyed the occasional company of men, and this was not the first time she'd greeted the sunrise from a man's place following a late-night hook-up. She always remembered them, until this morning. The migraine and the tequila played games in her head—loud, pulsing, and painful games.

The bedroom, where she did God-only-knows-what, was expensively furnished and decidedly masculine. Dark hues of burnished leather and deep mahogany dominated the space. A set of wooden horizontal blinds kept out some light, and in spite of her headache, curiosity demanded she open them.

The window looked out over Huntington Park in Nob Hill, some of the priciest real estate in San Francisco. From her vantage point, Jillian figured the room sat on the sixth floor, or higher, and commanded a view of the grey slate tile roof of Grace Cathedral and Mt. Sutro off to the South. The condo, or whatever this place was, offered the resident one of those "ten-million-dollar views" everyone wanted, but few could afford. Jillian's salary as a Vice President of Marketing for Dynalife Pharmaceutical wouldn't buy the dust in a place like this.

Another wave of nausea buckled Jillian's knees. She grabbed onto a dresser near the window and braced herself while the queasiness passed. As she opened her eyes, she focused on a silver-plated frame on the top of the dresser. Jillian peered at a photograph of her own image, a picture of her, with her boss, Jonathon Mattson, the CEO of Dynalife Pharmaceutical.

Confusion and panic clawed at Jillian's mind. Mattson was thirty-five years her senior and married to one of the city's society matrons. Jillian supposed some women found him attractive, with his swagger and the ease with which he flaunted his wealth. There were lines Jillian did not cross; never, ever, get involved with someone at work, and married men were off-limits.

What was she doing here, naked in Mattson's apartment? Had Jillian broken both rules? The thought of a relationship with Mattson was unthinkable. The photograph meant they'd been together before. The two looked at ease with one another in the photo, and it hinted at a close personal relationship, her hand on his chest. *When the hell was that taken?* She had no recollection of an evening with Jonathon Mattson, let alone posing for a photo.

"What have I done?"

Jillian staggered to the chair with her wadded-up clothes, slid into her panties, quickly stepped into her dark blue dress, shoved a bra in her purse, and grabbed her shoes from the floor. With an ear to the door, Jillian listened. Filtered by the thrum of her heartbeat, she heard voices deep within the apartment. She felt her face blush thinking about who she'd meet as she snuck out. Her hand trembled on the doorknob as she turned it, a fraction of an inch at a time until the lock slid back with a muted click. The door opened inward a few inches, the voices became more distinct—a television.

Shoes in hand, Jillian crept down the hallway. The hardwood floor felt cold under her bare feet as she made her way to the large open living space. A flat-screen television blared the financial news from CNN to an empty room. Jillian glanced at the kitchen, and she exhaled when she realized she was alone in the apartment. The veil of swirling bright spots in her vision started to clear, and she needed to head home for her migraine medication. She desperately wanted to leave before Jonathon Mattson returned. She couldn't face him with the cocktail of anger and shame whirling inside her.

Slipping on her shoes, she listened as the CNN anchor, a carefully coifed and airbrushed young blonde reporter, delivered her monologue.

"The market opened with a quick rally this morning," the anchorwoman said.

"Today's Saturday and the market isn't open, bimbo," Jillian said. "Where do they find these people?" She found her jacket folded over the back of a sofa.

Jillian tucked the jacket under her arm, reached for the apartment door, and stopped when she heard the woman's voice drone on.

"In other financial news, the death of Dynalife Pharmaceutical CEO, Jonathon Mattson sent the mega-pharmaceutical company's stock prices plummeting in early trading. Authorities are looking into the matter and haven't disclosed any details about the death."

Jillian froze when the screen flashed a photo of Mattson, with a banner under the image proclaiming, "Billionaire Pharmaceutical CEO Dead."

The television news turned the page and droned on about other financial news. Mattson was a mere footnote in the market ledgers. Business goes on.

"That can't be. Jonathon, dead?"

Another cramp of nausea hit her, and she wrapped her arms around her midsection as if she held her insides together. The apartment space closed in on her, and when the spasms subsided, Jillian darted for the door and flung it open. She ran across the hall to an elevator and stabbed the down button repeatedly, willing the car to appear. The hallway space was foreign; nothing in the décor sparked a memory of how she got here. But here she was, and it wasn't like she magically appeared in Mattson's apartment. Jillian didn't know Jonathon kept an apartment on Knob Hill. It must have been a secret rendezvous pad for Jonathon and his rumored affairs. A wave of

4

nausea swept over Jillian at the thought she was now among his conquests.

The whir of the elevator stopped, and a light electronic bleep sounded the arrival of the conveyance. She slid into the empty elevator before the doors fully opened and punched the lobby button. The cool wall of the elevator car soothed the back of her head, the first comforting thing since awakening in this bad dream.

She couldn't shake the nightmare off. Questions without answers cascaded through her mind. *What happened? Where was she? Who was she with?*

"Come on–come on," she urged the doors as they closed at a slow agonizing pace.

"It's not possible. Today is Saturday, and I saw Jonathon at a board meeting yesterday–Friday. It has to be a huge mistake." She drew in a deep breath and tried to center herself.

The elevator chimed, and the doors opened into the building's lobby. Jonathon wasn't there to expose some elaborate practical joke. Instead, Jillian found the marble-tiled lobby empty, except for a doorman who gave her a smirk and a nod signaling, "I know what you did last night." The man leered and stroked his short stubble beard as Jillian passed his station.

Jillian stepped outside to the curb and raised her hand for a taxi. She glanced at a newspaper rack on the sidewalk next to her, and the headline caught her breath short.

Billionaire Jonathon Mattson Murdered.

The date jumped off the page. It was the Monday edition.

Mattson was dead; she'd met with him on Friday and woke up in his apartment this morning. Jillian's knees buckled with the realization that two days passed without a single lingering memory. Two days erased without a trace.

Chapter Two

A red and white taxicab pulled to the curb where Jillian stood, transfixed on the unreal newspaper headline. She didn't hear the driver call out, or hear the doorman step from behind and grab the taxi door. His appearance startled her, and his lecherous smirk did little to calm Jillian's growing anxiety.

"Tough night, huh?" the doorman said.

Jillian slid into the back seat without comment and pulled the door closed, separating her from the sleazy doorman. It looked to her like he enjoyed her discomfort.

The cabbie watched Jillian in his rearview mirror, and he simply nodded at the address she gave him in the Sunset District, South of Golden Gate Park.

She leaned her head against the window and closed her eyes, exhausted even though she'd pulled herself out of bed only minutes ago. The damn migraines always drained her and made her want to crawl into a dark, quiet place. This headache was especially bad. It was a struggle to stay awake. The blank space in her memory worried her. She'd never experienced a blackout. She'd lost an entire weekend.

A buzzing sensation ratcheted up her panic level until she realized it came from her cell phone. The sound rattled through her skull and set off a frantic search through her handbag. Her fingers found the phone beneath her bra. She clutched it, punching the green connect button, mercifully ending the noise.

"Jillian Cooper," she responded. Her voice sounded as rough as she felt, graveled and raw.

"Where are you?"

Jillian knew the voice on the other end of the call. It was David Paulson, Dynalife's Chief Operations Officer, the number two in the company, after Mattson.

"I'm heading—"

"Doesn't matter. Come to the office. The Board called an emergency session to address the mess left in the wake of Jonathon's death," David said.

Jillian paused.

"You heard about Jonathon, right?" he asked.

"Yes. Yes, I heard. What happened?"

"Time to sort Jonathon's story out later. Meeting starts in fifteen minutes. You need to be here Jilly." He abruptly hung up before Jillian could reply.

She leaned forward toward the cabbie. "Change of plans. Could you take me to Battery and Pine?"

The cabbie nodded and looped the taxi East through Chinatown, where whole pig carcasses were unloaded from refrigerated trucks to dozens of restaurants through steel grates in the sidewalks. Jillian typically enjoyed walking through the spice shops, fortune cookie bakeries, and crowded gift shops. The collections of sights and aromas in the streets and alleyways were never the same, always a new and exciting discovery. This morning, however, the bright colors and gilded storefronts seemed garish and oppressive. The rows of smoked duck displayed in market windows made her stomach flip. City block boundaries marked changes, cultural and economic. Some communities flourished while others struggled to exist. Jillian wasn't sure where she fit today.

Minutes later, the cabbie's quick stop jolted Jillian back to the present. She got out of her taxi, in the heart of the city's Financial District, and headed into the Dynalife Pharmaceutical headquarters. The company held its offices in a tall glass corporate tower in the shadows of the sixty-one story SalesForce Tower dominating San Francisco's skyline.

The Dynalife lobby swarmed with frantic energy. On the occasion of a Board of Directors meeting, the pace in the office bordered on manic, but

Jillian felt an undertone of urgency and desperation this morning. In the center of the bullpen where the analysts worked in fabric-lined cubicles, David Paulson directed a score of underlings before his eyes caught Jillian.

"Jesus, Jillian, you look like shit."

"I got here as soon as I could," she said.

David glanced at his watch. "The meeting's about ready to start. Main conference room." He pointed down the main hallway. "Go clean up."

Jillian nodded and ducked into the women's restroom, off the main lobby. The sight in the mirror surprised her. Black circles under her eyes from smeared mascara, pale cracked lips, and smudged, worn makeup, all conspired to paint Jillian older than her thirty-three years. Her dark brown hair hung limp and tangled around her face. A few brush strokes weren't going to help, so she pulled it back into a ponytail and secured it with a barrette from her purse.

Rinsing the faded makeup from her face helped. The warm water relaxed her tensed jaw and allowed her a deep breath as she regarded her reflection. Jillian noticed a dark stain on her jacket sleeve, a few inches above her wrist.

"Great. What else can go wrong?"

She dabbed at the spot with a wet paper towel. The running water turned pink and grew dark crimson as she wiped. The paper towel in her hand came away soaked with blood; Jillian's hand recoiled at the sight. The towel fell into the sink, and Jillian watched the blood circle the drain. Though she couldn't recall a single moment from the missing forty-eight hours, she knew the blood was Jonathon Mattson's.

Jillian covered the bloody towel with another dry one and pitched them both into the trash. She scrubbed her hands until every trace disappeared and her hands felt raw from the effort.

The face in the mirror; Jillian felt removed from it. She couldn't make eye contact with the other woman in the reflection. Jillian was afraid one of them killed Jonathon Mattson.

Chapter Three

The board meeting started before Jillian entered the conference room. She found a seat in the back, away from the long polished table occupied by the board members and corporate officers. As one of Mattson's team, Jillian usually sat at the table and participated in the discussions guiding the company's course. Today, there was a change in the air. Jillian's twisted gut and migraine hangover weren't helping her unsettled mind.

A few heads lifted; faces flickered with recognition as Jillian found a seat among other lower-level Dynalife employees. A rail-thin man, with grey eyes, occupied the spot where Jonathon Mattson usually stood at these meetings. Jillian nodded at William Comstock, an investment banker with a reputation for running his firm with all the warmth and compassion of an old Soviet gulag.

"If we can continue," Comstock said, commenting on Jillian's tardy arrival.

Jillian looked away sharply and busied herself with the notes scribbled in her day planner. The handwritten highlights from last Friday's meeting opened a wound in her chest. Jillian's day planner summarized a meeting, one ending on a sour note. The last thing she recalled, with any clarity, before her blackout was a failed marketing proposal on a promising new HIV drug. Jonathon Mattson didn't let Jillian finish her pitch and rejected her approach with an uncharacteristically harsh dismissal. He chastised her for delaying the drug's release and claimed her project was nothing but a waste of time and company resources. She felt the sting of his rebuke as if the words dripped with venom. She remembered trembling as Mattson berated her in front of the executive team. She'd worked hard to establish her reputation as a tough, no-nonsense corporate shark, and he threatened to strip it all away and leave her bare. Bare, like she'd found herself in his apartment hours ago. What had she done?

As she sat in the conference room, Comstock droned on about the corporate mission, vision, and values. Then he started in on how Dynalife was bigger than one man. The last interaction with Jonathon Mattson was stuck in a painful replay in her mind. Anger. It finally registered with her what she felt, simmering beneath the uncertainty, was anger and resentment.

"Miss Cooper," Jonathon said in his last meeting, "Dynalife Pharmaceuticals is in the business of manufacturing high-grade medical pharmaceuticals. Business, Miss Cooper, not some save the world social cause. Distributing Bosphizion in third-world nations, at cost, is unacceptable. It's utterly unthinkable. This HIV treatment protocol will position the company at the top of the industry. We can name the price. Bosphizion will go to those who can pay for it, and pay for it they will. Besides, those 'third-worlders' you care so much about are going to die anyway."

Before Jillian responded, Mattson cut her off. "This has been a total waste of my time. It seems *you* are a waste of my time."

Stunned at Mattson's reaction, Jillian left the office, embarrassed, crestfallen, and incredibly angry. It was the last thing she remembered until she awoke this morning in Mattson's bed.

Her thumb rubbed against the wet spot on her sleeve, and the slick tactile sensation snapped her back to the present. From her perch in the rear of the conference room, she only half-listened to Comstock. He blathered on about getting the ship righted, staying the course, finding a safe harbor, and a half dozen other nautically themed metaphors for Dynalife Pharmaceutical.

"This ship needs a new captain, and we will make the assignment within the next few weeks. Until then, David Paulson will serve as Acting Chief Executive under the direction of the board," Comstock said.

Paulson nodded from his seat at the table.

"Our first priority is the strategy for pressing the Food and Drug Administration handwringers for approval of Bosphizion. Mr. Paulson has presented a few preliminary concepts to the board and has an interesting take on the future of our company. As I understand the matter, we experienced a few setbacks delaying the release of one of our feature products, but I've been assured our compass has since been recalibrated," Comstock said and glared at Jillian.

She lowered her head, pretending to take notes. A sliver of thick paper stuck out from the planner pages. She flipped the pages and discovered another copy of the photo of Mattson and her. Jillian's breath hitched. *This can't be happening. This isn't real.* She quickly turned the photo over before anyone seated next to her saw the image. On the back, scrawled in red felt marker were three words that sent a chill up her spine. "I did it."

Jillian didn't hear the next few words over the thrum of her increased heartbeat, but the meeting ended, and she found herself alone in the conference room. Another time slip. She hadn't noticed the meeting finish, or the procession of board members and executives leave the room. The lapse probably saved her from the pain from a score of judging glances and muttered condemnations. A voice pulled her from a trance.

"Jillian," a voice sounded.

"Jillian, David needs to see you." It was Lucy Travis, Paulson's Executive Assistant.

"I'm sorry. What?" Jillian said.

"David needs you."

"Give me a minute, I'll be right along."

As Lucy disappeared out the door, Jillian considered leaving the office and going home. She was in no mood to deal with David in her current state. This must be a bad dream; she'd take some Imitrex for her migraine, drink some hot tea, and go to bed. Jillian tucked the damning photo with the self-confession in the day planner and slammed it closed on her lap. She dropped the planner into her bag as she stood. She swore the planner felt hot—like a witch fire.

Overcome with doubt and increasing anxiety, Jillian made for the door and bumped into a man in a dark blue suit. From the cut of the suit, she judged it Italian, and pricey. The man, she figured, was one of the minions who followed on the heels of the Board Members.

"Excuse me, I wasn't watching," she said.

"Miss Cooper?" the man said.

"Yes." Wariness tickled at the base of her spine.

"I need a moment of your time."

"And you are?"

"Inspector DiManno, San Francisco Police–Homicide. We need to talk."

Chapter Four

"I need some answers," DiManno said while he pulled his identification and badge from his jacket pocket.

"We all need answers, Inspector." Jillian clutched her bag and angled for the exit.

Inspector DiManno blocked the door to the conference room, and in spite of his thin build, he presented an imposing figure. Not a person to be toyed with and not one who wasted his time on pleasantries, or pointless conversation. The stubble of gray-black beard darkening his face betrayed the long hours since he last went off duty.

DiManno gestured to the vacant conference table. "Take a seat, Miss Cooper." The words came out as a command, not a request.

An icy ball formed in her stomach. She didn't know what happened to Jonathon Mattson, but obviously, Inspector DiManno did, and it led him here, to her. She perched on the edge of one of the chairs, her back straight, her hands crossed in her lap, with one hand covering the bloodstain on her sleeve.

DiManno pulled out the chair next to her and faced her. He remained silent for a moment, staring at Jillian.

"How well did you know Jonathon Mattson?" he said.

"I don't know how much help I will be. I really didn't know Jonathon well. He was a private person," Jillian said.

"How long have you worked at Dynalife?"

"Five years."

"How long did you know Mattson?"

"Five years. He hired me."

"Who, would you say, was he particularly close with?"

Jillian thought for a moment. "I don't know. He didn't seem to have any close relationships with anyone here."

"Anyone he showed an interest in? Professionally, that is?"

"He didn't involve himself in staff matters," Jillian said.

"Yet, you told me he hired you," Inspector DiManno said.

"Yes…"

"With no appreciable marketing experience. How would you explain that, Miss Cooper?"

"What are you insinuating?"

"I'm saying the word among the staff here is you were the Golden Child."

"Hardly," Jillian said.

"Handed the plum accounts, fast-tracked to a senior position, then quickly appointed as a Vice President. Some say you didn't deserve the—"

"I've worked hard for everything I've achieved. I've sacrificed for this company," Jillian said.

She felt her face redden at the inspector's accusation. A flash of confusion washed over her. The photo in the purse at her feet and the gap in her memory ate away at her conviction. The unknown. The unthinkable.

"I'm certain you *worked* for everything," DiManno said with an insinuating smirk.

"I've given up my private life to ensure this company is positioned where it is today. Nothing was simply given to me, or to any other employee here."

"It must've come as a shock, getting dumped for bungling the company's largest account."

"What? What are you saying? I haven't been removed from…" Jillian's head throbbed with her rapid heartbeat.

"Oh my, did I speak out of turn? My bad. I guess Mr. Paulson hasn't gotten around to telling you. Apparently, a presentation you were responsible for didn't go too well. When was this?" DiManno's lip curled. He enjoyed taunting her.

"This can't be happening," Jillian said.

14

"So, Miss Cooper, when did you experience this crushing career failure?" DiManno fiddled with a notebook and settled on a page. "Friday, I see."

"Yes. But…"

"I understand Mr. Mattson's reaction to your marketing proposal for a new drug was devastating?"

Jillian paused.

"Miss Cooper?"

"He wasn't happy," she said.

"In fact, didn't he trash your approach and say Dynalife wasn't in the charity business?"

"Yes. He didn't see the big picture?"

"You put a lot of work into a presentation, no doubt."

"I did. We all did."

"How did his rejection make you feel?"

"I wouldn't call it rejection. He expressed opposing views."

"Loud, differing views, from what I've heard. You were outraged with Mattson for his lack of appreciation? I totally understand."

She shook her head. "I was disappointed. It's the nature of the job. I present possible marketing solutions for the company. Jonathon can't choose my favorite every time. It wasn't the first time in my career, and I'm certain it won't be the last."

"The last time Mr. Mattson opposed you, it was the last time."

"I'm saying it's the nature of my position."

"Or was," DiManno reminded her.

DiManno turned a page in his notebook, put down his pen, and looked at Jillian. She hadn't noticed the piercing dark brown eyes before.

"Where were you Saturday evening, Miss Cooper?"

There it was–the question. Jillian needed the answer as much as DiManno. But she feared the gap in her memory—and the hidden truth. Life as she knew it, would never be the same.

"I was home," she said. Jillian fervently hoped she was.

"Anyone who can verify your claim?"

"I live alone."

"That's not what I asked. Were you with anyone?" DiManno said.

"I said I live alone."

"So, no."

"No," Jillian said.

DiManno regarded Jillian silently for a moment, closed his notebook, pulled a clear plastic evidence baggie from his jacket pocket, and placed it on the table between them. "Does this look familiar to you?"

The baggie held a single dark purple Tanzanite earring. Reflexively, Jillian reached for an ear. Her fingertip grazed the bare lobe where an identical earring resided last Friday. Instinctively, Jillian knew the earring was hers. She quickly lowered her hand when she noticed DiManno watching her gesture.

"It's similar to a pair I own," Jillian said.

"Similar–huh. How do you think this one ended up in Jonathon Mattson's bedroom?"

Jillian felt a tremble in her hand. She clutched her arm tighter and hoped it didn't show.

"I couldn't tell you." It sounded hollow, but it was the truth. Jillian couldn't remember removing the earrings.

DiManno pocketed the baggie and stowed his notebook in another pocket without taking his eyes off of her. He slid a business card toward Jillian, said, "We know Mr. Mattson was with a woman the night he died. Anything you need to tell me, Miss Cooper?"

Jillian shook her head.

"You're holding back on me Miss Cooper."

"I'm not, I swear. It's just…"

"What? You suffered a career-ending blowup with your boss, and by your own admission, you were angry with him. You have no alibi for your whereabouts at the time he was murdered, and the office gossip is you were sleeping with him."

"That's outrageous!"

"Sure is," DiManno said.

Jillian felt tears build up. God, she didn't want to turn on the waterworks in front of this pretentious ass. She wouldn't give him the satisfaction. The frustration of the unknown exploded within. Her missing hours were entwined with Jonathon Mattson's death. The murky certainty wasn't comforting. Not knowing was the most disturbing feeling. Somewhere, lost in her broken mind, shattered fragments of truth and sanity lay buried in a dark, inaccessible place.

Jillian steeled herself, fought off the tears, and said, "I wish I had answers for you Inspector, but I don't." All Jillian held were more questions, bloodstains, and photographs.

"Have it your way, Miss Cooper. I'll find the truth here, with or without your help." DiManno stood and looked down at Jillian. "I'll be in touch."

She felt DiManno's eyes peer straight through her. She broke off eye contact, fiddled with her purse, and made sure the day planner with the compromising photograph was out of sight. When she regained the nerve to stand, she saw DiManno halfway down the hall huddled with David Paulson. The two men spoke in low, hushed tones and both turned in her direction. The conversation abruptly stopped. Inspector DiManno whispered a humorous comment to Paulson and nodded toward Jillian before chuckling and walking away. Another example of the 'ol boys club, but this one with life-altering consequences.

Paulson gruffly motioned for Jillian and waited in the hallway. Paulson served as Mattson's hatchet man over the years, and Jillian recognized the expression on David's face. A conversation loomed, and it was destined to end up one-sided.

"Jillian—inside," Paulson said, as he strode into his office.

Jillian followed and stood in the center of the room. She shuddered when the office door slammed after Paulson.

"Where the Hell were you?" I called you on your cell, and it kept going to voicemail," Paulson said.

"You're pulling me off the Bosphizion project?" Jillian said.

"You can't be surprised after your meltdown in the meeting on Friday."

"Meltdown? Mattson didn't like the approach, that's all. There was no fucking meltdown."

"You positioned the company to lose billions in revenue in exchange for some goodwill in a dark, meaningless corner of the world. Sounded like a meltdown as far as the board was concerned."

"You knew the direction and you approved our approach. We discussed it last week, and you didn't say a damn thing in the meeting. You left me twisting in the wind after Jonathon disagreed."

Paulson shrugged and turned his back to Jillian, facing the window overlooking the city.

"I told you it was a risky approach and you were on your own," Paulson said.

"You said no such thing. You said you were going to take it to Jonathon and make sure you had his buy-off before the meeting. You never did, did you?"

"None of it matters now..."

"It matters to me!"

Paulson turned and Faced Jillian, "The decision's made—you're off the Bosphizion project, and we need you to distance yourself from the company."

"Why did the police know already? Mr. smug detective threw it in my face, and he knew I hadn't gotten the message yet."

"The company is cooperating fully in the investigation..."

"Don't give me that crap, David. Save it for your public relations pitch. This is me we're talking about here," Jillian said.

"The board has lost its confidence in you, Jillian."

Jillian knew the point an executive lost the confidence and backing of the board, it led to corporate exile, or worse. The thousands of hours and hard work she invested, the personal sacrifice and isolation she endured, and this is how her rising star darkened?

She slumped in one of the overstuffed leather armchairs in the room and choked on the anger rising in her throat. Betrayed, confused, and wounded, Jillian's fingers gripped the arms of the leather chair until her knuckles turned white.

Paulson crossed to his desk and tapped the intercom button. "Lucy, send her in."

Seconds later, Ashley Raymond opened the door and strolled inside. Ashley ignored Jillian and strode to Paul's desk where she perched a slender hip on the edge and tossed her blonde hair over her shoulder. The woman finally acknowledged Jillian with a curt nod; a smug and superior air hung over her. Mid-twenties, no graduate school behind her, but Ashley worked a designer size four wardrobe and an athletically trim figure to make up for it. If a potential client was a lecherous old fart, Dynalife dusted off Ashley, twirled her around, and closed the deal. Ashley was the kind of woman who made it hard for other women to be taken seriously. She was all surface and show with no substance.

"Ashley has the Bosphizion project now. I need you to brief her on the details of the product and get her jump-started," David said.

"I'm sorry it happened like this. I didn't ask for it," Ashley said for Jillian's benefit.

Jillian pictured Ashley lurking in the office corridors, a sleek, young office lioness waiting for wounded, weakened prey. Jillian wasn't usually the weak, straggling gazelle in the pack and this turn in circumstances disturbed her more than she cared to admit. Ignoring Ashley's insincere remark, Jillian focused on David.

"How do you expect her to lead this project? Ashley's never managed any project, let alone one tied to the company's future."

Ashley slid off the desk to her feet, approached Jillian, and sat next to her in another chair. She leaned forward, unexpectedly took Jillian's hands in hers, and said, "I know this must be horrible for you. I can't replace you with your vast years of experience…"

Jillian heard, *blah, blah, blah; you're old and washed up, blah, blah.*

"The board thought it best in light of the circumstances," Ashley continued.

Jillian pulled her hands away from the younger woman. "Circumstances?"

"Well, certainly you can understand the board's position. You and Jonathon…"

"What are you implying? Jonathon and I were sneaking around having an affair?" Jillian said. "Ridiculous."

David chimed in. "Dynalife needs to separate itself from any hint of scandal or inappropriate behavior. This firm has a rock-solid reputation, and we need to make certain it stays intact while we recover. Now the police are involved. If it ever got out you and Jonathon were…"

Jillian jumped out of the chair. "There was no me and Jonathon, or some illicit relationship! You're talking about my reputation here!"

David rose from his chair. "Dammit Jillian, you're worried about your reputation at a time like this?"

"You're damn right I am."

"Jillian, the police interviewed you this morning. You are a 'person of interest,' and I tried to warn you they wanted to talk to you. I called you all day yesterday. You never returned any of my calls. I stopped by your apartment and left a note and I heard nothing back from you. What would you have me do?"

A person of interest. It served as a polite term for a suspect, not far from accused. Is that who she was now? Jillian fell silent.

David stepped toward Jillian and spoke softly. "Where were you?"

Jillian's eyes welled, fear and frustration boiled within her. "I can't say," she said.

"What?" David's face gave no reaction, but Jillian saw a glimmer of recognition in his eyes. It was hurt, anger, or relief, perhaps.

Jillian shook her head, unwilling to repeat her fears to a man she once trusted. Now it seemed she lost that small refuge.

"I've seen to it you'll receive your full severance package if you leave without a scene," David said.

The words cut Jillian. She felt sick to her stomach. A host of emotions whirled through her, betrayal, hurt, loss, grief and it left her empty and hollow.

"I haven't done anything," she whispered.

"Don't," David said. "Don't say another word. Take your severance and start over. I'm sorry Jilly, but it has to be this way."

"It's for the best," Ashley said.

Jillian desperately wanted to slap the bitch, but she didn't retain the strength in her body. For the first time she could remember, Jillian Cooper faced failure. With a hand instinctively clutched over the bloodstain on her sleeve, she felt certain the price of her failure included a future in a concrete prison cell.

Chapter Five

Numbness enveloped her. The cab ride from the Dynalife building to her apartment felt like a funeral procession, the last moments of a life-long career rendered to dust. She felt deep, dark loneliness after the cab dropped her at the curb. No throng of mourners waited for this procession, Jillian stood alone.

She fumbled for her key, and her hand trembled, requiring three tries before the key slid into the lock. Jillian pulled open the heavy lobby door of her apartment building and let it slip closed behind her. It was less of a lobby than it was a hallway with mailboxes, an elevator, and a stairwell, but the quiet, familiar confines comforted her.

Out of habit, Jillian took to the stairs and climbed the three flights to her floor. A pungent trail of stale perfume and hairspray warned her neighbor, Mrs. Tillman, lurked behind the peephole of the door across the hallway.

Jillian reached her door, keyed the lock, and picked up an accumulation of three days' worth of newspapers on her doormat. She balanced the papers in one arm and used her hip to open the apartment door. The rattle of Mrs. Tillman's security chain preceded the click of a deadbolt as it unlocked. Jillian wasn't up to a confrontation with the building's eighty-seven-year-old gossip and tried to hurry inside, but she dropped the stack of newspapers to the floor. A second deadbolt clacked open, followed by a wisp of menthol cigarette smoke wafting through a crack in the door. A dour-faced Mrs. Tillman peeked around the gap in her doorway.

"Miss Cooper," the old woman said. A pair of narrowed, judgmental yellowed eyes assessed Jillian's wrinkled, unpolished appearance. "How do you expect to land a young man looking like that?"

"Good morning, Miss Tillman."

"In my day young lady, if I flitted about like a common tramp, I would not have married Mr. Tillman, God rest his soul."

Mr. Tillman died ten years earlier when, "his brain stroked him," as Mrs. Tillman told it. Jillian hadn't known the Tillman's then, but she'd grown certain Mrs. Tillman's incessant nit-picking, gossip-mongering, and scolding hastened her husband's demise.

Lucky Mr. Tillman, Jillian thought. "All the good ones are taken, Mrs. Tillman."

"All the same, you lie down with dogs, you get fleas." Mrs. Tillman cracked the door open a few more inches, revealing a faded, floral patterned housedress, along with another wave of menthol-scented smoke. "What have you been up to Miss Cooper?"

"I've been–out. Out of town for a couple of days. Thank you, Mrs. Tillman, you take care now." Jillian slipped inside her apartment and closed the door.

From out in the hallway she heard, "Don't think about subletting your apartment while you're away. We won't allow it." Mrs. Tillman's door closed, followed by the clank, clack, and rattle of the security features protecting the old woman from the ravages of the outside world.

Jillian leaned against the inside of her door. She hated lying to the old woman about being "out of town," but Jillian told herself it was a little white lie. It was the kind of fib that didn't hurt anyone. Besides, what was she going to tell Mrs. Tillman? She'd slept around with her boss, gotten blackout drunk, and apparently killed him over the weekend?

The holes in her memory hadn't filled in. The lost time worried her. She couldn't murder Jonathon. It was unthinkable, but the drying bloodstain on her sleeve screamed Jillian was with Jonathon during the weekend—and he was dead. The frustration and confusion left her like a tightly wound clock spring; one more turn and she'd snap apart. Jillian went straight for the shower, turned up the water as hot as she could stand, and tossed everything she wore into a wicker laundry hamper. Steam filled the small bathroom, and she leaned against the cool tile wall while the water pummeled the knots in her neck muscles.

After the water turned cold, Jillian turned the shower off, got out, and roughly toweled off. She strode to the bedroom with a damp towel wrapped around her and pulled a set of fresh underwear from her bureau. She felt more refreshed and clear-headed, but the shower didn't uncover bits and pieces of memory to unlock the lost time. Her reflection in the mirror above the bureau looked like a worn version of her usual self.

At first, she nearly missed it. Among the cosmetics, hairbrushes, and assorted knick-knacks, one item, was unexpected—a small silver frame. The photo in the frame caused a hitch in Jillian's breath. Jonathon Mattson smiled back at her.

"What the hell?"

Jillian took the photo in her hand and noticed a circle of dust around the frame. This frame highlighted her lackluster housekeeping and confirmed the photo hadn't moved for some time. An uncomfortable tingle of familiarity crawled up her spine at the sight of Mattson's image. With a trembling hand, Jillian tore the backing from the frame and removed the photo. She unfolded the photo and saw her face next to Mattson's, identical to the photo this morning in Mattson's apartment and the one in her day planner.

Jillian pulled at her damp hair. "No, no, no. This isn't right!"

She gathered up the frame, the torn backing, and the photo, marched into the bathroom, and deposited the mess into a trashcan. She grabbed her purse and pulled out the day planner. She shook the pages until the other photo fell out with Mattson's image looking at her from the floor. Out came the white plastic trash bag liner with the frame remnants, and in went the photo and the clothes Jillian tossed in the laundry before her shower. The white blouse, skirt, and the bloodstained jacket filled the bag. Pausing a second, Jillian dug down into the bag and pulled out one of the photos.

She found the one resting on her dresser and looked for a date on the back to jog her memory. No date on the photo and nothing in the photo itself showed when or where this happened. This one didn't leave a confession printed on it either. There was no black-tie event she attended with Jonathon

Mattson, yet here was photographic proof she led another life. In the lower right-hand corner, a small stamp spelled out Carson Arts Photography, 8749, and nothing more.

She committed the number to memory, as fragile as it was, and tore both photos into small bits. The tiny pieces were added to the trash bag and clad in nothing more than her bath towel, Jillian carried the bag through her apartment, out her door, and stuffed the whole thing into a trash chute in the hallway.

Jillian knew she was a murderer, or insane. A killer, or paranoid delusional schizophrenic, either one meant a life behind bars. The name of the place wouldn't matter, prison or "hospital," the result was the same. She faced a slow withering death, locked away and discarded.

Chapter Six

Shelly Mattson abhorred waiting. Worse, Mrs. Jonathon Mattson hated crowded public places, where all manner of vagrant, sex worker, and brute criminal collected. She'd carefully constructed and curated her image as a society matron and patron of the arts. Shelly Mattson viewed the entrails of the Hall of Justice as a sign of blight in her city, where the wretched refuse of San Francisco circled the drain into faraway jails and prisons.

She stood in a small room within the Major Crimes Unit, where she supposed confessions were born from the likes of child killers and rapists. Waterboarding was too gentle for those predators. The scratched metal table held a heavy ring bolted to the surface, and Shelly conjured an image of a man covered in prison tattoos chained to the table where he coldly recounted his crimes. She'd seen enough of men like that in what seemed like another lifetime, one filled with violence, and shadows. The woman she'd become was above those gutter dwellers. She'd made sure of it.

Shelly pulled a compact from her Gucci handbag and checked her eyeliner. Deep brown eyes, olive skin, and shoulder-length lustrous black hair reflected back. Flawless and ready. She returned the compact to her bag at the sound of someone approaching. She straightened her shoulders and drew a deep breath.

From the open doorway, Inspector DiManno entered with two Styrofoam cups of coffee and a file tucked under one arm.

"Mrs. Mattson, thank you for coming down."

"It seemed my coming here was the only way to make sure I have your attention, Inspector."

"I assure you we are following up on a number of leads on your husband's death. Let me again say I'm sorry for your loss."

"Murder," Shelly Mattson said.

"Pardon?" DiManno put the coffee on the table.

"Murder. My husband was murdered; his death wasn't some unexplained heart attack or random car accident. Someone killed him, Inspector."

"Yes, again, I'm sorry for—"

"Save it," Shelly cut him off. "My husband was a miserable son-of-a-bitch. He cheated anyone with a nickel and screwed anyone who twitched her ass in front of him."

DiManno cleared his throat. "Coffee? Please take a seat. When we spoke this morning at your home, you said you didn't know who your husband was..."

"Entertaining? Please, it was obvious Jonathon allowed one of his playthings over for a romp. Always young, always vacuous. Made him feel powerful. As if he didn't need his little Viagra pick-me-up." Shelly ignored the coffee and couldn't force herself to take a seat in the worn, grime-covered chair.

"Do you know who he was with?" DiManno asked.

"No. But I did find this." Shelly Mattson opened the clasp of her Gucci handbag and pulled out a long, delicate gold chain and pendant. The gold basket pendant encircled a large deep purple Tanzanite stone.

"Where did you find it? The crime scene technicians searched every square inch of the bedroom."

Shelly placed the necklace down on the table. "It wasn't in the bedroom. I found it outside in the rear garden. The clasp is broken, so perhaps it fell off when his little whore snuck out the back door."

DiManno saw the bent clasp and an inch of fine gold chain dangling from the broken end.

"How did you happen to find this, Mrs. Mattson?"

"I take my morning tea in the garden. It hung on a Rhododendron branch near my table."

"Have you ever seen this before?"

"No. Not my taste–a bit too modern for me, but the Tanzanite is nicely cut. You'll probably discover it was a gift from my husband to one of his conquests."

"Any idea how it came to rest in your garden?"

"You tell me, you're the detective. Now, if you will pardon me, I must be off to an emergency board meeting at Dynalife. Jonathon was equally reckless in his business dealings as it turns out."

Shelly turned to leave the interview room and regarded DiManno for a moment. For a flickering instant, the widow's harsh exterior softened.

"Inspector, when will my husband's body be released?"

"If the Medical Examiner gets everything he needs, you should expect a call after the autopsy this afternoon."

"I see. Thank you, Inspector," she said, and the woman's face transformed into a cold hardened shell once more.

Shelly Mattson left the Major Crimes Unit, clipped down the stairs, and strode out onto the steps in front of the Hall of Justice. She paused, dug her sunglasses from within her sleek handbag, and hid behind them.

Inspector DiManno trailed behind and stopped next to her. "Mrs. Mattson, you mentioned Jonathon was reckless in his business affairs. How so?"

She turned and faced DiManno. Bright sun glinted off the designer frames, her eyes concealed behind dark oversized lenses. With a quiver in her lip, Shelly said, "Everything we built–everything we struggled for, my cheating bastard of a husband put in jeopardy. Five hundred million dollars in Dynalife's holdings–gone. The board suspects Jonathon siphoned the money off somewhere. They suspect him and by association–me."

"Do you suspect him?"

"He held the ability and the means to do so, but thievery was not among the long list of Jonathon's character defects."

"Has the loss been reported to the S.E.C.?"

"Not yet. The board has a team of forensic accountants tracking down the funds. An announcement at this time is premature; the accountants must complete their work and confirm the loss. I'm taking a huge risk by confiding this in you, Inspector. I hope you appreciate my trust."

"A rush to sell off stock before the loss becomes public," DiManno said.

"Quite so. Dynalife would not survive the scandal of financial malfeasance and insider trading if the information leaked. The board has a limited window to bolster the company's position."

At the curb, the rear door of Mrs. Mattson's limo swung open. The interim Chief Executive Officer, David Paulson, stepped out and waved for Shelly Mattson.

She sighed, said, "Someone's getting comfortable in their new role. I must be off, Inspector." She didn't wait for a response, turned on her heel, strode off toward Paulson, and ducked into the open limo door.

"Did you give him the necklace?" Paulson said while he looked at the police Inspector at the top of the stairs."

"Of course."

"Can he connect the dots to Jillian?"

"He wouldn't be much of a detective if he couldn't."

Chapter Seven

Dressed in a favorite pair of worn jeans and an old CSUSF sweatshirt, Jillian pulled herself into a tight ball in the corner of her kitchen floor. Knees hugged close to her chest, she slowly rocked back and forth, numbed from unfathomable events threatening to send her life into the toilet. It didn't happen. She couldn't have–but everything pointed at the fact it did and she was in the center of it all.

A cup of untouched chamomile tea rested next to her on the tile floor. The bits of tea settled to the bottom. When Jillian was a young child, in the good years before her mother took her own life, Jillian and her mother held elaborate tea parties where they pretended to read fortunes from their tea leaves. Jillian's mother always told little Jillian wondrous things were about to happen for her. In truth, Jillian held onto those precious moments because there were few of them.

Jillian and her older sister, Hannah, were raised by a single mom. There was a ten year age difference between Jillian and Hannah, ten years of resentment. To hear Hannah tell it, Jillian came along and kicked Hannah aside—soaking up every bit of their mother's love and affection. Jillian got the attention all right. Young Jillian was always compared to her older sister, and never fully measured up, in her mother's eye. The sisters never really shared anything in common. They never attended the same schools or shared any common interests.

Hannah moved out immediately after high school, enrolled in junior college, and got pregnant before the end of the first semester. She dropped out and tried marriage for a while, but it didn't take. Hannah wasn't about to come running home to mommy, so she couch-surfed with a toddler until she burned all of her bridges.

Jillian reached out for help when their mother started down a steep depressive episode. Her mother started experiencing memory lapses—a precursor, the doctors said, to a slide into dementia. Hannah told her she didn't care what happened to the woman. Jillian remembered how the conversation ended, when Hannah said, "Maybe I'll come and see her when she doesn't remember who I am." Those were her final words until the funeral.

Jillian gave up hope that Hannah would change after their mother's suicide. She was as caustic and jealous of what Jillian accomplished—graduation from college, securing an executive track position with a Fortune 500 company, and the fact Jillian could afford to live in the city.

The few happy moments of her childhood with her mother were all she had left, and those promises of a wondrous future seemed hollow now. The tea leaves in the cup on the cold tile floor held no promise and no explanation for what was happening to Jillian. A dark, brooding weight fell over Jillian, her breath hitched. She picked at a stray thread which started to unravel a thin spot on her jeans. Unraveling. This is what it felt like to lose your mind. Did her mother start like this?

The three unread newspapers lay stacked on the kitchen counter where Jillian placed them after her hallway encounter with Mrs. Tillman. The headline was visible on the bottom-most paper. *Pharmaceutical Giant Murdered.*

Everything Jillian knew about Jonathon's death came from her boss. The fancy-dressed police Inspector wasn't particularly forthcoming on the details.

She unfolded her legs, stood, and stretched to let the blood flow back into her muscles. Jillian pulled the bottom paper from the pile, snapped off the green rubber band, and unfolded the newspaper onto the counter.

The front-page article held the by-line of Kevin Anderson, a reporter Jillian met a few months ago. They tried dating a couple of times, but their schedules and his more conservative orientation didn't mesh with her decidedly liberal bent. Jillian admitted she could have tried harder to make the relationship work, but at the time, her priorities, her life really, was devoted to Dynalife. Every waking hour poured into researching, planning, and developing advertising copy for the release and marketing of the HIV drug, Bosphizion. The painstaking clinical trials promised a revolutionary new HIV treatment protocol with the potential to save millions of lives.

She scanned Kevin's article for more than the basic, who, what, when, and where of Jonathon Mattson's murder. The billionaire's bio described the corporate executive in glowing praise as if he was a combination of Albert Schweitzer and Mother Theresa, who tended to the sick and downtrodden.

"What a load of crap," Jillian said to Kevin's small photo next to his by-line.

The newspaper print smudged under her tight grip as she read the account of his death. Kevin's article contained limited detail on the cause of death, only one line reported Mrs. Shelly Mattson found her husband's blood-soaked body.

Blood-soaked body–blood on Jillian's clothes. A chill crept up Jillian's neck.

Kevin claimed sources close to the investigation revealed Mrs. Mattson returned home and discovered her husband's body sprawled across their bed.

Jillian froze.

Bed?

Their bed?

Then where the hell did I wake up this morning?

The article referenced the Mattsons' Pacific Heights residence. The apartment, where her trip down the rabbit hole started this morning was in Nob Hill. Not far away as the crow flies, but the point was, the apartment was not Mattson's home. It should've provided some relief, but it was another malformed puzzle piece in the jigsaw puzzle of her life.

Jillian folded the paper and tossed it aside. She needed answers, not more questions. She paced in the kitchen, nibbled on a thumbnail, and tried to connect the fragments. Nothing fit. Unless she was out of her fucking mind.

In mid-pace, Jillian kicked over the tepid cup of tea she'd left on the floor.

She grabbed a wad of paper towels from the counter and blotted up the pool of tea before it managed to stain the grout between the porcelain tiles. She'd put off sealing the floor because she didn't have the time. Months ago, she'd purchased gallons of penetrating sealer and sponges. Now she was without a job and no excuse to delay that chore. She wished there was a sealer that kept the unconnected images of Mattson out of her head.

A wad of tea-soaked paper towels was pitched in the trash bin. If cleaning her memory was only as easy–wipe it up and toss it. Maybe that was it. Find the dirtied images tucked away in her mind and wipe them up. It was better than the alternative, slowly inching toward insanity, the path her mother chose. Better to run headlong into it and face your fears, she thought.

But, fear has its own terms–terms that grab you by the throat and squeeze the living shit out of you, while you stare into its eyes, terms.

Chapter Eight

Aten-dollar taxi ride put Jillian at the steps of Grace Cathedral in Nob Hill, a half a block away from the room where her nightmare began this morning. Clusters of visitors milled on the broad steps outside the grand cathedral, waiting for the next tour. Jillian joined the throng because it offered her a chance to watch the front of the apartment building, without being too obvious.

The crowd gave Jillian a sense of anonymity until it evaporated as their tours commenced. The surroundings failed to spark any recognition. Nothing came to her before leaving the apartment building this morning. Everything transpiring in the forty-eight hours in between the Friday meeting with Mattson and waking up in the apartment building entrance was erased.

A few people entered the apartment tower's glass doors, none of them familiar. Her answers were hidden inside an apartment on the building's topmost floor.

She doubted she could walk up to the doorman, the dark-haired, greasy man who leered at her and say, "Hey, I might've killed somebody. Mind if I go and check?"

A FedEx delivery truck double-parked in front of the apartment entrance and its orange hazard lights flashed on. The deliveryman bounded out of the blue and white truck, and fast stepped to the apartment door. Jillian watched as the man balanced the boxes in his arms and pushed an intercom button. A few moments later, the deliveryman yanked the door open, took a half step inside, and twisted his back to the door, easing it closed with his parcel-laden body. Seconds later, the door opened, and the Fed-Ex deliveryman appeared in the doorway.

Jillian screwed up her courage, left the cathedral steps, and ran to the apartment building, cutting across the park, where she startled two old men who knocked their domino tiles off the cement bench.

"Sorry," she said without a break in stride.

"God-dammit, Harry. You did that because I was winning."

"Did what?" Harry said.

"You got your granddaughter to run through here and muck up our game."

"She ain't my granddaughter, and you weren't winning."

"You arranged a–a distraction, Harry."

"I don't need no distraction to kick your ass."

Jillian couldn't hear the rest of the argument because she focused on the apartment door ahead of her and the deliveryman's hand let go of the handle.

She quickened her pace. "Hold the door, please."

The deliveryman heard the pounding of shoes on the pavement and noticed the woman running toward him. He reached, holding the door open for Jillian.

"Thanks so much. I left my key upstairs," Jillian said.

"Happens all the time," the deliveryman said as Jillian slipped in through the opening.

The apartment lobby was as she remembered, narrow, small, and sparsely furnished. The station where she encountered the leering doorman was vacant. The elevator bank lay straight ahead, and Jillian made a beeline for them, the tread of her running shoes squeaking on the tile with each step. The sound echoed in the small space. Jillian gritted her jaw and tried to step light and fast.

The distinctive whoosh of a toilet flush came from behind a door to her right. Jillian rushed to the closest elevator and jabbed the up button. A rustle sounded from behind the restroom door, and Jillian hit the call button again, urging it open. The button didn't light, then she saw the thin horizontal slot–she needed a key card to use the elevator from the first floor.

Oil starved hinges on the bathroom door cried open, and Jillian made a dash for the stairwell door on the far end of the lobby. From the corner of her eye, she saw a dark figure step from the bathroom as she tugged open the stairwell door. She ducked inside and paused, her ear against the metal door, listening for the doorman.

She waited. She listened but heard nothing other than the pounding of her heart.

The greasy doorman hadn't seen her. Jillian bounded up the stairs to the second-floor landing. She remembered she didn't need a key card when she used the elevator from the upper floors this morning. She'd use the second-floor elevator to reach the sixth-floor apartments. The answers were here. She was certain of it. Her confidence buoyed with movement and a goal.

The funny thing about confidence is it demands feeding, like a hot air balloon. No heat, no lift, and you crash on the rocks of your own self-doubt.

A locked stairwell door started letting the air out of Jillian's confidence balloon. By the time she found the third, fourth, fifth, and sixth-floor doors tightly locked down, the heady air of confidence leaked away, leaving her balloon in shreds. She rested on the sixth-floor landing and considered her next move. Wait for someone to open the door? Little chance of that happening, and if someone did, they would surely recognize she didn't belong here.

"Little lady? You're gonna need to come down sometime," said a voice from a speaker mounted above the door.

Jillian turned and craned her head to the left and saw a small camera box trained on the landing. The doorman watched her all along, as she failed in her entry attempt. She stared back at the small black camera lens.

"That's right. I see you. Now come on down. Don't make me call the police on you."

Police involvement was the last thing Jillian wanted. How could she explain why she was in this apartment building? *Oh yes, Officer, I was just here to find out if this is where I killed Jonathon Mattson.* A one-way ticket to the funny farm.

Jillian got up from her perch on the sixth-floor landing and trod down the stairs until she saw the lobby door propped open. She didn't see the police or anyone else there but expected someone ready to pounce on her the moment she reached the doorway. No one accosted her, but Jillian's anxiety fluttered at the thought of the sleazy, grease-ball doorman waiting in the hallway. She tucked her head through the door, and the tension in her shoulders let go when the only person in the lobby was a grandfatherly seventy-year-old man planted behind the doorman's desk.

Nick, according to the name on the brass-colored badge clipped on his navy-blue blazer, weighed in at a whopping one hundred and ten pounds, stretched over a five-ten frame. Reed-thin, with a crown of wispy hair the shade of a copper penny, the man was as threatening as a declawed kitten.

"Now, young lady, let's do this the proper way. How can I help you?" Nick said with a brilliant smile that melted the rest of Jillian's apprehension.

She left the shadows of the stairwell and felt more like a child called to the principal's office than a grown woman caught trespassing in an apartment stairwell. Her eyes darted to the front door and then back to Nick.

He read her expression. "How about we start with names? I'm Nick."

"Jillian," she said and immediately cursed under her breath for giving him her real name.

"So Miss Jillian, you must have an important reason for you to sneak in and prowl around."

"I did not prowl."

"Do you know what prowling is?" His smile widened, and he leaned back in the chair, not in a manner that threatened Jillian, but one that playfully challenged her.

Jillian stood in front of the doorman's desk, hands on hips, said, "I imagine cat-burglars and jewel thieves prowl."

"Sinister types, out to hurt good people. Anything sinister about your lurking in my building?"

"So, now I'm lurking?"

Nick seemed to enjoy the banter, leaned forward, bony elbows on the desktop. "From where I sit," he pointed to the small bank of cameras racked on the desk, "Yes, young lady, you are a lurker–one who lurks. What are you lurking for?"

"I left something in an apartment upstairs. It's a watch, and it's kind of embarrassing. The other doorman saw me leave this morning. He can verify I was here; ask him. I only need a minute to go up and grab my watch." Jillian hated lying to Nick.

"The other doorman?" Nick asked. His eyes narrowed and suddenly locked on Jillian's own.

"Yes, the guy wore a blazer like yours, younger guy, short, clipped black hair, a beard, or stubble passing as a beard these days, and dark eyes." Jillian couldn't forget those judgmental leering eyes.

"When was this?" Nick's demeanor changed in a flash. He didn't seem as playful.

"This morning, a little before eight." Jillian noticed Nick's personality shift. "Why?"

"I've worked here for eleven years. There is no other doorman."

Chapter Nine

"What do you mean there's no other doorman? I saw him this morning. He sat right where you are now."

Nick rolled the chair closer to the desk. "I'm the only doorman in this building. I think they keep me on out of pity. They really don't need me. It's not like I can help the tenants carry anything heavier than a milk jug." Nick leaned closer and in a conspiratorial whisper said, "You may've noticed, I'm not an imposing figure."

"I swear. I saw a man here this morning. He wore a jacket like yours…"

"This jacket?" Nick grabbed the lapels of the blue blazer. I hang it on the back of the chair when I'm off. Makes people think someone is always around. Now that you mention it, it wasn't where I left it last night. Somebody folded it up and left it on the desk."

"Why would someone pretend to be a doorman?" Jillian said.

Nick shrugged his pointy shoulders. "Don't know. I'm telling you whoever you saw doesn't work here."

Jillian's dark cloud of self-incrimination gathered on the horizon. She surprised herself, pressing on. She came here for answers, and by God, she was going to find them.

"Who lives in 6B?" she said.

"I'm not supposed to give out that kind of information."

"Please, Nick. It's important."

"I'm sorry, I can't. Don't you know? You said you were up there this morning?"

"I can't explain, but I need to know."

ook"You can call them on my phone," Nick said.

Jillian gathered Nick's withered hand into hers. She felt his surprise at the gentle gesture, but he didn't pull away.

"Please. Tell me who lives in 6B."

Nick's eyes broke away from Jillian. He pulled his hand away from her grasp and cleared his throat.

"You could get me into a lot of trouble, you know?"

"I don't mean to."

"6B, you say?" Nick shifted in his desk chair. Jillian felt a spike in the doorman's interest.

"Yes."

"I think you got that wrong."

"What…what do you mean wrong? I know where I was," she said. As soon as the words were out of her mouth, she felt the nagging doubt bubble up from the dark recesses of her mind. This field trip to the apartment was supposed to jog her memory, but perhaps some memories are best left buried.

Nick pushed back from the desk and pressed his gaunt frame from the chair. The blue blazer hung loosely off his shoulders, and his khaki pants were equally ill-fitted. His belt tightened well past the last hole, where the buckle bit into a makeshift slit on the surface. Nick circled around his desk, hitched up his pants, and ambled toward the elevators. He didn't bother to glance back.

"Well, come on."

Nick's grace surprised Jillian. She expected slow, shuffled, uneven movements from the aged doorman. Instead, she found a smooth, balanced efficiency in his gait. She hurried to catch him in front of the elevator cars.

Nick pulled a key card from his blazer pocket and shoved it into the slot before he pushed the up button with his bony finger. In seconds, the closest elevator car's doors slid open, and the two of them stepped inside. The doorman pocketed his key card, tipped his head down, but eyed Jillian with grandfatherly pity. He sighed and stabbed the button for the sixth floor.

"So you believe me?" Jillian said.

"I believe you think you visited someone in 6B. Thing is–you didn't."

The elevator doors parted into the hallway on the sixth floor, and a wave of relief hit at the familiar colors, wall décor, and heavy polished doors. She bolted from the elevator, ran down the hallway, the carpet soft underfoot, as she remembered.

She wasn't losing her mind. It was real. Jillian found the apartment door, the apartment door she recalled from the beginning of her nightmare. She pulled on the brass lever and found it locked. Frustrated, her breath grew shallow, and she started pounding on the door with the palm of her hand. The smack of her flesh against the hardwood door stung as it echoed in the hallway.

Nick watched her for a moment. "You sure this is the apartment?"

Thin droplets of nervous sweat collected on Jillian's forehead from her exertion. She smacked the door again.

"This is the one. I'm sure of it," she said and kept pounding.

Nick fished a ring of keys from his pocket and nudged Jillian aside. He selected a key, slid it in, and unlocked the apartment door.

Jillian rushed past the doorman into the space. Once through the door, Jillian faced a vacant, unoccupied space. She stopped in her tracks. Plastic sheeting hung on one wall where bare wooden studs bore evidence of a kitchen renovation in progress. Crates of cabinets waited for installation. The damp faint acidic odor of freshly grouted tile permeated the apartment.

She ran to the window and caught a glimpse of the cathedral tile roofline. It seemed more distant now. It was the same view, but different. Everything felt out of reach.

She collapsed to her knees. "No. I was here. I swear. This wasn't here before," she said tugging on a plastic sheet."

Nick took her by the hands and with unexpected strength, pulled Jillian to her feet. He placed his hands on her shoulders, partially to steady himself, and faced her.

"No one lives here Miss Jillian."

"But, I swear I was here."

"I'm afraid it's not possible. The Marquez family owns two units in the building and 6B is unoccupied. She's remodeling 6B before she moves in. The contractors have been tearing this place apart for two weeks."

Jillian's head started to spin; pinpoints of light filled her vision. She couldn't catch her breath.

"This can't be. I'm not going crazy. I was here." Jillian heard the faint call of her dead mother's voice. *Like mother like daughter...*

She couldn't breathe. Jillian felt the walls press down like a rusty claustrophobic vise. Lightheaded, she turned, retreating to a safe refuge outside of this mind-bending apartment. Woozy and off-balance, Jillian fought off the urge to collapse in the hallway. Her mind finally snapped and convinced her of an elaborate fantasy where she'd awoken in this apartment. The construction debris, dust, and materials proved differently. There was no way she slept in this place. Only the most broken of minds could conjure up a hallucination with such vivid detail. Especially, a mind that might be suppressing murdering Jonathon Mattson. Her unconscious created the false memory to shield her from the truth. Now, Jillian's truth crashed down upon her.

"Air, I need to get some air." She trundled past Nick, shouldering him out of her path.

The old man's eye's narrowed, and he reached out to guide Jillian, but she pulled her elbow away from Nick's hand, recoiling as if his touch burned her flesh.

"Let me call someone to help you," he said.

"Leave me alone." The words came from the back of her throat and startled Jillian with their venom. She felt trapped and pushed away from the aging doorman.

Nick shuffled back from Jillian and her sudden rage. His trembling hand fished a cell phone from his pocket, and he held it at arm's length, squinting at the nine, one, and the one keys he needed.

Jillian reached the elevator and jabbed the lobby button, and the doors closed, drowning out Nick's voice.

The moment the door parted, Jillian edged through the gap and raced across the lobby to the entrance doors. Her lungs burned because she forgot to breathe. A step into the open air, she dropped to her knees and drew deep shuddering breaths. She cursed herself for letting her mind become feeble. *Who forgets to breathe for shit's sake?*

The fresh air helped her thoughts crystalize, but those crystals turned to jagged-edged paranoia. *Why was this happening? I'm not crazy.* Jillian recalled her mother saying the exact same words in the months before she killed herself.

This is different. This is real. Jillian thought her mother must've felt the same uncertainty in her downward spiral into insanity. An adrenaline-fed jolt of fear of following in her mother's footsteps overwhelmed her and threatened to drown her in a waterfall of unanswerable questions. She needed to run, far from this building, from Mattson's death, and whatever hand she played in his murder.

Jillian rose from the landing and set a frantic pace away from the building. She jostled pedestrians along the sidewalk, drawing a few watch-the-fuck-where-you're-goings, in return. A car horn broke her trance as she stepped off the curb in the path of a taxi.

The taxi driver parted his hands in a "what now" gesture. Jillian jogged to the rear passenger door and sank into the seat. "Take me home," she said.

"And where would that be, sweetheart?" the driver said.

She gave him the address, and the cab circled around Grace Cathedral and cut south toward Golden Gate Avenue.

As the cab slowed for a streetlight, Jillian caught the eyes of strangers, with their damning glances. They knew what she'd done. They knew.

When the driver pulled in front of her building, she tossed the fare in the front seat and bolted from the cab. She made it to the lobby door before she caught sight of the police officer standing at the elevator. Jillian's blood ran cold as she looked past the officer and locked eyes with Inspector DiManno. The door handle felt like ice against her palm, a warning of what waited for her within.

If she bolted, they'd think she was guilty. Maybe, they already knew she was Mattson's killer. For a glimmer of a second, she embraced knowing what was real and what was a psychotic nightmare. The police Inspector wouldn't skulk about in her apartment building to pass on good news.

The Inspector nodded toward the door, and the officer turned, registering Jillian's presence. He spoke into a radio clipped to his shoulder while keeping eye contact with her.

Jillian released the door handle and took a step backward. The Inspector and the man in uniform made no move to close the distance between them. A moment passed before Jillian sorted out why. A shoe scuffed on the cement walk behind her. Another policeman blocked her retreat on the sidewalk. He stood at a distance, not threatening Jillian, but she was boxed in—trapped.

A car horn sounded in the street, voicing some commuter discontent and it was the distraction she needed. The officer on the sidewalk glanced away, toward the sound, and Jillian bolted in the opposite direction.

"Shit," the cop said.

She didn't look back but heard his footfalls on the sidewalk behind her. He gained on her.

Jillian couldn't outrun him, so she darted into the traffic on Golden Gate Avenue. Drivers swerved avoiding her, but two cars sideswiped one another in the confusion. She stepped in the path of a city bus and the heavy tires barked as the lumbering vehicle shuddered to a stop. Faces marked with panic peered out the windows, sorting out the reason for the sudden rough stop. Jillian shot across the remaining two opposing lanes, and the snarl of traffic shielded her escape.

A half-block away, Jillian leaned against a store window front and forced a deep breath. Inspector DiManno emerged from behind the stalled bus and turned, searching. He threw his hands up in frustration, and the uniformed cop who lost her got an earful from the Inspector.

Jillian hunched her shoulders, it didn't really make her smaller, but it felt like she was trying to blend in with the others on the sidewalk. She let the flow carry and conceal her.

She knew she'd face the Police Inspector at some point, but not until she held her own answers. Even if the path to those answers proved she was irretrievably mad.

Chapter Ten

A squat concrete hole of Hallidie Plaza served as the opening to the underground workings of the Powell Street BART Station. The escalators funneled passengers below street level for the trains to the far reaches of the city or access to the East Bay through a claustrophobic trans-bay tunnel. The crowd provided the instant anonymity Jillian needed. Here, a ticket out of the city didn't require any identification.

She used cash at a kiosk, and the machine spat out a paper ticket. Jillian joined the flow of people down the escalators to the train platforms. At the turnstiles, the line bogged as passengers slid their tickets through the reader. Jillian's stomach knotted at the sight of a BART officer, the transportation district's version of a transit cop, monitoring the lines.

The officer listened to a radio call and stepped in Jillian's direction. He stared at her, continuing his approach, and closed the distance between them. Her legs trembled but didn't respond to her impulse to run after the fear clamped down.

"Hey lady," a bearded man in skinny jeans, said from behind her. "Sometime today?"

The BART cop reached Jillian, and she clenched her eyes tight. She'd lost the battle with her fear. She held her hands out, expecting the cool steel of handcuffs, but the officer brushed past her and kept moving. Jillian opened her eyes when the hipster behind her shouldered by on the way to the turnstile. The officer wasn't interested in her. His attention focused on rousting a pair of panhandlers from the platform.

At her turn, Jillian slid her ticket through the reader and bumped the turnstile with her hip. Inside, past the barrier, she didn't feel as comforted as she hoped. The press of the crowd amplified the tension. Unfamiliar faces came with their own set of worries. Street thugs slithered through the crowd, searching for young runaways, lost in the big city, or inattentive pickpocket marks.

Jillian pressed against the wall. This was a mistake coming here, trapped like a rat underground. She felt the incoming train from the vibration against her back and the subtle change in air pressure on the platform. The pitch of the electric engines lowered as the train slowed at the platform. Jillian waited until the loading area was empty before she jogged to the train door.

The car was half full, and Jillian found a seat toward the rear of the car, next to an older man. Among those who rode, several freshly released prison inmates celebrated their newfound freedom with loud, raucous accounts of their exploits in prison, retold in exaggerated tales casting them as gangsters, or shot-callers on the yard. Brown cardboard boxes tattooed with prison identification numbers held each man's meager possessions. A change of clothing, family photos, a few magazines, and collected letters from the outside filled the boxes.

The man next to Jillian silently held his prison box on his lap and watched the petty criminals swap stories from the "Big House," with tired eyes.

"Young fools," he said with a deep, coarse voice that Jillian thought was likely a rich baritone twenty years earlier.

She nodded.

The man coughed into a handkerchief, accompanied by a labored wheeze. A small spot of blood stained the yellowed linen in his hand. He quickly folded it and stuffed it in a blue chambray shirt pocket.

"I'll move," he said. His eyes cast down and away from Jillian.

"Don't bother." Jillian spotted a brown envelope on the bench between them. The swollen envelope bore the man's last name, Johnson, and his prison number. Open on one end, folded papers poked out among what Jillian believed was the man's personal effects.

Johnson shifted his weight, knocking the envelope to the floor and eight prescription medicine bottles spilled onto the dirty floor, and rolled in different directions.

He jumped from the bench, grabbed two bottles at his feet, and reached for a third rolling down the aisle.

Jillian grabbed another from under her seat. Pills rattled inside the white pharmaceutical bottle when she picked it up. The familiar Dynalife Pharmaceutical label on the unopened bottle caught her attention. This bottle bore the company label, but it was black and white, rather than the usual blue and red lettering. The same logo affixed to the label, but in different colors. She approved every marketing decision and branding strategy for the company, and this was a product label she'd never seen cross her desk. The black and white bottle shouldn't exist.

According to the label, the bottle contained Bosphizion. The HIV medication wasn't in circulation and as far as pharmacies were concerned, the drug wasn't available for distribution. Jillian knew everything about Bosphizion, the next-generation HIV medication, which promised increased CD4 counts from 100 to 1,200. The completion of clinical trials and Federal Drug Administration approval for release was, at best, twenty-four to thirty-six months out. She'd emphasized the timeline during the Friday meeting with Mattson. Yet, she held a bottle of the untested Bosphizion in her hand.

Scuffed brown shoes stepped into the edge of her vision. Jillian looked up and saw Johnson's face more clearly, tired jaundiced eyes, thin face, and a slight rash on the side of his neck. She recognized the HIV drug side effects and the telltale markers of low CD4 blood cell count. The CD4 blood cells were the "helper" blood cells that fight off infection. In people with compromised immune systems, low cell counts meant the body was vulnerable to opportunistic infection.

Jillian lifted the bottle for Johnson. "Who gave this to you?" she said as she shook the container.

"What's it matter to you?" Johnson said. He grabbed the bottle and stuffed it back inside the brown envelope.

"You shouldn't use this medication. Who gave it to you?" Jillian said.

"You a doctor?"

"No."

"Then leave me alone." Johnson turned and tried to leave, but Jillian grabbed him by the arm.

"Your drug may not be safe."

"You think I care? I'm a dead man walking. The prison doctors gave us this stuff, but it don't work."

"How did they have it? It's not supposed to be on the streets yet."

"How the hell should I know? There's closets full of the shit." Johnson held up the envelope of prescriptions. "I can't afford this on the streets, so when I'm sick, I violate my parole, and I go back inside. Since I'm HIV-positive, I get the meds I need. With the treatment they give me at Vacaville, I get better and go back home. Except, this time..."

"You didn't recover," Jillian finished for him.

"No. None of us did."

"Us? How many are we talking about?"

"One-hundred and twenty at CMF."

"CMF?"

"The California Medical Facility, the prison at Vacaville."

"All of you?"

Johnson nodded. "The strange thing is we have lower CD4 cell counts after taking the drugs than we did when we came in from the streets."

"What's your count?" Jillian asked.

"Mine's is 85. It was 120 when I got to CMF. It was like they was trying to make us croak. Five guys got moved out to hospice while I was there. Guess the State won't pay for them no more."

Jillian tried to sort out how an unapproved drug made it onto state prison pharmacy shelves without trials or FDA approval. She'd gotten fired for trying to accelerate the FDA approval for the drug and distribute it where it would do some good. It was impossible the medication was out on the streets, yet she saw the evidence.

"Where are you headed?"

"I got me a ticket to Stockton. Then I hit the Parole Outpatient Clinic for a refill of these."

Jillian dug through her purse and pulled out a notepad. She scribbled out a few lines, tore it off, and handed it to Johnson. "I want you to call this doctor the minute you step off the bus. He runs an AIDS clinic where you can receive the right treatment and it won't cost you a dime." Jillian recalled meeting the Stockton-based doctor at an AIDS and HIV treatment conference a few months ago, and she was impressed with his commitment to his patients.

Jillian held the note out and abruptly pulled it back when Johnson reached for it.

"I need you to do me a favor first," she said.

Chapter Eleven

Jillian's grip on the world was fragile—the photos with Mattson she couldn't explain, the slips in time, and now physical proof Bosphizion was in production. Unable to come up with an explanation for this series of unconnected events, Jillian feared becoming her mother—paranoid, delusional, and disconnected.

The BART station map showed Lake Merritt and Fruitvale as the next stops on this line. Fruitvale wasn't far from her sister Hannah's place. Jillian wondered if her subconscious put her on this train to seek out family? As much as she didn't relish the "Hannah treatment" she would face if she showed up on her sister's doorstep, Jillian feared she was going down her mother's slow path of mental decline. Dementia, they called it. Did her mother suffer the same kind of memory loss Jillian was experiencing now? Hannah was older. She must've noticed the decline. What signs did Hannah see? It was a precarious test of her mental health, but one of the few options Jillian had left.

Jillian left the Fruitvale station and plodded through the blight-ridden commercial district to the residential section near 33rd Avenue. She thought it odd with her memory gaps, she could recall the address of a place she'd only seen on returned mail.

Hannah's address was the lower left side of a six-unit apartment building. Indecipherable graffiti tagged the side of the building, and a once green patch of lawn was now well-trodden dirt and strewn with trash. Jillian kicked away a syringe and climbed the steps, taking a breath before she knocked.

Hannah pulled a curtain aside and scowled. She'd aged, and not gracefully. Wrinkles around her mouth pruned as Hannah tightened her jaw. Her hair was half-grown out from an attempt to go blonde. Another reinvention of herself, Jillian figured.

A click of a deadbolt opening sounded, and Hannah stepped out onto the porch.

"I'm running late, you should have called," Hannah said.

"Hello to you too. You changed your phone number, and I don't have the new one."

"What do you want from me, Jilly?"

"I need to talk with you—it's about mom and—"

"I don't have time for this. Father Washington is expecting me down at the rectory."

Jillian cast a skeptical glance at her sister and the threadbare housecoat she wore. The old garment was out of place—a garment an older woman would throw on while puttering about the home. Hannah wasn't the puttering type. Dropping Father Washington's name into the conversation told Jillian the flavor of the most recent incarnation—religion. False piety is especially ugly.

"Please, it's important," Jillian said.

"No, it's not."

Hannah started to turn and go back inside the house, and Jillian grabbed her elbow. Her sister pulled away.

"You haven't even heard what I wanted to ask you about."

"If it's about mom, then it's not important."

"It's important to me."

"Then you should have called. Really—I have to go now, Father Washington can't manage the youth group without me."

"Hannah, please…"

"What do you expect from me, Jilly? I'm supposed to drop everything for you because you show up on my doorstep? You got mom's attention growing up. I don't need to give you mine. You always demanded the center of attention."

"I need—"

"You need. It's always about you, Jilly. I told you I don't have time for this. Come back in a couple of hours."

"Can I wait inside?"

Hannah looked at her sister, pursed her lips, and said, "I don't think so. Come back in a couple of hours if you need to."

The door slammed in Jillian's face, and she backed off the porch, stepping on a pile of cigarette butts with smeared pink lipstick, the same shade she'd noticed on Hannah a moment ago.

She'd spotted a small mom-and-pop coffee shop a few blocks back. It was nearly empty, and Jillian figured it was a place to park for the next couple of hours until Hannah would agree to see her.

Two older men sat at one of the three tables, reading their newspapers. One would occasionally point out some news story fact to the other. The response was always, "You don't say."

Jillian took the table closest to the window where she could watch the smallest corner of Hannah's building.

An older woman came from behind the counter and tossed a laminated menu on the table in front of Jillian.

"Coffee?" the woman asked.

"Yes. Yes, please."

The woman poured and asked, "What can I get ya?"

"Coffee and a muffin."

"Hon, we don't have no muffins. What we do have is pie. You want you a piece of strawberry pie?"

"That sounds good."

"It ain't," one of the old men said.

"George Francis Davis, you keep to yourself, you hear?" the woman chided.

"Trying to do my civic duty, warnin' the girl," he said.

"I'll bring you the pie," the woman told Jillian.

"Don't say you weren't warned," the old man mumbled into his coffee cup.

Jillian sipped at her coffee and kept an eye on the street in front of her sister's place. If she walked to the church, Jillian might be able to see her.

The waitress slid a plate of pie in front of Jillian. The slice covered the tan-colored plastic plate and steam rose from the strawberry filling. It reminded her of a Saturday morning when she was young—before the bad times came. Jillian and her mom would sit on the porch swing and eat apple pie, fresh from the oven.

Over pie and coffee, Jillian kept watch on the street for Hannah and the police. By now, the Inspector would've pulled up the street camera feeds and videos from inside the BART stations—according to the television shows she'd seen.

Jillian paid her bill and complimented the woman on the strawberry pie.

"You're most welcome, hon. You hear that George? The lady liked my pie."

Jillian couldn't hear the rest of the banter as she left and walked back to Hannah's apartment. She climbed the steps, and her sister opened the door, dressed in the same threadbare rose-colored housecoat.

"You came back."

"I told you I needed to talk," Jillian said.

"Fine." Hannah didn't invite Jillian in but left the door open as she retreated back inside.

Hannah parked on the sofa and picked up a cigarette from the ashtray. "So talk."

Jillian moved a stack of celebrity gossip magazines from the sofa and sat next to Hannah.

"I need to know what mom started to act like when her problems started."

"Problems? Like her, I don't care about Hannah, problems?"

"It wasn't like that."

Hannah blew a smoke ring. "Like hell, it wasn't. You didn't see it. I did."

"Did mom have memory problems or blackouts?"

"She always blamed memory problems when it came to school plays and parent-teacher conferences."

"You know what I mean, Hannah."

"She had dementia, Jilly. Of course she had memory problems. Why are you dredging up the past?" Hannah stubbed out her cigarette in the overflowing ashtray.

"Please, be honest with me."

Hannah shrugged in response.

"I need to know about her. I suffered a blackout. I can't remember what happened the day before. I'm scared."

"Were you out drinking again? You're not twenty anymore, Jilly."

"No—yes—I don't know. I've never experienced this before. I'm scared. They're saying I did things."

"You think you're losing your mind like mom did—how ironic."

"Hannah, please. I'm asking for help here."

"I haven't seen you in years. You don't send me a birthday card, and now you literally show up on my doorstep and demand time from me."

Jillian stood. "Listen, you're the one who ran and hid when mom got sick. You're the one who abandoned me when I needed you. You think I wanted to come here? You were there when mom's problems started, and I thought maybe you'd use some of your newfound religious compassion you like to throw around and talk to me."

"You should leave. I want nothing to do with you. My mother is dead, and the memories are buried with her. If you're having blackouts, then you're going crazy like she did."

"They—they say I killed someone. I didn't. I couldn't."

"If you're so sure, then go to the police."

"I can't."

"Listen to yourself, Jilly. Get help. You sound insane. You sound like Mom. She was delusional too."

Jilly dug in her pocket and pulled out the white prescription bottle. "It's real."

"So, you're a drug addict now. I shouldn't be surprised. Mom self-medicated too."

"Aren't you listening? I found this. It doesn't exist. But, it's real. People think I—"

"Jesus, Jilly. Get some help. Maybe go to church and ask for forgiveness—"

"Forgiveness? I haven't done anything! Aren't you listening to me?" Jillian's hands were balled into tight fists.

"Calm down Jilly. I should call someone."

"Forget it. I should've known coming here was useless."

"Then leave." Hannah lit another cigarette.

"When did you become such a miserable human being?"

"When? The moment you were born. You ruined everything. It's only right I see your life take the turn you deserve."

Jillian left her sister on the sofa, and when she reached the door, she turned and looked at the woman who was once her sister. "I'm sure Father Washington would be proud of your fine Christian example of compassion."

"Bitch, get out!" Hannah hurled the ashtray toward her sister. It left a trail of lipstick-stained butts from the sofa to the living room wall.

Jillian hopped down the steps and hiked away from the building. She passed the coffee shop where the two old men took stock of the world from their table.

Jillian didn't know what to expect from a visit to her sister, but it confirmed two things in her troubled mind. First, Hannah couldn't recall their mother having blackouts erasing days of memory. And second, Jillian was on her own.

She shoved her hands into her coat pockets, and the hard plastic side of the prescription bottle gave a measure of comfort—it was a touchstone to reality. It meant there was a way out.

Jillian bought another BART ticket and boarded the first train back into the city. That's where the answers were and where the bottle in her pocket promised to unlock the truth.

Chapter Twelve

The thin metal siding of the moving train car didn't provide the slightest measure of comfort. Each minute on the tracks put her closer to the source of whatever torment pursued her. If a darkness crept from inside her soul, a genetic gift from her mentally ill mother, it was a curse she'd never outrun. She felt the pressure build with each passing station.

Passengers came and left, as the train moved through the route, and paranoia commanded Jillian to study each face, wondering which one posed the greatest danger. Of the people who rode in her car, two stood out among the single mothers with their kids, college students, and a handful of transient homeless. An emaciated drunk hung on the handrails as if he manned the deck of a foundering ship in a storm. Another man, held an overhead bar, his back to the compartment door. The black denim jeans, black t-shirt, and distressed leather jacket gave off a scruffy vibe. Dark sunglasses concealed his eyes, but Jillian felt his gaze land on her more than once. She hadn't seen him board, but his presence unsettled her.

Practiced paranoia made her take notice. Jillian acted on the warning and stood from the seat. She turned her back to the man and approached the exit doors as the train slowed for the upcoming station. She glanced over her shoulder and caught a glint from the dark lenses as the man scanned the car. He caught her movement, locked on, and stepped away from the wall. He moved in smooth, fluid strides, with no wasted effort, a man with strength and purpose. The gap between the two closed rapidly, and Jillian pushed out between the train doors as soon as they started to open. She made it to the platform outside and she felt a hand roughly grab at her shoulder. The sun-glassed man grasped the collar of her jacket through the door. Jillian twisted out of the man's grasp, and the door closed hard against his arm.

The sudden weight of the door dislodged the man's sunglasses. Jillian leaned against the door, her face separated from his by a thin pane of dirty glass. One look at the eyes, the uneven stubble on the man's chin and her knees buckled.

The man who pretended to be the doorman from Mattson's apartment, the one who leered at her the moment her life fell apart, glared back at Jillian.

He shouldered the door open a few inches, and Jillian's feet slipped across the cement. Inches away from his face, she saw a thick white scar running from the man's right eye to the corner of his upper lip. Distracted by the disfiguring scar, Jillian didn't notice his arm snake through the opening and grab her wrist.

"Let go," she said, as she jerked away.

The doors sensed the man's arm blocking them and parted. He stepped out onto the platform behind her, threw an arm around her waist, and lifted her off the ground. She felt his hot breath against her neck as he squeezed.

"I know what you did," he whispered.

Jillian struggled and flung her legs back until she caught his shin with the edge of her heel. Then she hammered on the spot, only to feel his grip tighten. The man pawed at her breasts, roughly grabbing them, and then reached down to her crotch. He cupped his hand between her legs, the heat from his touch, vile and repulsive.

Jillian looked to the people passing on the platform for help and noticed how they ignored her, another squabble between the vagrants who roamed the streets near the BART station. They were not about to become involved in street drama. But the struggle was getting attention.

She wriggled away from his offending touch and felt his hand dig into her pocket. He grabbed the Dynalife prescription bottle she got from the parolee on the train.

"You're going down for this, bitch. Run while you can."

After the warning, he loosened his grip and Jillian dropped to the sidewalk.

She stumbled and fell backward, landing hard on her tailbone. She expected a kick to her head and shielded herself with her hands, but the blow didn't come. The man simply shoved the prescription bottle in his leather jacket, put his sunglasses back on, turned, and fell into the flow of people on the platform.

Dazed, Jillian sat where she landed, people parted and flowed around her like water past a rock in a stream. She ran her hand over the ripped pocket where he'd grabbed the prescription bottle. Her evidence of sanity, of a tangible sign of the truth, was gone.

She got to her feet and craned her neck, expecting to find her assailant tucked away, watching. He'd disappeared—now she knew why. Four BART Officers jogged toward her position on the platform. They must've been alerted to the struggle by the nest of closed-circuit cameras above the train. With a surge of adrenaline, Jillian's mind cleared. She couldn't let them take her. The creep with the scarred face—if he knew what she did, then the police did too.

The BART Officers blocked the end of the platform, scanning the source of the disturbance. Jillian turned away from them and joined in with the throng of departing passengers heading for the escalator. One quick glance over her shoulder confirmed the police weren't following her escape. The final run of the escalator dumped her on the corner of Market and Drumm, and in spite of the gooseflesh prickling her arms; Inspector DiManno wasn't waiting for her.

Chapter Thirteen

Thoughts raced through Jillian's brain at a near-manic pace. The police chase, Mattson's death, the blood, her memory loss, it felt unreal, unnatural, and undeniably insane. The sole anchor in her storm of mental collapse was the prescription bottle with the black label. She didn't imagine the cool plastic container. It was solid, it was real, and she felt it. The bottle was physical proof hidden within a web of dark hallucination. It was also important to the scarred man who stole it from her. His dire warnings, "I know what you did," and "You're going down for this," meant he knew what happened during the missing chunk of time and what she'd done to Jonathon Mattson.

Only a matter of time until it caught up to her.

A throb in her temple provided an odd sense of relief. It was a headache, but not the migraine kind with the blinding kaleidoscope of painful dots. It felt like the pain from caffeine withdrawal. Painful, but soothing because it meant she'd gone without coffee for at least two days. The cup at the diner wasn't enough to make up for the caffeine depletion in her system.

Two days, a missing slice of time, during which her entire life imploded. Jillian never missed an opportunity for a cappuccino or an afternoon dark brew. The act of grinding, brewing, and savoring her first cup in the morning was ritual. Nothing would interrupt the habit if she were in control of her own body. If she hadn't been in control, who was?

Jillian ducked into a crowded Starbucks to deal with the growing throb in her temple, and to get off the exposed street. Inside, she was temporarily hidden from the police and her scar-faced pursuer. A fast survey of the coffee shop found no familiar faces, or threatening glances cast in her direction. Jillian ordered a dark brewed coffee, one promising more of a caffeine bump, but smelled of burnt gym socks.

She pulled cash from her wallet, handed a five-dollar bill to a barista with blue metal gauges in her distorted earlobes. The holes were large enough to shove a thumb through. Distracted by the quarter-sized skin flaps which looked like they would whistle in a strong wind, Jillian didn't sense the approach from behind.

She felt a hand grasp her arm. She wheeled around and freed her jacket from the grip of a small boy. Jillian expected a beefy cop with a Taser at the ready, not an innocent-faced child.

The boy's eyes grew wide, not expecting Jillian's sudden, aggressive move. Scared, but determined, the boy held up a scrap of paper. "You dropped this."

Jillian scanned the lobby for her pursuers, and the only face she found interested in her was the boy. She unclenched her fists, once she was certain she didn't need to claw, pummel, and fight off her attacker. She bent down on one knee and looked into the boy's soft features.

"Excuse me?"

"You dropped this," the boy said and held out the paper once more.

Jillian took it from him and unfolded the scrap of paper.

"Did someone give this to you?"

"No."

"Are you sure?"

"I saw it fall out of your wallet," the boy said. His thin finger pointed at the floor behind Jillian.

"Thank you," Jillian said.

The boy trotted back to a table with his parents and smiled back at Jillian.

Jillian looked at the paper once more. It held four words. Four odd scribbled words, the t's crossed high on their stems, the l's tall with wide loops she recognized were created by her hand. A handwritten confession, or a suicide note, she wasn't certain which, but the note's message chilled her spine.

I killed Jonathon Mattson.

She crumpled the note, stuffed it in her pocket, and searched the coffee shop for an accusing face.

"Jillian."

Her blood turned cold for a moment until she realized it was a barista who called her name, holding the coffee she ordered. She felt the fool for letting her anxiety overtake common sense. What did common sense know about a murder confession shoved away in her pocket? How many other confessions were out there waiting to be discovered?

She retrieved her coffee from the counter and found an empty seat at a table in the rear of the shop. Her perch allowed a view of the comings and goings on the street, giving her a few seconds' head start if her pursuers found her.

Jillian wrapped her hands around the white paper cup until the heat chased her fingers from the surface. The sensation against her skin reminded her this was real; she wasn't stuck in a dream world of imaginary demons.

A backpack nudged her elbow as a young woman tossed her belongings on the table next to Jillian at the only empty spot.

"Oh, I'm sorry. I didn't mean—I didn't spill on you did I?"

The girl's eyes were soft, warm, and unjaded by life. "No, I'm fine."

"Mind if I sit here?"

Jillian did mind, but sitting next to another person wouldn't make her stand out as much if someone was looking for a lone woman. Besides, every other seat was already occupied.

"Sure," Jillian said.

She rested the camera bag on the floor, with her legs pressed awkwardly around the equipment, keeping it from going missing. The new arrival's city survival skills were in play.

The woman extended her hand. "Kate."

"Jillian."

"I hope I don't bother you." Kate unfolded a laptop. "I really need to finish."

"No problem."

Jillian felt the caffeine work through her system. She was spent, and every part of her body felt the crash from the adrenaline high that pushed her for the last few hours. She caught a partial reflection of herself on Kate's laptop screen. There was little resemblance to a successful, driven, in-control corporate executive. With the superficial trappings stripped away, her soul laid bare, Jillian saw what remained; a scared, lonely woman who'd isolated herself to excel on the job. It left a terrible hole in her life she'd ignored until now. Gone was her steely determination and inner strength. As the laptop brightened, Jillian's image faded and dissolved, a disappearance she wanted to do as well.

Kate tapped computer keys, and dozens of photographs popped up on the screen in a random mosaic pattern. Most of the small thumbnail photos consisted of Kate with friends and family. A few shots stood out; a Golden Retriever with a gray muzzle, and a number of photos featuring an older couple. Parents, Jillian assumed, given the striking similarity between mother and daughter. On the right side of the computer screen, a single straight column of photos didn't mesh with the mishmash of assembled images. The photos on the right were formal, most in black and white and each was a familiar, if not historical, image. Among them, Martin Luther King, Jr., as he stood on the crowded steps of the Lincoln Memorial, Neil Armstrong's first steps on the moon, President Clinton embracing a young intern named Monica Lewinsky in another, F.D.R., Churchill, and Stalin gathered at Yalta during the Second World War, an iconic image of a solitary protester holding back a line of military tanks in Tiananmen Square, and United Airlines Flight 175, seconds before it knifed into the south tower of the World Trade Center.

Jillian watched as Kate swiped her finger across a touchpad and pulled the image of Martin Luther King Jr. to the center of the screen. Kate opened another software program and clicked on the photo again. From a menu at the side of the screen, Kate selected a function labeled Image Extraction. She began in the background of the historic photo and one-by-one, eliminated the people who converged at the Reflecting Pool on a day in 1963. After Kate finished, the civil rights leader stood alone, a small, insignificant, solitary figure against the massive grey steps of the Lincoln Memorial.

"What are you doing?" Jillian asked.

"Homework," Kate said, "for a photojournalism class."

Jillian pointed at the altered photo. "Why did you change it? I mean, why did you take out the people? It doesn't even look the same."

Kate smiled. "That is the point of this assignment—'what-if.' What if, two hundred and fifty thousand people stayed home and no one came to the Lincoln Memorial that day? Would it change history? Would the Civil Rights Movement happen? Would President Johnson sign the Civil Rights Act of 1964 or the Voting Rights Act?"

"How can you know what would've happened?" Jillian said.

"You can't. Not for certain. The point of this assignment is to believe the event didn't occur and prepare an alternate account of how history unfolded."

"Seems kind of…"

"Shady," Kate said.

"I was going to say odd. Why would a journalism class want you to report altered history? Isn't that 'fake news'?"

"It isn't so much about the history itself, it is more about where you can take the story without barriers. Besides, it happens all the time on social media."

"What do you mean?"

"Depending on the social media outlet, the reports are skewed to a liberal or conservative bias."

"But, changing the event itself?" Jillian said.

Kate turned slightly in her seat to face Jillian. "In 2001, after the attack on the twin towers, you remember the streaming footage showing crowds of Palestinians celebrating in the street?"

"Well sure. You telling me that was fake?"

"No. They were real people celebrating, but it was filmed months before the attack at a protest gathering in Gaza."

Sometimes looks are deceiving. Wasn't that what her mother said? Jillian looked at the edited photo of Martin Luther King Jr. once more. "Changing the photo doesn't change what happened…"

"Okay, okay, let me try and explain it from another point of view. A small number of people firmly believe the moon landing in 1969 was faked. So, 'what-if' it was really filmed in a top-secret government film studio and broadcast as the real deal? Huge profits for the aerospace industry, a sense of national unity in the middle of the Viet Nam War, and the public was completely oblivious."

"You're saying the networks doctor the truth?" Jillian said.

"Probably not the networks or legitimate affiliates, but some of the more unregulated fringe media outlets do it. Not the scale of faking a moon landing, but adding more smoke to a story about a fire, pasting in a few extra dead bodies into the scene of a disaster, that kind of thing. Most of the time it involves taking an object, or someone, out of a photo that distracts from their desired spin."

The hair on the back of Jillian's neck tingled. The photo of her with Mattson was a phony. *Sometimes looks are deceiving.* "How can you tell what's real and what's not? Can you put someone in a picture who wasn't there?"

"Couple of things," Kate said, as she tapped a series of commands on the laptop keyboard. "First off, you want to look for scale; the people must be sized appropriately. Shadows are a dead giveaway. One face has a shadow, and another doesn't. That's an indication. Then there is the pixelation around the image that shouldn't be there."

"I'm not following," Jillian said.

"Pixelation. It is the fine grain of the photograph. Any time there's editing done, there is usually a trace of rough edges around the image. Look here." Kate zoomed in on her Martin Luther King photograph where fine wisps like a ghost veil outlined where people existed in the shot before she cut them out.

Jillian recalled the photo of her and Mattson together, but never looked at it with this kind of detail in mind. She saw it at face value, as would everyone else. She cursed herself for destroying the photo.

Kate worked for another twenty minutes changing history when she glanced at her watch. She shut down her computer and stowed away her belongings in the backpack. She extended her hand to Jillian. "Nice to talk with you."

Jillian shook Kate's hand and thought of one more thing.

"If someone changes a photograph, what happens to the original?"

"Most programs, like the one I use, PhotoPlus, save the original in a separate file. You can delete the original, but why would you?"

To frame me for Mattson's murder. "Yeah, why would you?"

Jillian needed to tell someone, a person who would understand, and more importantly, someone she could trust. In spite of David Paulson's many flaws, including his belief she murdered Jonathon Mattson, he always protected the company. Whatever was happening to her was certainly not in the company's best interest. He would recognize the drubbing Dynalife faced and help her sort this out if only to save the value of his stock portfolio. Jillian plucked her cellphone from her purse and dialed.

"Paulson."

"David, it's me."

After a pause, "Jillian? Where the hell are you? The police are been swarming the offices bleeding us for information about you. You need to turn yourself in."

"I didn't do anything, David. Please believe me."

"Not according to the police, Jilly."

"I can prove it. I think I can, with your help I can prove I wasn't involved in Jonathon's death. I'm being set up. Bosphizion is out."

"What proof?" David's voice turned cold.

"Bosphizion is out in public and being sold."

"Jilly, the Board hasn't approved distribution, not to mention the FDA hasn't blessed our request to start drug trials, let alone approve the product for sale. We covered this topic in your Friday blowout with Jonathon."

"I saw it. I saw a bottle of Bosphizion. A parolee had it. But, it was different; there was a black and white label on it."

Silence from his end of the conversation.

"David, did you hear me?"

"Do you have it?" he said.

"No, I..."

"Where is it? We need to control—find out what it is you think you saw."

"I don't have it."

"Come meet with me, and we can work this out, Jilly."

"I can't. I'm scared."

"Come to Dynalife, the cops will be gone."

Jillian gripped the phone tight, the fear threatening to crush the phone. "What time?"

"Now."

She thought his tone carried a demanding edginess, and it didn't sit well after being pursued and assaulted. "I need to take care of something. I'll meet with you in the morning at the office before the place gets busy."

"Jilly, I need you to be careful and not tell anyone what you saw."

"Is that for me, or for the company's protection?"

David disconnected the call.

"You son of a bitch," she said, catching a few glances in her direction.

She needed tangible proof for her meeting with David. Without evidence, no one would believe her. The bottle with the odd black and white Dynalife label was gone. She'd ripped up the photo of Mattson and her, leaving her no way to examine it for shadows and pixelation like Kate described. A spark of salvation lit as Jillian recalled Kate explaining the original photo would exist in another file.

Jillian tapped a web browser app on her phone and retrieved two addresses. The first was Carson Arts Photography and the second was for a Parole Outpatient Clinic in the city where HIV patients, like the man on the train, could refill their prescriptions.

The phone felt hot against her palm. Initially, she chalked it up to the day's dose of warranted paranoia. Then her phone suddenly froze and the screen turned black, with a message claiming the phone was reported lost, followed by a phone number. Someone was tracking her phone. The police wouldn't use a find my phone app, but the greasy doorman might.

Jillian turned off the phone, pulled the SIM card, snapped it in half, and tossed the bits into a trashcan on the way out of the coffee shop. She wasn't going to risk waiting around to find out who was on her trail. The police, or the man who attacked her on the train platform—Jillian didn't know which one to fear most.

Chapter Fourteen

I f there was one bottle, she could find another. Parole Outpatient Clinics handed out mood stabilizers, antipsychotics, tranquilizers, and a rainbow-hued menu of psychotropic meds like Skittles. A sizable chunk of the pharmaceuticals ended up on the street, sold for pea-sized crack rocks. Self-medication muzzled the demons. The psychiatrists at the clinic didn't dabble in the medical end of the pharmacy pool and stuck to the gray world of mental illness. Parolees with medical conditions, HIV, and others, were siphoned off to crowded emergency rooms where those on public assistance competed for attention. Why then, Jillian wondered, was a parolee coming here to fill HIV prescriptions?

Jillian once submitted a bid for pharmacy contract services with the regional clinic, only to find a convoluted chain of procurement, questionable inventory controls, and expired medications. She pulled the bid after a media dust-up behind sex offenders getting erectile dysfunction drugs to "help out" their self-esteem hit the front page. The public was blissfully ignorant of the flow of felons, in and out of the clinic off of Mission, adjacent to one of the San Francisco Parole Units.

A streetwise knot of parolees gathered on the sidewalk outside the clinic; more than a handful twitched with tremors and drug-addled shuffles reacting to the unseen voices. The prison system had become the public depository for broken people, and the human evidence stained this section of pavement.

Jillian navigated through the maze of societal castaways and ducked behind two men pushing inside a busy waiting room. The noise level wasn't the leftover buzz from the prison yard, as she'd experienced on the train. Here, in this medicated place, the voices screamed on the inside. The lobby was silent enough to hear the phlegm-strangled breath of a man to her left. It was unnaturally silent for the number of bodies packed into the waiting room.

One of the two men she followed peeled off and collapsed in a dingy plastic chair, while the other approached a glass-fronted counter. He waited for a slight, black woman to hang up the phone and she didn't look like she was in any hurry. The man leaned to one side and grabbed his stomach, a painful grimace set on his face. He knocked on the glass partition and the woman put her hand up, palm out, in the universal symbol, wait.

A moment later, she hung up and addressed the man, not looking at him, but at her computer monitor.

"Name and number?" she asked.

The man responded, but Jillian couldn't hear, so she inched closer.

"Agent's name?"

"Grove," he said.

"Doctor?"

"I don't know. I'm supposed to pick up a refill of my meds. The doc at the prison told me to come here. I'm out of what they gave me."

She tapped a few keystrokes. "I don't find a prescription on file for you. Do you have the meds with you?"

"I said I was out. I took the last one yesterday. All I have is this." He withdrew a bottle from his pants pocket and passed it to the attendant. She raised her reading glasses from the limp chain around her neck bringing the prescription label into focus.

Jillian didn't need glasses to identify the strange black and white Dynalife label, visible from where she stood.

She jumped ahead and tried to snatch the bottle, but the attendant was wise to parolees who came to the clinic to steal prescriptions. The woman's icy expression forecast an ill temper, now directed at Jillian.

Jillian backed away as the woman picked up her phone. Jillian overheard the woman say, "Got another grabby one."

She couldn't risk waiting around for security, the police, or responding parole agents, so Jillian left the clinic and trotted across the street.

Jillian waited at the corner and watched. No one followed her, satisfied the problem was out of the premises. She waited until the man who demanded his prescription refill parted the door and stepped into the sunlight.

She followed him for a block and a half before Jillian crossed the street. Within a few strides, she pulled behind him.

"Excuse me," Jillian said.

The man kept shuffling ahead.

She tapped him on the shoulder. "Excuse me."

He whipped around, recoiling from her touch. His arms raised up in a defensive posture. This man was used to physical confrontation and ending up on the losing end.

Jillian stepped back, putting some space between her and the anxious man. She put her hands up and said, "I'm sorry, I didn't mean to scare you."

"What do you want?"

"You had a prescription bottle in the clinic. Can I see it?"

It was the man's turn to stutter back a step. He wanted to run, but he was in no condition to outrun anyone. "It's mine's, get your own."

"It's important. I need to see it. I promise I won't try and steal it."

The man searched Jillian's face and shrugged. He dug into his pocket for the medication. It wasn't in the black and white Dynalife bottle, or any bottle. The man held a small rectangular paper envelope, the side swelling from the refilled prescription.

Jillian's eye shot to the printed label affixed to the envelope. Bosphizion.

Jillian leaned in, studying the label, causing the man to shove the envelope in his pocket. "Hustle your own, for whatever good it'll do you."

"But..."

The man turned away, crossed the street against traffic, his way of ending the conversation.

The man was right about one thing. She needed to hustle her own.

Chapter Fifteen

J illian found the Carson Arts Photography shop, but the small business was closed. She tugged on the locked storefront, hoping to rouse someone from the back room. No response came from rattling the iron security gate. She backed away from the storefront and took a position at the mouth of an alley a half block away. On the street, shopkeepers tended displays and greeted customers. These buildings, on the edge of the Tenderloin District, started as single-room occupancy hotels and apartments. Over time, they morphed to match the population. Three buildings bore scars of the economy, boarded-up and vacant. A methadone clinic operated out of one storefront, a small mom and pop liquor store held the prime location on the corner, and wedged between two vacant storefronts was a combined photography and copy shop. Carson Arts Photography—the establishment printed on the back of the photo where Jillian looked so intimate with Jonathon Mattson.

A man in a blue polo shirt and surfer shorts paused at the door, and Jillian stepped out from the safe confines of the alley. Exposed and out in the open, Jillian ignored her inner alarm bells and approached the man from behind. He saw Jillian's reflection in the store window behind him and dropped his white Starbucks coffee cup on the sidewalk.

"Jesus lady, I keep telling you people I don't do handouts. Go hit up the folks at the clinic," the man said while he picked up the coffee-soaked *Chronicle*. His blue shirt bore a wet coffee stain above the Carson Arts Photography logo, and a few drops managed to drip from his nametag, which read, Brad.

You people? The words nearly escaped from her lips, but she caught her reflection in the window and silenced herself. A half-day on the run and she looked every bit like the leftover bits of society who wandered the streets.

Brad fumbled with his keys and unlocked the door to the shop, flipped a small orange neon "open" sign, and tossed his soggy newspaper into a trash basket.

Jillian followed him into the shop, mindful her appearance was going to make it difficult, she kept her distance and held back by the door.

"I told you, get out," Brad said.

"I need your help," Jillian said.

"No."

"Please–it's about a photograph."

Brad eyed her with suspicion and looked out the door for others who waited to rush in and steal the shop's cameras and digital memory cards while this woman distracted him with some crap about a photo.

"Let's see it," he said.

"I don't have it."

"I don't know what you're trying to pull..."

"I remember a number—a number from the back of a photo from this photography studio."

"Studio? We ain't much of a studio." Brad paced the circumference of the small store, turned on a half-dozen backlit displays with LED lights, and warmed two large digital copy machines. His initial apprehension level waned, but he kept Jillian in view while he prepared the shop for business after his coffee break. He powered up a computer terminal behind the sales counter. "Don't get any ideas. There's cameras in the place." He flicked a switch under the counter, and a twenty-three-inch flat-screen monitor blossomed with light.

Jillian's sleep-deprived, disheveled likeness appeared in four quadrants of the screen, each taken from a different angle within the store. She located a small black plastic dome on the ceiling directly over the cash register and from there quickly found the three others based on the point of view projected on the monitor.

"Don't worry about me. I'm not going to cause you any trouble. I'm only here to find out about a photo." Jillian eased closer to the counter and needed Brad to trust her if she hoped to unravel the truth behind the photograph.

"You said you have a number?"

"Yes. The photo I'm looking for had your business name and the number 8749 on the back. Does the number mean anything to you?" Jillian said.

Brad stepped to a computer keyboard on the counter. A flat rubber keyboard gave off no clicks or clacks as Brad tapped on the pad. "Could be–yeah, here it is. 8749—huh, been a popular item. Someone ordered six prints of the photograph."

Jillian's throat tightened. She'd seen three of the photos, which meant at least three more were out there, somewhere. Without realizing she'd moved, Jillian pressed against the counter. "Can you show me the photo?"

"You got ten bucks?"

Jillian dug in her purse, which looked less designer and more dumpster-diver from the scratches and grime ground into the soft leather. She pulled out a crumpled twenty-dollar bill, her last. She straightened and smoothed the wrinkles out of the bill and handed it to Brad.

He took the twenty, laid two fives in change on the counter, and printed out a small paper order form. "Fill in the top section."

Jillian grabbed a pen from a coffee cup with a camera logo and filled in the spaces on the form with name, address, and contact information. She paused and mulled over whether to use her real name. Then she glanced at the bottom portion of the form. The item number was as she expected 8749. The caption floored her. It read Jonathon and Shelly Mattson at the Botanical Garden Society Fundraiser.

"Are you sure you got the number right? Jillian asked.

Brad glanced at the screen. "8749, right?"

"Yeah." Jillian paused, "Who ordered the six prints?"

Jillian tried to appear calm and uninterested but combined with her scruffy appearance she appeared more like a junkie on the nod. She avoided looking at Brad because she feared she'd lose her nerve. The order form completed, Jillian slid it across the counter.

At the rubber keyboard, Brad tapped in the order history for the photograph. "Six copies were ordered last week. Kinda odd."

"Why's that?" Jillian said.

"The photograph was taken six months ago, and not a single order until last week."

Brad scooped up the order form and hit the print command on the keyboard mat. A few steps away, one of the large digital printers whirred to life. Within seconds, a glossy printed photo dropped into a tray secured below the printer. He slid the print into an envelope with a Carson Arts logo and handed it to Jillian.

"All six copies were ordered and picked up last week. No name listed, customer paid cash," Brad said.

Jillian pulled the photo partially from the envelope, still warm from the printer. Jonathon Mattson's head peeked out along with another face. It wasn't Shelly Mattson. Jillian's own face stared back.

"Did you take this photograph?"

"Me?" Brad said. "Hell, no. All's I do is print 'em and sell 'em."

"Then who shot this?" Jillian said, shaking the envelope in the air between them.

Brad tapped the keys on the rubber keyboard and pulled up the information on photograph number 8749. He swiveled the computer monitor toward Jillian.

"Linda Vanney. She's a freelancer. We take requests for coverage at some event or another, and we send out a freelance photographer."

"Who asked for her?"

"Says we got a call from the Botanical Garden Society," Brad said and tapped the spot on the monitor.

"How does it work? Someone gets in touch with you, and then you pick a photographer. How'd you choose her?"

"It was her turn in the rotation, most likely. We keep a list of freelancers and move down the list as we pull in new assignments. Some won't work weddings, others refuse to work with certain clients because of a bad experience, or they aren't 'green' enough. Really, I don't give a shit. I need someone to show up."

"Linda dropped off the negatives after the Botanical Garden fundraiser?" Jillian said.

"Negatives? Nobody uses film anymore. Everything is digital. The photos are e-mailed in to us, and like I said, all I do is print 'em and sell 'em."

"But this is what your photographer sent you?" Jillian said.

"Yeah, why? You got a problem with what Linda sent in?" Brad reached for the envelope, and Jillian pulled it away.

"How can I get in touch with the photographer?"

"Why, you the event planner at the methadone clinic?" Brad's demeanor snapped to a darker place.

Jillian knew she'd run this as far as she could. Either the questions about the photographer fell on deaf ears, or Brad realized Jillian wasn't going to purchase a second photo. The result was the same; she wasn't getting any more information from him. She tucked the photo envelope into her purse and turned toward the door.

"Never mind. Thanks," she said.

Brad watched as Jillian left the store. Instead of heading up the street, she held back, near the entrance and watched Brad hold the ten dollars in change she'd forgotten, surprised a street person would leave money behind. Uneasiness washed over his face. Brad tapped out a print command on the rubber keyboard, his fingers hammered out the keystrokes.

The printer whirred once more and spat out a copy of the image he sold minutes earlier. Brad grabbed the photo, and he must've recognized Jillian.

He pulled a cell phone from his pants pocket and hit a number stored on the phone's speed dial list. He squinted at the photo while he waited until someone picked up.

Jillian overheard "Hey, I was told to call this number if someone came in asking about your photo."

Chapter Sixteen

She found a name, an unfamiliar name, on the blank canvas of her faulty memory. She wasn't sure how the photographer and six purchased copies of the photo came together, but Linda Vanney was an edge piece of a jigsaw puzzle linking Jillian to Jonathon Mattson's murder.

Fifteen minutes after she committed the name to memory, Jillian perched at one of the three hundred computer terminals at the San Francisco Public Library in the Civic Center. As soon as her butt hit the chair, she wrote the name down on discarded notepaper, left behind at the terminal. She remembered the name now, but Jillian feared it would evaporate in the thin lace of her short-term memory. A mix of college students, moms with their kids, and street people were scattered throughout the expansive atrium. Jillian's appearance at one of the computers drew no more attention than any other homeless person who sought shelter from the cold.

Energized with a burst of adrenaline, Jillian typed Linda Vanney's name into a Google search page and pressed enter. Seventeen Linda Vanney hits returned and displayed on the computer screen. Jillian clicked on the links, one-by-one, until she pulled up Linda Vanney Photography on the eighth try. The website featured a picture of Linda in the upper right corner. The woman was twenty, to twenty-five years old, red hair, light complexion with blue eyes. If Linda tried to pull off a Julianne Moore look, she'd nailed it. Cute and memorable, but Jillian was certain she hadn't met this woman before.

"Who are you?" Jillian said to the screen.

Linda Vanney's website displayed examples of her work captured during portrait sessions, weddings, anniversaries, and corporate events. Jillian clicked on a menu of services available, and she scrolled down and drew a sharp breath. One of the services provided was "digital enhancement," where long-deceased family members could be inserted in a family portrait, or a serviceman on deployment in Afghanistan could be shown bedside at the birth of their child.

Jillian jotted down the phone number and address listed on Linda's website. She peeled back another layer of her missing memories. The photographer could tell her who paid her to change the photo and place Jillian in the frame.

Jillian closed the web browser and grabbed the note with Linda Vanney's contact information. The address was in Hayes Valley, an enclave of resale shops, cafes, and art galleries, between Gough and Fillmore Streets. She tucked the note into her back pocket and made for a restroom near the exit.

She leaned on the sink with stiffened arms. Someone was doing this to her. Why destroy her? Why? Her hands turned into tight, white-knuckled balls and pounded on the tile. She'd been used, framed for Mattson's death, and tossed out–yesterday's trash. Frustrating, but it meant she wasn't losing her grip on reality. They'd planted a fast-growing seed of fear in her faulty brain, and they counted on the roots choking her to death. Perhaps, urging her to follow her mother's example and end the pain.

Jillian grabbed the confession note and the address she'd written minutes ago from her pocket, spreading them on the counter. She rubbed a thumb over the confession she'd written, with the slim hope it would vanish on its own accord. Her handwriting remained, damning and absolute. The two separate scraps of paper were of the same hand, Jillian's unique slanted script. The address bore equally spaced letters under a hard pressure, which always indented the page. Jillian noted the confession note's letters were crammed tighter together and lighter on the page. Hurried, forced, or coerced, perhaps, yet written by her. There was no argument on her authorship, only how it was done and under what circumstances. She balled up both slips of paper and shoved them deep into her pocket.

Jillian sensed a shift. She'd felt the black and white labeled Dynalife bottle in her hand, she held a copy of the "enhanced" photo to prove it was digitally altered, and she knew who shot the original photograph. Combined, they proved, to her at least, she wasn't insane. She was done with avoiding, running, and hiding.

Jillian left the library and hit the sidewalk, scanning over her shoulder for someone following. It felt good to press for answers, but a healthy dose of paranoia couldn't hurt. Within an hour, from the public library, Jillian found the address listed for Linda Vanney's photography operation. It wasn't in one of the storefronts filled with handmade jewelry or splashes of acrylic paint that passed for art. Instead, Jillian stood on the curb in front of a green, and grey-trimmed Victorian residence.

The two-story structure, once an expansive home, was sectioned off into three apartments, two on the first floor and one upstairs. Jillian fished the note from her pocket, and the address for Linda Vanney's business was the space on the upper floor. A narrow staircase, installed after the apartment conversion, led to a small deck serving as an entrance to the office. Jillian paused at the first tread. What she needed to know was up there. Linda Vanney changed the original photo, and she could tell Jillian who paid her—who was responsible for Jillian's life coming undone.

The treads creaked under Jillian's footfall as she made her way up. The front door was ajar, and through the leaded glass inlay, the shadow of a person passed within the apartment. Jillian inched toward the crack in the doorway, remaining out of sight as she approached. Someone ruffled through file drawers and papers. A drawer slammed closed and another opened. The contents splashed onto the floor. Jillian edged closer to the narrow opening in the door and couldn't see who ransacked the apartment. With her fingertips, she touched the door and gently pushed the door until the intruder came into view. The unexpected cry of rusted hinges startled both Jillian and a smallish, puffy-faced woman.

"What do you want?" the woman said. She pushed a shock of grey hair out of her face.

Jillian stood in the doorway, no way to go but onward. "I'm looking for Linda Vanney."

"She's not here."

"When is she coming back?"

The woman looked hard at Jillian and then glanced back to the boxes at her feet. "Never. She died five days ago."

"What–what happened?" Jillian stammered.

"You don't look like one of Linda's friends."

Jillian stepped inside where boxes lay strewn on the apartment floor, hand-printed lettering on the cardboard cataloged the dead woman's possessions. In a hallway beyond the main space, a stack of boxes held clothes, bathroom items, towels, and sheets, according to the labels they bore.

"I'm Jillian," she said ending the awkward silence between the two women.

In spite of Jillian's appearance, the older woman was satisfied with the response. She seemed distracted and detached as she placed a bundle of papers into an open cardboard box. She wiped her hands on the front of her jeans and extended a hand. "Mary Vanney. Linda's mom. Nice to meet you. I didn't meet any of Linda's friends after she moved here."

"I'm so sorry. I didn't know–how did it happen?" Jillian said. She didn't dispel the mother's impression that Jillian was here as a friend. The grieving mother seemed grateful to talk to someone about her daughter.

Mary Vanney looked down at an empty box, tapped at it with a shoe. "I can't understand it. Linda goes out every morning, walks to Cup of Soul Coffee, and reads the newspaper. She's always careful, you know?"

Jillian nodded.

"She never even saw it. I guess it means Linda wasn't afraid before she—she died. The police say it was instant when the car hit her. She didn't suffer."

"What?" Jillian said.

Mary pulled a ragged hunk of tissue from beneath a sweater sleeve and dabbed her eyes. "It doesn't make any sense. A car jumped the curb, ran down Linda from behind. Then the driver stopped, got out, grabbed Linda's backpack, and left her in the gutter. Why would someone be so cold?"

A chill ran through Jillian's core. *To keep me from talking to her.* The bastards behind driving Jillian insane raised the ante. They were willing to kill someone to keep secrets.

Jillian noticed a spread of black and white photographs, framed and mounted, above a large IKEA worktable. Lights, two bulky photo printers, a docking station for a laptop computer, and an external hard drive back up took up much of the open space. The mounted photographs pulled Jillian's attention. Four black and white prints of Paris, Rome, Barcelona, and Prague, each taken at night; the effect was stark, yet elegant.

"Did Linda take these? They're breathtaking. She must have enjoyed the travel."

Mary stiffened slightly. "You didn't know my daughter very well, did you?"

Jillian turned, and one look at the dead woman's mother told her she deserved the truth. "Actually, I wanted to speak with Linda about a photograph she took. How did you know?"

"Linda hated to travel and even the thought of boarding a plane terrified her. Anyone who met her would know." Mary gestured at the photos, "Those were her dream vacations, for the day she got over her phobias. And you don't exactly look like someone she'd hang with."

Silence echoed the unfulfilled life of the young photographer. After a moment, Mary shuffled back to the open cardboard box, stuffed the contents of a file cabinet inside, and sealed another part of her daughter's life shut.

"Do you have anyone to help you?" Jillian said.

"I need to keep busy, or I think I'll go crazy. I don't understand why my girl died. Why her? The police said it looked deliberate like someone targeted her." Dappled sunlight, filtered by Linda's linen curtains, kept a mother's grief partially concealed, but the unexplained loss was clear in her voice, a voice worn from asking for a reason.

The mention of police involvement set off a spark deep within Jillian's nervous system. She expected the photographer's death would be under investigation, but somehow the thought of police involvement gave her a chill.

"Who would deliberately hurt your daughter?" Jillian asked.

"You sound like one of the cops," Mary said as she worked to assemble another cardboard box.

Jillian helped fold the box and held it while Mary taped it together.

"I don't know. Truth is, Linda didn't share too much of her personal life with me. I don't know if she had a boyfriend or anyone she was serious about. Other than her photography, the only other thing she did was work a part-time job at the Chronicle. Linda wanted to be a photojournalist and hoped the editorial assistant job would get her work noticed."

"Linda had a keen eye," Jillian said as she thumbed through a folder of photographs before she filed it away into another cardboard box. A label on the folder identified the contents as White-Hillson wedding, followed by a six-digit number, 052315. The photographs featured a young couple in the traditional bride and groom poses.

"A shame the Chronicle didn't believe in her. Linda told me they only let her touch up photographs; she never got to take any of her own. But, it paid the bills."

Jillian placed a thick bundle of similarly labeled folders into another box. As the manila folders settled to the bottom, one propped open and exposed a familiar face. Jonathon Mattson's face, but it was not the photo she purchased at Carson Arts Photography. This one caught Mattson behind a podium. Jillian recalled the occasion, a World AIDS Symposium where Mattson delivered a keynote address, which Jillian prepared for him. After the speech, Mattson leveraged grant funding from two private foundations for continued research and development of Bosphizion. Jillian thumbed through the photos in the file. There were dozens of him at the event, and several taken more recently. The collection did not include the photo Jillian wanted.

A disconcerting thought occurred to Jillian. "Why would the person who ran down Linda take her backpack?"

"Probably thought it was her purse and grabbed it hoping Linda carried cash around with her. Damn drug addict looking for a score, most likely." Mary pointed over to the small dining table in the corner of the kitchen. "She didn't take her purse. I guess they'll pawn off her laptop computer for a quick buck."

Linda Vanney died because of what she knew. Her laptop held the evidence. Jillian fished the copy of the photograph from her purse, pulled it from the envelope, and held it out to Mary. "Linda took this. Does it look familiar?"

Mary tipped her face toward the image of Mattson and Jillian together and then lifted her eyes to Jillian. A furrow creased her brow and wariness colored her voice. "How do you know my Linda took this?"

"Brad, down at Carson Arts told me."

"When was it taken?" Mary asked as she handed the photo back.

"I don't know," Jillian said.

Mary shot a wary glance at Jillian.

"I think Linda edited the picture. I—I wasn't there," Jillian continued.

Mary strode to a tall dented metal file cabinet. Apparently, Linda tried to reclaim the discarded steel office piece and applied a thick coat of bright yellow paint. The attempt at redemption only highlighted the dents. Jillian knew what it felt like to be tossed out on the trash pile.

Jillian held the photograph under a bright desk lamp and looked for the telltale signs of pixelization and shadowing Kate told her about. Linda Vanney was good. There was nothing that jumped out and screamed fake.

"The Botanical Garden Society holds two fundraising events a year, one in the spring and the big one in the fall." Mary pulled open the top drawer, and it released with a shriek from broken drawer guides. Her fingers walked across the labeled tabs on the folders until she found two files, one listed as, Bot. Gar. Soc. 100520, and one with Bot. Gar. Soc. 032220. Mary pulled the files and laid them on a worktable near Linda's desk.

"This one is the fall fundraiser back on October Fifth, " Mary said.

Jillian recognized the number system on Linda's files referred to the date she snapped the photos. The October file was an inch thick, and Linda painstakingly listed each photo by name and number on a sheet attached to the inside cover of the folder. Jillian ran her finger down the list and stopped on photo number 8749. Linda referred to the photo as Mr. and Mrs. Jonathon Mattson, the same way Brad at the photoshop pulled it up on his computer.

The photos lay, numerically sorted, and began with 8700. Each photo was in its designated place, with the exception of 8749. It was missing. The one Jillian needed wasn't there.

Jillian slumped into a desk chair, her search blocked. Every avenue she uncovered twisted into a bottlenecked dead end, the noose gathering tighter and tighter, with nowhere to turn.

"Shit!" Jillian slammed the file down on the worktable surface, the contents spilled onto the table and floor.

Mary dropped to her knees and gathered the photos from across the scuffed wooden floor. "I don't know what your problem is, but you need to leave."

Jillian watched a mother retrieve a lost daughter's possessions as if they contained a spark of her soul, some essence she could hold onto. "I'm sorry, Mrs. Vanney. Linda was killed for something she saw."

From her knees, Mary turned toward Jillian. The mother's face bore the creases and furrows of exhaustion mixed with confusion. "You need to leave."

Jillian rose from the chair and couldn't think of any consolation capable of erasing the pain caused by the loss of a child. She watched Mary gently sort each of the photographs into a neat straight-edged pile.

Jillian needed concrete evidence she wasn't connected to Mattson's murder and each time she came close, the proof evaporated. The prescription bottle at the bus station hustled away by the scar-faced thug, the missing original photo, the photographer's stolen laptop, and the sudden death of the photographer herself, systematically removed in a calculated fashion. Stitching the bits together revealed a dark hand at play. The noose pulled slowly at first until the trap was set; now it was suffocating.

A bolt of recognition hit Jillian. How did she miss the signs? They, whoever *they* were, were ahead of her at every step. They expected the photo might lead her to Linda Vanney. The photographer was killed to stop Jillian from unraveling their plans. The hairs on her arms tingled with the realization she acted like a pigeon to their breadcrumbs. They wanted her here.

Jillian pulled Mary by the shoulders from the floor.

"We have to get out of here," Jillian said.

"Let go of me," Mary said and jerked away from Jillian's grasp.

"We need to leave now. The people who killed Linda are coming."

Mary backed against a bookcase away from Jillian. "Get away from me. I'm calling the police." Mary reached for a phone on the desk.

Jillian snatched the phone out of Mary's grasp and threw it across the small apartment. Mary recoiled from the crack of the plastic phone against the wall.

Mary grabbed a computer cable from the workstation and cracked it toward Jillian. Attached to one end was the external hard drive Linda kept next to her computer docking station. The hard drive flew off the cable and thudded on the floor at Jillian's feet. Mary whipped the cable in the air between them and caught Jillian on the arm, raising a long angry red welt from her wrist to her elbow.

"Get out of here!"

"You need to leave too," Jillian said as the end of the cable snapped inches from her face.

Crouching while she kept her distance from the sting of the cable, Jillian picked up the compact external hard drive and backed toward the door.

"Put that down. It doesn't belong to you," Mary said, punctuated with the whistle of the cable as it cut through the air.

Mary snapped the cable at Jillian, and the wire opened a gash on the back of her hand. The pain made Jillian wince, and her hand opened on reflex, sending the hard drive clattering to the floor. Mary charged again.

Jillian grabbed the hard drive, tucked it into her waistband, and ran for the door. She tripped on the landing but regained her balance slamming her hip into the stair railing. She nearly pitched off the landing onto the concrete patio below if not for the sturdy wooden post. She dashed down the stairs, and her hip ached with each step.

A block away Jillian turned a corner, paused, and looked back at the converted house. Mary Vanney dashed to the bottom landing and searched for the direction Jillian fled in her escape. Jillian watched the woman trot to the front door of the home next door.

Jillian knew Mrs. Vanney was calling the police and soon the area would swarm with cops looking for her. Jillian passed the coffee shop where Linda Vanney died. A scream drew her attention, and she glanced over her shoulder. Frantic people gathered near the stairs leading to the Vanney apartment.

A dark tendril of smoke wafted from the open front door at Linda's office. Through the windows, Jillian saw orange and red flames lick at the linen curtains. The smoke grew darker as it consumed the contents of the photography studio. A shadow emerged from the flame-tipped doorway. Jillian started running toward the house. Mrs. Vanney needed help. Halfway there Jillian stopped in mid-stride. The shadowed figure wasn't Mary Vanney, it was the man who threatened her at the train station.

The crowd watched the old timbers ignite and waited for the fire trucks to deal with the inferno. As they gawked at the destruction, the man slipped from the building's landing and blended with the crowd. Jillian lost sight of him until he bobbed above the crowd, searching. She patted at the hard drive jammed in her waistband and headed away as the first fire engines roared up to the building.

Her tormentors anticipated Jillian's every move, calculated to make her appear guilty. However, they hadn't counted on Jillian getting her hands on the photographer's hard drive. The secrets behind the original photo of Jonathon Mattson were tucked away inside a digital file. It was a risky move, stealing the hard drive, but Jillian felt there was little choice to keep the fragment of evidence to prove she wasn't a murderer. It was a bet which she'd pay with her life. If the evidence wasn't in the drive, she was as good as dead.

Chapter Seventeen

Jillian cut through the crowd gathering to watch a small slice of the world burn. She craned her neck for a glimpse of the scar-faced creep. The man was relentless, everywhere she turned, there he was. Dumping her phone, she hoped to become a more elusive prey. She used the throng of a curious crowd to cover her retreat and put some distance between her and the burning building.

When the last rays of evening light retreated for the marine layer, Jillian's skin felt the cool damp air while the fog dampened the sound around her. It made her feel isolated and alone, a foreshadowing of the night-long vigil awaiting her. Her apartment was off-limits. She harbored no doubt Inspector DiManno kept the place under close watch. She smiled at the thought of her neighbor, Mrs. Tillman, pressed against the peephole, phone in hand ready to call DiManno the second she spotted Jillian.

With nowhere to hide, Jillian roamed the city streets until she found the encampments and makeshift homeless cardboard condos dotting the sidewalks in the area. She parked on an empty patch of concrete and blended in among them, one more anonymous victim of circumstance. Two black and white police cruisers passed during the night. The first police sighting nearly made her bolt into the street until she realized the police weren't interested in the clusters of homeless unless the street-dwellers got out of hand; drunk, high, or violent.

Without a word spoken, nightfall created a shift in activity on the sidewalks and alleyways. Life retreated from the streets as scores of homeless wriggled into their cocoons of cardboard, tarps, and blankets. Most silently carried out their rituals, unpacked their belongings, recounted and resorted them into shopping carts and bags. One man sat on his haunches; a small trail of tears stained his grime-crusted face. Once more, his plea to God to die in his sleep delivered to the heavens.

After a few hours hiding in shadows and dark streets, Jillian moved to a gathering of homeless people she spotted along a stretch of Golden Gate Avenue. While others wandered throughout the night, this place was for sleeping. Makeshift bedrolls, made of discarded blankets no longer holding their original color, sleeping bags, and cardboard comforters dotted the sidewalks. Two men stood watch, discouraging others from preying on those who sought out a few hours of respite.

Jillian's instinct told her to keep moving, but a mix of pain, fear, and frustration welled within, and there was nowhere to turn, no one to trust, and no place to disappear. The homeless encampment offered an opportunity to hide in plain sight. After all, who really looked at the face of a homeless person?

The bearded man, who served as a sentry, blocked her path as she got close to the sleeping area.

"Move on," he said.

He stepped in Jillian's way a second time and barred her from moving forward.

"Please, I only want to rest," Jillian said.

The sentry eyed Jillian for a moment; his gaze paused on the oversized UCSF sweatshirt she wore. "You wanna give up the sweatshirt?" he said.

"My sweatshirt?"

"Nothing's free, sugar."

She exchanged the sweatshirt for a barren square of concrete sidewalk. Clad in a thin t-shirt, the wall behind her retained a small bit of warmth collected during the daylight hours. Her body soaked up the heat as if she were on a remote Caribbean beach, a beach reeking of human waste and urine. Under different circumstances, Jillian would avoid eye contact with these people, or crossed the street to skirt around the social unpleasantness of the encampment. Now she hoped everyone did–pretend the wretched human refuse didn't exist.

Jillian found the place sheltered from the dampness by the buildings to the north and the slight rise in elevation pooled the cooler air down the hill toward the Embarcadero. The selection of a sheltered location and the way this group posted sentries, meant they knew what they were doing, and the goal was simple—survival. Nothing else mattered.

For a moment, she forgot about the photographer's hard drive tucked in her waistband, the police detective, and her scar-faced pursuer, and slipped into a light sleep. She stirred as two of the sentries argued over Barry Bonds and if his homerun record was juiced or not. No one else in her pack of sleepers seemed to care. Jillian dozed, and within a few hours, the last ember of warmth from the concrete wall dissipated, turning the surface as frigid as the night air. Someone slipped a few scraps of cardboard next to her while she slept. She placed one behind her back, between her thin shirt and the building surface, and saw others wrapped their legs with blankets of cardboard pieces, so she did the same.

She could hide amongst the street people for a while. It wasn't much of an existence, but it was better than rotting away in some shitty prison cell. Her tormentors convinced everyone who mattered that she'd lost her mind and murdered Jonathon Mattson. Her anxiety settled in her chest. What would they do after they caught her? Kill her? Lock her away? Fear was no way to live. Jillian noticed her breath, rapid and shallow from the internal terrors nibbling at her mind. Her mother lived a fear-based existence and look how she died. Jillian was determined to break the cycle and needed someone who trusted her–believed in her. David Paulson didn't believe in her anymore. It was clear his priority was protecting his own ass. He was once her mentor and friend, a man she confided her hopes, fears, and dreams in. Jillian hoped she could nudge him back in her corner after their meeting in the morning. She'd convince him it was in his best interest. This was going to be the biggest sales presentation of her life.

Chapter Eighteen

At daybreak, the enclave of street sleepers broke camp and drifted in the general direction of the soup kitchens near St. Anthony's, dodging crack dealers along the path. Jillian left their ranks and headed East toward Union Square and the financial district. She caught the glances from a few business types on their way into the vast warren of corporate offices in the district. The curled lips, disapproving eyes, and wide paths cut around her made judgments clear without a single uttered word. She didn't belong here. A woman with her grimy t-shirt and nest of tousled hair would've put the old Jillian on edge. A social pariah—unclean, now an outsider in the only place she felt at home.

In front of the Dynalife building, four black and white San Francisco Police Department squad cars blocked the entrance to the parking garage. A crowd formed at a thin ribbon of yellow crime scene tape and onlookers craned their necks for a view into the open maw of the garage.

Jillian edged her way to the back of the crowd.

"What's happening?" Jillian said.

"Someone's been killed," a portly man next to her said. He didn't look away from the garage as he spoke.

"Who was it?" Jillian said. Her mouth dried as she spoke.

"I dunno. They ain't letting nobody in or out of the building," an older woman next to Jillian said. The woman's worn clothing and trash bag satchel marked her as another street survivor, like Jillian.

The spectators lined the crime tape with their cell phone cameras ready to capture some important detail or a salacious nugget. A red and white local television news van skidded to the curb behind the gathering. Bystanders turned to assure themselves they weren't about to be mowed down. The news van's doors flew open and a young reporter, impossibly thin, adjusted her dark hair in the side view mirror.

"Oh crap. Not her," a voice said a few feet away from Jillian.

A uniformed San Francisco Police Officer stood less than ten feet to Jillian's right. Jillian hadn't noticed him as he kept the crowd on the other side of the yellow tape. The officer's attention swept from the people in front of him to the news van.

"Tell Inspector DiManno the media showed up. And tell him it's Lopez from Channel Five," the officer said.

The mention of DiManno's name sent chills up Jillian's spine. She backed away from the front of the crowd and hid in the middle of the pack.

Jillian noticed the officer keyed a transmitter clipped near his shoulder when he spoke. An earpiece threaded from under his uniform shirt to his right ear, muffling his response.

Pia Lopez shouldered her five-two frame through the crowd and used her microphone like a polar icebreaker as she moved toward the tape. Pia lifted the tape and ducked under the barrier with her cameraman in tow.

"Whoa, whoa, whoa. Miss Lopez. Stop. You know you can't go in here," the officer said. He moved in the reporter's path blocking her access to the parking garage.

"Officer, the public has the right to know what's happening," Pia replied.

The cameraman positioned behind her, shouldered his camera, and pointed the lens at the officer.

"Behind the tape, please."

"Have you confirmed the identity of the dead man as another Dynalife executive?"

"I have no comment. You'll need to wait for the Public Information Officer. Now, stay behind the yellow tape."

Jillian's ears pricked up when the reporter claimed the victim was a Dynalife executive. She edged toward the tape, closer to where the officer held the reporter and her cameraman. The reporter reversed course and ducked under the tape, scowling at the sight of a competing news van pulling onto the scene.

"Will the PIO issue a statement soon?" Pia asked.

"You'll have to ask the PIO and Inspector DiManno."

"Tell DiManno I need to see him. I want an exclusive, and if he blows this for me, I'll make it miserable for him."

"I thought you guys were supposed to report the facts," the officer said.

"You think the Chief and the Mayor will like a story about the inept investigation into the deaths of corporate executives at a time the city is begging for new business investment? You can't even protect the business leaders we have, so what's the message to new investors? Not a warm and fuzzy picture, huh? Report the news? I make the news."

After the officer turned away from Pia, Jillian wormed her way closer to the reporter and tapped her on the shoulder.

"You know who was killed?" Jillian said.

Pia expected to see one of her adoring fans and her expression hardened because all she saw was the disheveled woman in jeans and a grimy T-shirt. "Of course I know." The reporter looked back to the mouth of the garage where a handful of police officials stirred.

"Who was it?" Jillian asked.

"You'll need to watch my report."

Pia nudged her cameraman and tipped her head toward the garage. The cameraman looked to the far right of the tape where the uniformed police officer chatted up an expensively dressed young businesswoman. The cameraman lifted the tape for Pia, they both shot under and trotted down the garage ramp.

The officer caught the movement out of the corner of his eye. "Goddammit! Back behind the tape." He ran to the garage entrance and tried for an angle on the cameraman, slowed under the weight of a camera and battery packs. Pia ran ahead unimpeded by her three-inch heels, which chattered off the cement ramp as she ran.

Pia stopped at the garage entrance only because two officers blocked her progress. Inspector DiManno appeared from the darkness of the garage with protective covers over his shoes and latex gloves on his hands. From Jillian's distance, she couldn't read DiManno's face, but his tight shoulders and stiff manner screamed he was not pleased with Pia Lopez and her pushy style at his crime scene.

DiManno ignored the reporter's questions, rolled the protective gloves off his hands, and tossed them into a biohazard bag next to the crime scene entrance. The protective booties followed.

As DiManno ambled up the ramp into the sunlight, he was unshaven and wore the same suit, now rumpled and creased.

"Do you have a suspect in the murder of yet another Dynalife executive?" Pia said with a microphone jammed inches from DiManno's face.

"Miss Lopez, please clear out of my crime scene," DiManno said.

"What can you tell us about the connection between the deaths of former Dynalife CEO Jonathon Mattson and the murder of interim CEO David Paulson?"

Jillian froze, her hands involuntarily clutched onto the yellow plastic crime scene tape.

DiManno's exhaustion turned to visible irritation. He stopped walking up the ramp and looked at the reporter. He spoke through a tight jaw, "We haven't released or confirmed the identity of the victim."

"My sources reveal David Paulson was stabbed to death in the parking garage of his building. How could a horrific attack happen in a secured building? Why did the San Francisco Police Department allow this brutal murder?"

"Miss Lopez, we have no comment for you. You know we don't comment on a matter under active investigation," DiManno said.

"What can you tell the citizens of the city about this apparent serial killer?"

"No one has mentioned a serial crime here, Miss Lopez."

"Are you saying the murders of Mattson and Paulson aren't connected?"

"I'm only saying the matter is under investigation at this time and we have no comment."

"Once again the San Francisco Police Department stands by and does nothing to stop a serial killer hunting in our city streets. The people of this city deserve better, Inspector."

Pia Lopez didn't wait for a response from DiManno and wheeled toward her cameraman for her money shot. "This reporter has learned one person is, in fact, responsible for the deaths of the two pharmaceutical executives." Pia pulled an eight-by-ten black and white glossy photo and held it for the camera.

"This is Jillian Cooper, a former Dynalife employee, named by sources as the jilted lover who murdered Jonathon Mattson. My sources characterize Cooper as shrewd, ruthless, and mentally unstable. She is reported to have sought out David Paulson and apparently killed him after he refused to help her evade capture."

The reporter removed Jillian's image from in front of the camera and glanced over at DiManno. "While our law enforcement agencies sit on their hands, we ask you, our viewers, to take action. Channel Five has received a donation of ten thousand dollars as a reward for information leading to the arrest of Jillian Cooper. Call Channel Five at the number shown on your screen at home, if you have any information relating to the whereabouts of this murderer. Don't approach Cooper directly; she is obviously dangerous. Please call the Channel Five hotline for assistance. A strike team of fugitive apprehension professionals stands ready to take Cooper into custody.

"This is Pia Lopez, Channel Five, live in the city, reporting for you."

Pia signaled her cameraman she was done with a circle drawn in the air with a finger.

"We're clear," the cameraman said as he unshouldered his equipment.

"Jesus, Lopez. That was reckless," DiManno said.

"You have your job to do, Mario, and I have mine."

"Bounty hunters? For Christ-sake, you're gonna get someone killed."

"Look around Inspector. People are getting killed, and you aren't doing anything about it. My sources will let me succeed where you and the entire San Francisco Police Department failed."

"Speaking of sources, where did you hear Paulson was the victim here and who put up the reward money?"

Lopez smiled and wagged a finger at the inspector. "I cannot divulge my sources, Inspector, you know better."

"You are obstructing a murder investigation."

Lopez extended her slender wrists together in front of her. "Then arrest me. That would be great for my ratings."

"If anyone gets hurt behind your nonsense, their blood will be on your hands," DiManno said before he turned and retreated into the garage bay.

"I could say the same to you, Inspector," Lopez called out after him.

The murmur of the crowd around Jillian grew stronger, fueled by the call for vigilantes from the reporter. Energy surged through the bystanders with the prospect of a quick buck.

Jillian held back the instinct to run. The feeding frenzy set off by Pia Lopez threatened to release the hounds if someone recognized her. The photo Lopez used came from her Dynalife identification card and the well-groomed woman broadcast across the city bore little comparison to Jillian's current disheveled state.

"I could use ten grand," one voice said.

"Me too. Wonder if it's dead or alive, like in the Old West?" another person said.

"I'd turn in my mother for ten thousand," a middle-aged man in a business suit next to Jillian said.

"Jesus, Gary, that's no way to talk about your mother," said a man with him, similarly dressed.

"You met my mother."

"I know. Once they meet her, you'd be lucky to negotiate for five hundred."

The two men laughed and strolled away from the garage, back to one of the office buildings nearby.

Jillian slipped away as the crowd evaporated and one word tucked in the last snippet of conversation struck a chord. Negotiate.

Chapter Nineteen

The Embarcadero, a bustling thoroughfare near the city's iconic Ferry Building, hosted a combination of moneyed tourists in the boutique shops, green-minded locals picking through organic produce at the farmer's market, and a collection of street performers. The blend of offbeat rhythms from plastic buckets repurposed as percussion instruments, wild guitar riffs, and whiskey-throated lyrics, wove a manic fabric without any real identity, like the performers themselves. Faceless, anonymous, background figures in a larger world.

Stunned by David Paulson's murder and the bounty announced by the Channel Five reporter, Jillian bumped and threaded her way through the crowds into the Ferry Building. She needed to hide from the scores of watchers on the street. The reward hit the airwaves only minutes ago, yet Jillian felt the psychic noose tighten. Which of the faces she passed would be the one to spot her and call in for their blood money? Jillian wondered what David Paulson did to earn his fate? He and Jonathon Mattson were in lockstep during last Friday's HIV drug marketing proposal, shutting Jillian down. On the surface, the reporter's bounty on her head appeared reasonable. The reporter cast her as a woman scorned, taking out anyone who stood in her way. In her fragile mind, Jillian couldn't explain where she was when Jonathon died, but she knew she wasn't accountable for David's murder. Someone wanted her in the crosshairs, and they were doing a dammed good job. She knew she was blamed for the murders, but she wanted to find out the "why" behind the setup. A whisp of a plan formed. And it was a risky one. If "they" wanted to find Jillian, fine.

Jillian scanned the crowds inside the Ferry Building and spotted what she needed in less than a minute. A small coffee shop inside the Ferry Building set aside seating for their patrons at a collection of black metal patio tables in the main corridor. A woman in a bright blue dress and matching heels placed her slim clutch purse on one of the tables, with her latest generation iPhone on top, while she waited for the barista to steam her latte.

"Catherine, non-fat caramel latte," the barista called.

The woman strode for the coffee bar, and Jillian passed the table, sliding the purse and phone off the tabletop, and kept moving to the street. Jillian glanced over her shoulder as she ducked out the door and caught the confused look on the face of the woman in blue, returning to her empty table.

Outside, Jillian pushed her way through the farmer's market with the stolen items clutched in hand. The theft triggered an unexpected rush. Exhilarated, scared, and surprised by the ease with which she added petty theft to her burgeoning criminal resume, Jillian kept moving until she found an isolated bench on a pier two blocks north of the Ferry Building.

Jillian shoved the iPhone under her thigh while she opened the slim Coach purse. A wallet with a California Driver's License said the woman in blue was Catherine Delio.

"Sorry Catherine," Jillian said and rummaged through the purse.

Catherine carried three credit cards and one hundred forty in cash. Jillian grabbed the cash, tucked it in her bra for safekeeping, and left the credit cards in the wallet. It wouldn't be long before Catherine reported the theft, canceled the cards and turned off service to the phone. There was little time to put her plan in motion.

Catherine was the trusting sort without password protection on her phone. Jillian used the phone's Internet browser and pulled up the Channel Five webpage. A few taps on the screen brought her to the "on-air personalities" link, then on to the bio page for Pia Lopez. Below the glamour shots of the reporter and her puffed-up history of "reporting action news as it unfolded," the station's hotline number displayed for her followers. Jillian tapped the screen, and the phone dialed the number.

On the third ring a male voice answered, "Five hotline, Gary speaking."

Jillian cupped the phone close keeping her conversation unheard by those who passed her bench. "Gary, I need to speak with Pia Lopez."

"If this is about the reward, you need to give me the information, and if it pans out, I'll pass it on."

"It's important I speak with Pia, personally."

"Listen, lady, this is the way it works. If you want a shot at the reward, I'll take down your information, and *if* it checks out and *if* Jillian Cooper is taken down, then you'll get your money."

"Tell Pia I can give her Jillian Cooper on a platter," Jillian said.

"How are you different than every other whack job calling in saying they know where she is?"

"Because I'm looking at her right now."

A pause on the other end of the line.

"Gary, are you listening?"

"Yes. Where are you? We'll come to you."

"No Gary. Like I said, I want to talk to Pia. Is my number on your caller ID?"

"Yes, it is—Catherine," Gary said, using the name of the phone's owner.

"Good. Get Pia to call me in ten minutes."

Jillian disconnected the call and waited on the bench.

The farmer's market crowd thinned after the selection of fruit and vegetables shrank to a few soft apples, bruised strawberries, and wilted bok choy. One by one, the vendors boxed up the remaining produce and took down their plastic tarp canopies.

A trio of homeless men stood off from the market area, their eyes tracked every movement of one of the vendors as she stacked heavy boxes onto a dolly. Five boxes stacked on the dolly, and two other boxes brimming with unsold fruit waited on the sidewalk for a return trip. She rolled the dolly, laden with apples and mandarins, toward the parking lot where the sellers loaded their trucks. The saleswoman wheeled her produce past the homeless men, and one of them dipped his head, looking away.

Jillian picked up on the man's attempt to appear disinterested. It was too practiced, a street smooth move. The men targeted the woman. They'd waited until the farmer's market ended and the woman pocketed her sales proceeds. The men wanted her money. Jillian, like other women in the city, developed a certain instinct chilling the flesh on the nape of her neck whenever a group of shady men suddenly appeared. Where were her instincts when Jillian fell into the quagmire with Jonathon Mattson, David Paulson, and Dynalife?

As the vendor wheeled past the men, they made their move. Jillian sprang from the bench, a warning to the other woman caught in her throat, but her intent was clear. The vendor looked back in the direction of the shuffle of feet on the sidewalk behind her. The men swarmed over the unattended boxes of fruit and shoved as much as they could carry in the pockets of their tattered overcoats and pants. A grin spread on the vendor's face as she continued the trek to her truck.

Jillian misjudged the men and their intentions. They never planned to rob the vendor—they wanted the food.

"You thought they were comin' after me, didn't you? You were tryin' to warn me?"

Jillian nodded.

The woman parked her dolly near Jillian. "Well, thanks anyway. But, Tracy and I have an informal agreement of sorts. He and the boys are too proud to beg. I 'inadvertently' leave some stuff I can't sell, and they take care of it for me."

"You knew they were going to take it?"

The vendor tipped her head toward the curb. "Whatever's leftover after the market, I take to the shelter down off Hyde. They save me and my back another trip, and they get a little somethin' in return."

"I'm–I'm sorry if I frightened you," Jillian said.

"You didn't know. Most people would've looked the other way, but you wanted to warn me." The woman quickly reached into the top box, grabbed two smallish apples, and held them out to Jillian.

"Here—take them," the woman insisted and thrust the fruit into Jillian's hand.

Before Jillian responded, the woman hefted her dolly back on its wheels and pushed off.

The men stuffed as much of the leftover produce in whatever pockets, makeshift bags, and folded cloth they came with. One of the men, Tracy, Jillian supposed, looked up, and yelled, "Thanks, Miss C."

The vendor simply waved a hand over her shoulder as she wheeled around the corner.

Jillian regarded the apples in her hand and realized she hadn't eaten since yesterday. Now she was aware of it, the small slightly blemished apples sparked hunger pangs.

She retreated to the bench and dove into one of the apples, devouring it in four quick bites. Sweet, cool juice dripped from her mouth, and she wiped it away with the back of her hand. A bite into the second apple, the iPhone vibrated under her leg.

Jillian spit out the apple, pulled the phone from under her, and tapped the screen to connect the call.

"Hello," Jillian said.

"Hold for Miss Lopez," a tired voice droned.

"This is Pia Lopez. You have information for me on Jillian Cooper?"

"I do."

"Well, what is it?"

"I want to tell you in person."

Pia sighed. "That's not how we do things. You tell me what I want to know and if I like it, you get your reward. You want the ten-thousand, right?"

"Who put up the reward money?"

"What?" Pia hadn't expected a potential street snitch to question the money's origin.

"Where did the money come from?"

"What do you care?" Pia said.

"Because if you want Jillian Cooper, you're going to have to act like the investigative journalist you pretend to be and find out."

"Who do you think you are? You don't get to tell me what to investigate. If you want the reward, tell me what I want to know."

Jillian paused and considered her next move. The partially eaten apple rolled off the bench and plopped into the cold gray water lapping against the old pilings under the pier. The apple bobbed and floated out with the current.

"Here is how it is going to go down, Pia. Meet me at the benches at the end of Pier 39 at Fisherman's Wharf in twenty minutes. Come alone, and I'll give you Jillian."

Jillian sounded more confident than she felt, and her hand shook as she disconnected the call.

She watched the apple float lower in the water until it disappeared, sucked beneath the surface by unseen currents. Jillian wondered if she was destined for the same fate.

Chapter Twenty

Tourist-heavy traffic clogged the northernmost end of the Embarcadero near the string of souvenir shops clustered at the pier. Beyond them, salmon and crab fishing boats motored to their moorings after their morning runs in the crisp, cold waters outside the Golden Gate. Blue and white tour buses disgorged wriggling masses of sightseers into the plaza in front of Pier 39. Children ran, camera shutters clicked, and voices in a dozen dialects filled the air with an electrified thrum.

Jillian arrived at her vantage point, a bit out of breath from the distance she covered in fifteen minutes. Along the way, she deposited the purse, along with the unused credit cards and identification, lifted from Catherine Delios, in a mail collection box. She regretted taking the woman's cash and phone and slipped a note in the purse promising to reimburse Ms. Delios for the trouble. Jillian hoped she survived to make good on any future commitment.

On time, exactly twenty minutes after the call to Pia Lopez, a boxy news van, emblazoned with the Channel Five logo, pulled to a stop in front of the pier. The funnel-shaped entrance packed the crowd together, forcing them past the shops and storefronts. It also left few exit options for people trying to leave the tourist attraction. The van's side door opened and the reporter hopped out, pulling a light jacket over her shoulders. From one of the jacket pockets, Pia lifted a cell phone and appeared to dial a number.

Jillian watched the reporter from the top level of the parking structure across the street and felt the iPhone vibrate in her hand.

"Yes," Jillian said.

"I'm here, in front of Pier 39. Are you here with Cooper?"

101

"Yes."

Pia raised a hand in the direction of a dark sedan, Jillian hadn't noticed the vehicle at the end of the plaza, in front of the ticket lines for the Alcatraz boat tours. Three men got out of the car and headed for the Pier 39 entrance. One man, thick-necked with a slick bullet head was clearly the leader. He gave his two subordinates assignments, and they split off, one toward the left and the sea lion viewing deck and the other to the right, into the crowd.

"Did you come alone?" Jillian asked.

"I did," Pia lied.

"What did you find out about the reward money? Who put up the ten-thousand?"

"Let's talk later. Why don't you and Cooper meet me at the bistro near the performance stage? You know it?"

"I know where it is," Jillian said.

Pia looked over to the bullet-headed man and signaled him into the Pier. Jillian watched him raise a small radio and presumably ordered his capture team in place.

"Good. Breakfast is on me." Pia quit the call, shoved the phone into her jacket, and stood her ground at the news van.

Ten minutes later Jillian saw the bullet-headed man emerge from the crowd and shrug his shoulders. He hadn't found his target was the message.

Once more, Jillian's phone vibrated. She answered, "Hello, Pia."

"I can't seem to find you." The agitation in her voice was palpable.

"That's because you lied to me, Pia."

"Where are you? I don't have time for this bullshit." A more demanding tone crept in.

"We were supposed to meet alone, not with your crew of thugs."

Pia swiveled around and surveyed the crowd around her. Bullet-head noticed the reporter spin around, and he scanned the faces of the people who milled in the plaza.

"Lose your friends, and we'll talk," Jillian said from her perch in the parking garage.

"What makes you think I trust you? Cooper is a fugitive, and if you want your money, you're gonna have to play ball. Now turn her over to me, and I'll be sure you're paid."

"Trust is a two-way street, Pia. Did you find out who posted the reward?"

A pause, followed by a sigh. "I did."

"Who?"

"Dynalife Pharmaceutical. The company put up the reward."

Jillian held the phone down as she considered why the firm would put up the money.

Then, Jillian said, "This is how it is going to go, Pia..."

Jillian finished the conversation, she dropped the iPhone to the asphalt garage surface and stepped hard on the touchscreen. After several hard blows, the screen cracked, and the thin metal band along the side of the device sprang apart in pieces.

The reporter and her bounty hunters crammed into their vehicles and pulled away from the wharf, cutting off a line of tourists in the crosswalk.

Jillian fast walked down the staircase of the parking garage and disappeared into the crowd. The reporter needed a story, and Jillian wanted to make sure the story was the corporate downfall of Dynalife Pharmaceutical, not Jillian's own demise. The hard drive in her waistband would blow the story wide open.

Chapter Twenty-One

Exposed on the street, Jillian's paranoia made her feel vulnerable and alone. No one to trust, and the reporter weaponized the city population in her manhunt. Every face she saw posed a new risk and it chilled Jillian's marrow to quicksilver. Which face among the masses on the streets and sidewalks would be the one to betray her? She needed off this dark ride and make her own path, one her tormentors would not anticipate. She patted the photographer's hard drive in her waistband for tangible proof of the lies and manipulation. The device was a touchstone to her sanity and hopefully, it contained the evidence the reporter needed to publicly clear Jillian.

From a block and a half away, Jillian spotted the black and white police sedan parked at the curb in front of her apartment building. The outline of one officer filled the passenger side, which meant his partner must be inside the building. The second officer was probably posted right outside her apartment door. She needed a distraction, and one living across the hall would do.

Jillian wished she kept the stolen phone. Mrs. Tillman called her at least once a week to complain about her aches and pains and pass along the tenant gossip. There was no doubt in Jillian's mind the informal apartment building phone tree now considered her a murderess and, a whore. Worse yet, by their values, Jillian once received a letter of reprimand from the tenant's association after she left a Christmas wreath on her door past New Year's Day, an unpardonable breach of proper decorum.

Public payphones were few in the city, but they existed, if you knew where to look. She passed one in her apartment lobby every single day, but the police presence in front of the building ruled the phone off-limits. Jillian ducked into an apartment building across the street from hers and exhaled when the officer in the car kept his butt firmly planted in his seat. Her hunch paid off, a relic of a payphone was mounted opposite the elevator. She dialed Mrs. Tillman's number from memory. On the fourth ring, an impatient voice picked up.

"Hello," Mrs. Tillman said, competing with the loud television broadcast in the background.

She'd interrupted her neighbor's soap opera time. "Mrs. Tillman, it's Jillian Cooper. I need your help."

The television sound instantly muted. Jillian grabbed her attention.

"Jillian, I'm hearing bad things about you—unspeakably bad things."

"Don't believe everything you hear. I need you to meet me at the Ferry Building."

"Coming and going at all hours; keeping the company of *several* men. I'm not at all surprised where you've ended up."

"Meet me at the Ferry Building," Jillian repeated.

"Why would I do such a thing? You're nothing more than a common criminal."

"I'll turn myself in to you. You'll be a hero, maybe on the television news. You might even earn the reward money Channel Five is offering. I'll meet you in front of the entrance under the Ferry Building tower in thirty minutes," Jillian said and disconnected the call.

With the patience of an angler, Jillian set the hook. She knew Mrs. Tillman's sense of drama and her constant need for self-centered attention would prove irresistible. Less than two minutes after the call, Mrs. Tillman paraded down the front steps, escorted by a uniformed police officer.

The officer opened the rear door for Mrs. Tillman, who slipped inside for her moment of celebrity. The officer closed the door quickly and trotted to the driver's door. He paused, appeared to look in Jillian's direction, and spoke into a radio microphone, clipped to his uniform collar. Jillian held her breath until the officer turned, got into his patrol car, and drove east toward the Ferry Building.

A half an hour, perhaps a few minutes more, was all the time Jillian bought. As soon as the red taillights of the police sedan faded, she sprinted for the apartment building doors.

At the building, she moved with more tentative steps, half expecting another officer tucked in the shadows of the lobby, or one hidden in the elevator. Paranoia ratcheted up each second as Jillian crossed the small lobby and made for the staircase. Footfalls echoed within the cramped space and Jillian froze, pressing against a wall. The sound stopped as suddenly as it began and Jillian realized the phantom steps were her own. She felt foolish, but Jillian couldn't relax until she finished the climb to her floor.

Without Mrs. Tillman at her usual post at the peephole, Jillian unlocked her apartment door and slipped inside unseen. Her tidy living space showed signs of careless occupation, fast-food wrappers, and white Styrofoam coffee cups strewn over counters and floors. Strong cigarette smoke clung to the walls mixed with the smell of rancid food from her open refrigerator. Someone moved the appliance away from the wall, pulled the plug and left the door ajar. Cabinet doors and drawers hung open, the contents tossed on the counters.

Jillian looked at her flat-screen television, DVR and stereo, surprised they remained in place. They were not top-of-the-line models, by any stretch, but the fact the electronics were as she left them said the place was ransacked, not robbed. What did they hope to find, and who were *they*?

Jillian found the answer on the middle of her dining table. Pinned under a half-empty plastic water bottle, an officially prepared document announced a search warrant for Jillian's apartment and common areas. The fact the police left her apartment in this condition did not lessen the sense of violation. People pawed through her clothing, food, books, and personal items. They knew what she ate, her literary preferences, and were now acquainted with her bra size.

She pulled the warrant from under the water bottle paperweight and read the affidavit on the face of the warrant sworn by Inspector DiManno. The warrant authorized a search for evidence related to the murder of Jonathon

Mattson, the murder of David Paulson, conspiracy to commit fraud, and grand theft.

"You're a one-woman crime wave now, aren't you Jilly?" She shook her head in disbelief. Someone was going to a great deal of effort to bury her. "Grand theft—right. Like I have the crown jewels tucked away in my sock drawer."

A second page attached to the warrant listed dozens of items seized by the police during their raid. According to the inventory, nearly every stitch of Jillian's clothing was taken for fiber and blood trace analysis, her phone answering machine confiscated, tax returns and her credit card statements, seized for a forensic audit. Her laptop computer, storage devices, and business files were among the last items on the list. Without the laptop, Jillian couldn't access the storage device she seized from the photographer's studio.

"Dammit." She crumpled the warrant and tossed it to the floor. Exhaustion intertwined with frustration seized Jillian, and she leaned against a wall. She slid down the wall until she collapsed on the floor with sagged shoulders and wept.

She felt beaten, with nowhere left to turn. She'd never been one to give up on a fight, but dammit, they were making this hard. A twinge of panic sparked in her belly, molten and white-hot. She wanted to close her eyes and make everything stop. Thoughts her mother must've experienced in the seconds before she ended her own life.

A scuffling sound came from beyond the door in the hallway. Muffled voices with sharply spoken words carried on for a few seconds, followed by the abrupt, yet distinct clunk of Mrs. Tillman's apartment door. The neighbor and her escort returned from their trip to the Ferry Building.

The blue LED clock on the kitchen range displayed the time; her thirty-minute window hadn't expired. The police couldn't have searched the water-side building in the time they were gone. Jillian tensed as keys scraped in the lock at the front door.

Jillian ducked down the short hallway and stepped into her bedroom as the front door opened. She didn't know who used a key to her place, but she didn't want to hang around to find out. There wasn't enough time to open the window and kick down the old fire escape stairs. Even if she did, the metallic racket they created would call attention to her escape attempt.

Shoes scuffed in her kitchen, someone opened a drawer and slid it shut with a bang. The sound moved from the kitchen to the hallway, closer to the trap Jillian set for herself.

The footfall sounds grew closer, Jillian lay face down on the wood floor and slid under her bed frame. Even with her small build, there was barely enough space for her underneath the bed. With a gaggle of dust bunnies around her, Jillian craned her neck toward the bedroom door.

Preceded by a scuff, the tips of the shoes shone in the doorway. Brown scarred work boots hemmed by frayed blue jeans; definitely not police issue. They paused at the doorway and worked their way around to the opposite side of the bed, at the window with the fire escape.

Pinned in tight, Jillian couldn't turn her head to watch where the boots stopped. However, she heard the curtains part and fall closed. Apparently, the person was satisfied whatever he looked for wasn't out on the fire escape. The boots moved away from the window and paused at the foot of the bed.

Two strong hands grabbed Jillian by the ankles and jerked her from beneath the bed. Grasping and clawing at the floor as she slid, Jillian flailed to free herself from her attacker. She kicked as hard as she could, but the hands tightened their grip and pulled harder. Jillian's head crashed into the bottom rail of the bed frame. The blow stunned her, stopping her resistance long enough for her attacker to drag her from her hiding place.

The weight of one knee on the back of her neck and another in the small of her back pinned Jillian to the floor, immobile and unable to see her attacker. She shuddered as a gloved hand brushed the hair from her face, a strangely soft and intimate gesture. The weight above shifted, lips grazed her ear.

"You are going to pay for what you did." The voice was cold with an edge of anger. His hot breath caressed her neck.

In front of Jillian's face, the tip of a stainless steel boning knife plunged into the floor. A shudder coursed through her body. The knife loomed inches from her eyes as the weight shifted above her once more. Jillian felt the touch of a gloved hand again. This time it grabbed her jaw and forced her mouth open. It came with a handful of pills, and he cupped her mouth, and a knee to the back made certain she swallowed.

"No, not like this," Jillian said through the attacker's grip.

Everything around her faded and darkened with each successive heartbeat. Confusion and panic tore at her.

Jillian felt the weight from the above release, but she felt no control of her muscles, and her mind slipped from sharp contrasts to hazy shades of grey. The last sensation she noticed was the sound of clothing as it ripped off her body.

Chapter Twenty-Two

"There we are. Welcome back." A voice hovered over her.

Anxiety ratcheted up, and Jillian tried to move away from her attacker. Her arms and legs wouldn't respond and seemed as if they were filled with concrete. They weren't numb, but even though she forced them to move with all her strength, her legs wouldn't budge. Jillian tried to lift her dead arms, but they were equally frozen. *What pills did this asshole shove down my throat?*

The shadows shifted around her as the man changed positions. Instinctively, Jillian turned her head away from his approach. She found the only part of her body she could control was her head. Tension against her arms and legs held Jillian in place, immobile and vulnerable.

There was a musty, faint, unfamiliar industrial odor in the air. The edges of Jillian's vision cleared bit by bit. Dull fixtures and a cloying clinical staleness marked the unadorned muddy beige walls. Clinical, but not hospital-like with plain laminated brown furnishings better suited at a low-budget motel. Where was she? *Another blackout.* This one wasn't born in the untrustworthy reaches of her brain. She was attacked.

A touch on her shoulder and Jillian recoiled. An angry moan escaped her lips. The sound was animalistic, a cry from a trapped defenseless creature.

She caught movement alongside and Jillian tensed, the effort shot pain down both arms. Instead of the foreign, malignant touch she expected, she heard the squeak of a vinyl chair cushion as someone shifted. Jillian turned to the source of the sound and her vision cleared enough for her to make out the face of Inspector DiManno in a chair at her bedside.

110

"Where am I?"

The inspector removed a pillow from an end stand next to the bed, placed it behind Jillian's head, and tucked it gently under her.

"Hello there, Miss Cooper."

Jillian's eyes reacted to the voice and shuddered tight. The voice boomed inside her head and echoed against Jillian's skull. Light carved a slit between her eyelids; searing white light poured in around the outline of the Inspector above her. Another migraine. *God, they've never been like this.*

"I didn't have you pegged as the desperate sort, Miss Cooper," DiManno said.

A tinge of claustrophobia nagged at Jillian when she spotted a uniformed cop and woman in medical scrubs joining DiManno.

The Inspector moved his chair closer to Jillian's bed. He nodded toward the cop who followed his suggestion and stepped outside. DiManno leaned back and unbuttoned his jacket. "You know why you're here, right? Feeling guilty and want to come clean?"

"I don't know where *here* is."

"It's a place to find help. For others, it's a place for the guilty to hide."

Jillian hadn't noticed a heart monitor until it quickened its pace and announced the increase with a rapid series of beeping sounds. The medical equipment acted as a makeshift lie detector and betrayed her.

A slight grin came from DiManno. The expression looked out of place on the Inspector, a man who seemed humorless and droll. "Looks like I struck a nerve there..."

"Miss Cooper needs to rest," the nurse said as she released the straps from Jillian's arms and legs. Jillian rubbed her sore wrists as the nurse released her bindings.

DiManno ignored the nurse. "What were you running away from? Another 'blackout'?"

"I wasn't running. I'm being set up," Jillian said through chapped lips.

"Who would do that?"

"I don't know."

"Is that why you tried to kill yourself?"

111

"I—I did no such thing. The last thing I remember is being in my apartment, then he grabbed me."

"Someone 'grabbed' you? You expect me to believe a mysterious stranger suddenly appeared, attacked you, and forced you to take a lethal dose of pills? Kinda sounds like, forgive the term, crazy talk, to me."

Beep-beep-beep sounded the heart monitor.

"I didn't try to kill myself." Her voice came out more uncertain than she'd hoped.

"You threw up most of them. That's the only reason we're talking. You must have been pilfering the stores at Dynalife for all those sedatives."

"No, I wouldn't…"

"How about we talk about you killing Jonathon Mattson?" DiManno said.

Beep-beep-beep-beep-beep.

"I've already told you. I didn't do it. I can't tell you what you want to hear."

The heart monitor's pace increased.

"Let me tell you what I know," DiManno said. He reached into his jacket and retrieved a small brown envelope. "I know you were with Mattson the night he died."

"No—"

DiManno put up his hand. "Let me finish," and unclasped the brass clasp on the back of the envelope. He pulled open the flap and shook the contents out onto the thin sheet over Jillian's chest. Against the white sheet, another copy of the damning photograph of Mattson and Jillian laid alongside a gold and tanzanite necklace.

Jillian's breath shuddered at the sight of the damning photo, one more gift from Brad at Carson Arts. She hadn't paid attention to the details in the photo before. Around Jillian's neck was a unique tanzanite necklace. The fine gold chain and six deep purple stones were a one-of-a-kind piece made for her at a small jewelry shop in Mendocino. She recognized her necklace on the bedcovers and reached out to pick it up.

"Mustn't touch the evidence," DiManno said as he grabbed up the necklace and the photograph.

"Where did you find it?" Jillian asked. Her voice quivered. She pulled the sheet up close to her chin, a thin cotton barrier between her and the police inspector.

"You left it at Mattson's house after you killed him."

"I didn't kill him—I couldn't have," Jillian said. Her words sounded hollow, empty of hope, uncertain of their truth.

"I know, I know, you were at home alone, with no one to verify your alibi. You have to admit everything we have points at you alone. The relationship with Mattson, the chummy photo of the two of you together at an intimate dinner, the humiliating business presentation, and your jewelry left behind at the crime scene." DiManno ticked each of the points off on his fingers.

"And then we found this next to your unconscious body at your place." DiManno selected a photo on his phone, one that Jillian recognized as her apartment bathroom. On the tile floor, next to the tub, lay a blood-stained knife.

It looked like the boning knife Jillian recalled plunging into the floor before she blacked out.

"We have the lab testing the blood against Jonathon Mattson. Any guess to what we might find?"

Tears flowed from Jillian's tightly shuttered eyelids. She hated the fact she showed weakness in front of DiManno. The tears were not born of sadness, or fear, but of anger. A deep, dark, and foreboding feeling welled up inside. The emotion surprised her. Jillian felt anger—anger at her failing mind, anger at the unknown, and anger at the unanswered questions threatening to suffocate her.

"This isn't real. The knife ,the photo, all of it. The photo, it—it was faked. I can prove it."

"What were you doing at the apartment owned by Renee Marquez?"

"Who?" The question startled Jillian.

"You visited an apartment on Nob Hill. The doorman reported you demanded to see Marquez's apartment, and then you scared the bejesus out of him, pushing past him running from the building. An old man, you could've hurt him."

"I didn't mean…"

"Why did you go to the apartment, Miss Cooper?"

"I don't know anyone named Renee Marquez," Jillian said as she searched her porous memory.

"Who did you think lived in the apartment?"

"I don't know. That's why I had to go there. To. Find. Out!" The heart monitor gave a rapid staccato series of beeps. Jillian's hair stuck to the cold sweat gathered on her forehead. The thin hospital gown clung to her damp chest with each ragged breath. She looked the part of a caged animal, feral and guarded.

"The 'I don't know,' line isn't working for you anymore, Miss Cooper."

"Why am I here?"

Inspector DiManno leaned forward, his eyes locked on Jillian's. "Really? We've already established you are a danger to yourself and others. You tried to kill yourself with an overdose of pills in the bathtub."

Inspector DiManno rose from the chair and circled the hospital bed, his rubber soles squeaked with each measured step. He bent down to Jillian's ear and whispered, "As soon as the doctors here do their evaluation hocus-pocus, I'll see you're booked where you belong, in jail. You'll spend the rest of your life in prison, so enjoy this while it lasts. It's not getting any better for you."

"Someone did this to me. He's after me."

"You're safe here, Ms. Cooper," the nurse said.

"Where's here?"

"PHF." DiManno pronounced it "puff."

The confused look on Jillian's face prompted him to continue. "Psychiatric Health Facility."

"Psych...why am I here?"

A furrow deepened in DiManno's brow. He leaned forward in the vinyl chair, his gaze locked on her. "Your family had you committed, Miss Cooper."

"What do you mean?" Jillian pushed herself up looking DiManno in the eye.

DiManno leaned back slightly. "Your sister filed an affidavit expressing concern for your welfare. She believes you are a danger. I hear there's a family history."

"I can explain it. Wait–did you find a computer hard drive?" Jillian's blood chilled at the recollection of the device.

"A computer what?" DiManno responded.

"A portable computer hard drive. I got it from a photographer who shot Jonathon Mattson's picture at a fundraiser."

"Let me guess, the same photo where you and the late Mr. Mattson look so comfy together?"

Jillian nodded. "That's the one, except for the fact I was never there."

Inspector DiManno's glare darkened. His patience had worn thin with Jillian's story.

"Look, Miss Cooper, I get it. I really do. If you need to continue to play out some not guilty by reason of insanity deal, fine. I'm telling you, you can't keep up this fraud. You're gonna slip up, and when you do, you won't be in some cozy mental hospital." DiManno gestured to the bare walls of the room.

"I'm telling you the truth. I don't know anything about Jonathon's murder," she said.

"Please, Miss Cooper, save me the drama. You were overcome by guilt after you murdered Mattson you went off the rails—a dissociative state—I think they call it. You killed David Paulson, then tried to kill yourself. Or, you wanted to prove you were insane. It's one or the other."

"I wouldn't do that!"

DiManno leaned forward once more; a strange, angry smirk crossed his thin lips. "I did some checking, Miss Cooper. I know about your mother–about how she shot herself. You found her, didn't you?"

Jillian nodded.

"It's the kinda thing that would screw up a kid. Makes you wonder if her kind of crazy is genetic. You know, like mother, like daughter?"

Tears welled in Jillian's eyes, but she didn't want to give him the satisfaction of seeing her cry, again.

"Did you find the hard drive?"

After a pause, Inspector DiManno shook his head. "No, Miss Cooper, there was no reason to search for an imaginary computer drive."

"Go to Hell."

"I think you'll be there before me." DiManno rose from the chair and hitched up his pants. "I'll see you tomorrow. You're set for an arraignment in the morning. Lucky for you, your attorney got the court to order you held here instead of the jail. The D.A. is gonna see to it you go where you belong, behind bars."

"Attorney?"

"Yeah. Dynalife Pharmaceutical kicked down for an attorney–go figure."

DiManno turned and left the room. As the door hung open on the self-closing hinge, Jillian saw DiManno approach another man in the hallway outside her room. She recognized him immediately.

William Comstock, the Chairman of Dynalife's esteemed Board of Directors, listened to Inspector DiManno. From the distance, Jillian couldn't make out what the Inspector said, but the look on the Chairman's face held worry. Comstock didn't worry about trivial matters like her fate, he was concerned about his stock price.

Comstock's face flushed and he poked a finger in DiManno's chest as the door closed. Jillian overheard raised voices from outside; the two men argued, but Jillian couldn't make out the muffled conversation.

The rumble from the voices quieted, and the door swung inward. A tall, well-muscled man entered Jillian's room. He appeared to be the type who looked more at home on a rugby pitch than a corporate boardroom. His slicked-back dark hair and expensively cut suit marked him as a backroom hired gun, a guy more accustomed to billing hours as opposed to defending criminal defendants.

"I'm Ryan McGowen. I'm your attorney, and you are not to speak with the police or anyone else on this matter without me. Are we clear?"

"How did you...?"

"Are we clear on that point, Miss Cooper?" McGowen said. A scowl emphasized his thick jaw.

"Yes, yes. I hear you. Don't talk to anyone. Why are you here? I don't know you."

McGowen glanced at his new client, and a flicker of disgust crossed his face. "Mr. Comstock asked me to come. He told me you needed help."

Jillian tugged at the neck of her hospital gown. "I'm not crazy," she blurted.

McGowen held out a hand as if to stop her. "I don't care. We have a few things to get straight before your court hearing tomorrow morning. The District Attorney has filed three separate charges. First, the Mattson murder..."

"I didn't..."

Again, up shot the dismissive hand from McGowen. "Let me do the talking. Consider it practice; you don't utter a single syllable tomorrow at the hearing. The District Attorney is willing to make a deal."

"What deal?" Confusion etched on Jillian's face.

McGowen leaned forward; his cologne was as abrasive as his personality. "The D.A. is prepared to offer Voluntary Manslaughter to make this go away. My advice to you is take the deal."

"If I don't?"

"You face twenty-five to life in prison if they proceed with one count of First Degree Murder; fifty-to-life if they double up the charges with Paulson's murder. With a Manslaughter charge, your exposure is down to eleven years, you'd be out in six, maybe seven years. Take the deal."

"I won't. I'm not spending seven years in prison for a crime I didn't do."

McGowen looked as if he was dealing with an ill-tempered child. His jaw muscles tightened and a thick vein throbbed on the man's forehead. He glanced at a bulky, white gold wristwatch and stopped himself from banging it against the bed rail in response to the insolence of his newest client. "Let's assume, for the sake of argument, you didn't murder Jonathon Mattson. What am I supposed to present as a defense? Deny you and Mattson had a falling out over a business proposal? A scene witnessed by a dozen people in the room, by the way. Or, you had an extracurricular relationship with the man, who was old enough to be your father? Juries eat up salacious gossip. Then, we have to explain away the evidence, including your jewelry at the murder scene, dropped when you fled. Let's not overlook the alleged murder weapon found in your apartment. Am I leaving anything out?"

Jillian started to speak, but once more McGowen dismissed her.

"Oh, how could I forget? You turn up in a hospital psych ward because your own family thinks you're a public menace. All you have is a bullshit amnesia claim and fantastic conspiracy tales. You see where this is heading, Miss Cooper? There is nothing I can present as a defense. Frankly, the D.A.'s willingness to allow you to plea to Voluntary Manslaughter is an act of charity. Not to mention the matter of David Paulson's murder will not be pursued."

"What's in it for the D.A.? Why are they in such a hurry to make this—to make me, go away?" Jillian said.

"You have Mrs. Mattson to thank. It seems the widow and the district attorney are old college buddies. Mrs. Mattson didn't want her late husband's indiscretions aired in public. The D.A. could've gotten a lot of political mileage out of a high-profile case like this, but he's giving you this deal as a favor to her."

Jillian fell into stunned silence while she mulled over McGowen's last comment. Shelly Mattson only cared about keeping Dynalife afloat. Fast-tracking Jillian to a prison cell was the widow's play to keep the company's reputation out of the gutter.

The awkwardness between attorney and client evaporated the second William Comstock pushed open the door and strode into the room. He looked from Jillian's face to McGowen's and saw the layers of tension.

The attorney puffed up with the self-importance of a high school gym teacher. "You need to have a come to Jesus meeting with your little friend here," McGowen said.

"What's going on?" Comstock asked.

"What's going on is she insists on continuing with this nonsense," McGowen said. He headed for the door. "I'm gonna get some coffee," and he disappeared outside.

"I swear I didn't have anything to do with Jonathon's death," Jillian said.

Comstock's eyes drilled into Jillian. This man was direct and never shy about conflict. "It doesn't matter what I think. This has gone too far. You have to end it now." His gaze shifted to the stained ceiling, "You need to take the deal, put this behind you, and after, you can try to claim some semblance of a life down the road."

"You think I should roll over and say I'm guilty when I'm not?"

"I don't think you have much of a choice. Take the deal, and you're out in a couple years; otherwise, you die in prison."

"Doesn't the truth matter to you?"

Comstock's expression hardened. "Don't be a child. There is no such thing as truth. It's all about perception, and the perception is you are a vindictive bitch who killed her lover when he didn't give her what she wanted."

"You can't possibly believe him," Jillian said.

"Like I said, it doesn't matter what I believe. Jonathon disrespected you during the board meeting. Has anyone ever dared say no to you Jilly? You whored yourself out and got what you deserved."

Jillian's hand darted across her body and slapped Comstock. The sharp echo of the blow reverberated off the walls in the small room.

"What the hell did I ever do to you?" Her face was tired, drawn, and flush with anger.

Comstock rubbed his cheek where the pink outline of Jillian's hand welted against his tanned and toned skin. "Quite some anger problem you've got there."

The door swung open and framed a portly man with shoulder-length grey hair secured back into a thick ponytail. The hair, coupled with a wrinkled grey tweed sports coat and high-water khaki pants portrayed a man who fell off the professorial tenure track at a small liberal arts college. He saw Comstock's pink cheek, and he stiffened in the doorway.

"Visiting hours are over," the man in the tweed jacket said. He held the door open to emphasize the point.

Comstock glared back at Jillian and said, "You don't hold any other choice. Take the deal tomorrow and move past this. It isn't only about you."

"Seems like it to me," Jillian said.

He bent toward Jillian, and she shrank away as if she expected a backhand.

"You do this, and you'll be taken care of."

Jillian's face betrayed her confusion. "What do you mean?"

"There is too much risk in allowing you to play out this childish charade. Admit what you did and I'll make sure you are taken care of while you're–gone, and after you get out."

"Risk? What the hell are you talking about?"

Comstock looked over his shoulder at the tweed-coated door monitor and lowered his voice to a whisper. "The longer you draw this out, the more Dynalife comes into question. The Board is concerned about the implications of this negative attention. The stock price..."

"This is about money? You want me to sacrifice my life, so Dynalife's shares don't fall a couple of pennies?"

"Of course it's about money. And, a lot of it for you, if you go along. I'll meet you in court tomorrow morning. Sleep on it. I know you'll make the right decision."

The Chairman backed away from Jillian's bedside and strode out into the hallway.

Money. It always came down to money.

Chapter Twenty-Three

T he tweed-clad man looked relieved watching William Comstock exit the room. Once the Chairman left, the gray-haired man stepped away from the door and came to Jillian's bedside. He jotted a notation in a file and set it on the bed next to her.

"I don't like that man much," he said.

"I'm not too fond of him either."

"I'm Sheldon." He extended his hand toward Jillian.

Jillian took his hand. "Jillian Cooper."

"I'd ask you what brings you to our fine establishment, but it seems kind of obvious," Sheldon said.

"Are you a doctor?"

"I'm one of the social workers here. Want to leave this room?"

Jillian nodded. "Where are we going?" Cautious.

"Out on the floor. This room is for intake and detox when it's necessary."

"I don't need detox," Jillian responded and swung her legs off the bed. A pair of clean navy blue sweatpants and a gray t-shirt lay, folded on the end of the bed.

"Go ahead and change and meet me out in the hall."

"I understand you claimed to have a blackout. Have you experienced a memory lapse before?" Sheldon asked.

"No." The lie spilled out easily. She broke off eye contact.

"Change and let's take a walk." Sheldon closed the door and waited outside until Jillian appeared, dressed in the oversized clothing.

In stocking clad feet, Jillian padded to the doorway and peered out onto a long hallway, lined with doors that Jillian assumed were patient rooms. At the end of the hallway, a large Plexiglas barrier separated the sleeping spaces from an open dayroom where a dozen patients sat in an arranged circle of chairs. The men and women in the circle wore the same sweatpants and shirts as Jillian, the uniform of the broken people.

Sheldon and Jillian reached the barrier and Sheldon pulled a magnetic card from his jacket pocket, swiping it across a card reader. A buzzing noise preceded a loud click, and the Plexiglas barrier swung open a few inches. Sheldon entered the room first and held the door for Jillian.

When the door clicked open, the group fell silent, and heads swiveled in Jillian's direction. Eyes assessed the newcomer, some looking for the threat she posed, while others sought out vulnerabilities to exploit. One slight woman never looked up. She held her head low, her face hidden behind a curtain of long dark hair.

A staff member sitting in the circle gathered the group's attention. One by one, with their inventory of Jillian's strengths and weaknesses completed, they resumed their group discussion.

Jillian noted narrow glass windows letting in a modest amount of light, but prevented patients, she presumed, from getting out. Two other Plexiglas doors with card readers led away from the dayroom.

"Is this a prison?" Jillian said.

"No–but it is a locked facility. The patients here pose a danger to others, or themselves," Sheldon said.

"I don't need to be here."

"Well, the judge and your family said otherwise."

"What judge?"

"The judge who committed you here for a seventy-two-hour observation. Seems your sister reported you came to her home and starting spouting off about murders and blackouts. She informed the court she was concerned for your safety."

"Hannah's never concerned about anyone but herself. Don't I have any say in what happens?"

"That's kind of the whole purpose. You can't make decisions for yourself

122

right now," Sheldon said as they headed for a small sofa in the corner of the room.

"What happens after seventy-two hours?"

"It's up to you. People come here to hide from what they've done, some have nowhere to go, and a few are here to get some help." Sheldon stopped, turned, and looked at Jillian. "Which one are you?"

"I don't know."

Sheldon considered her for a moment. "At least that's an honest answer."

Jillian shrugged. "Does it really matter?"

Sheldon sat on the sofa and gestured for Jillian to join him. She selected the far end and pressed into the cushioned corner as far as possible.

Beyond the group of patients in the center of the room, a few loners parked themselves in small chairs and activity tables arranged along one wall. A middle-aged man nervously thumbed through the pages of a worn copy of Field and Stream, a twenty-something woman worked a jigsaw puzzle exposing the upper half of a wild animal, and a woman who looked like a soccer mom, with bandages on her wrists, sat isolated from the others.

The soccer mom sat, back to the wall, with eyes betraying fear, loneliness, and incredible sadness. She clutched a pendant made up of two intertwined silver hearts.

"What's her story?" Jillian asked.

Sheldon glanced across the room. "I can't talk about other patients, Jillian. This is a safe place, what you tell me here is protected by therapist-patient privilege. I cannot repeat what you tell me, any more than I can tell you what any other patient says."

"How do I know you aren't working with the police to pull information from me for their case?"

"I'm not going to ask you about it."

"Nothing?"

"Nope. It really doesn't matter. I'm more interested in the blackout you mentioned. You've experienced these episodes before?" Sheldon said.

Jillian nodded.

"When did it happen?"

"Once before, a couple of days ago," Jillian said.

"Anything prior?"

"Never. I've never experienced a sensation like this. Hours missing—missing and I can't explain it. Holes—huge gaps in time. I woke up in a strange place and have absolutely no memory of what happened, or how I got there. I don't remember a thing."

"Nothing like this before a few days ago? No head trauma, no injuries in childhood?"

"No. Nothing. It suddenly happened, and I don't know why."

"Tell me, what can you remember right before the blackout? Were you drinking? Drugs?"

Jillian closed her eyes, and disconnected images filled her mind. Waking in what she thought was Mattson's apartment, coming to in an asylum facing murder charges. In between, only dark caverns of nothingness.

"What's the last thing you remember?" Sheldon said in a soft voice.

With her eyes shut Jillian said, "I remember the awful meeting with Mr. Mattson, then I'm sitting at Slosek's. It was after work, and I sipped on a vodka tonic. Only one, and I wasn't drunk. David Paulson came in, and we talked about the meeting. He was trying to make me back down or change my proposal to come in line with the company's new direction. Then, nothing. Next thing I know the weekend disappeared."

"David Paulson. He a friend, co-worker?"

"Yes. Why do you ask?" Her eyes popped open.

"I'm trying to put the pieces together. Why do you think you experienced this episode?"

"That's what I'm trying to tell you! I have no fucking idea what's happening to me."

"Can this Paulson help you piece your memory together?"

She shook her head. "He's dead."

"He's dead?"

"And I didn't fucking kill him."

A few curious patients in the group turned in Jillian's direction.

She lowered her voice, "One minute I'm having an after-work drink, and the next, I'm in a strange apartment."

"Why?"

"What do you mean?"

"Why did this happen to you? There has to be a reason. The results from your medical screening this morning showed no organic cause. No tumors, lesions, or signs of stroke…"

"Someone is doing this to me."

"Someone? Who'd want to hurt you, Jillian?"

Silence thickened the space between them. Jillian pulled her knees up, and she hugged them tightly. With her chin resting on one knee, Jillian said, "Someone's gone through a whole lot of trouble to do this to me."

"Over the years, I've found the simplest answer is usually right. Who would have the most to gain from you being in this position?"

Jillian tilted her head toward Sheldon and considered his question for a moment. Her career path was on course and not without a handful of bumps along the way. Jillian became a corporate warrior, with countless battles waged in the boardroom where she bested her opposition. Results mattered and revenge always simmered under the surface.

"There are a few who wouldn't mind if I disappeared from the face of the Earth."

"A few enemies along the way, huh?"

"It's the way of life in big business."

"Not much of a life, if you ask me. Has a pretty high price tag to go along with it."

"Apparently," Jillian said.

The group of patients in the circle stood from their chairs, the session over. Chairs scuffed back into place at tables and scattered along the wall. Patients either waited near the corridor doors or loitered about in front of a television where a staff member fiddled with a DVD player.

A woman with short auburn hair and pale blue eyes came over to the sofa where Jillian and Sheldon talked. The woman shot a side-eye at Jillian, then to Sheldon, said, "This the new gal?"

"Annette, this is Jillian. Why don't you help her settle in and show her around?"

"Sure thing. I'll show her the ropes," Annette said.

Sheldon's jaw clenched, and he exhaled a sigh. "That's not funny, Annette."

Annette spoke to Jillian. "He has absolutely no sense of humor. I tried to hang myself last week."

"We talked about this, remember?" Sheldon added. "We agreed you wouldn't joke about it."

"Relax. You don't have to be so serious all the time. Gawwd. Lighten up, would ya," she said.

Underneath the surface of casual attitude and behind a hint of a sparkle in her blue eyes, Jillian saw a flicker of pain. The secret hidden within the young woman added years to her face, evidenced by premature lines and wrinkles. Jillian recalled her mother said they were "worry lines," and blamed most of them on fretting over Jillian.

"Come on, I'll show you around and set you up in your room. And, we'll stay away from ropes and sharp things," Annette said.

Sheldon shoved his hands into his pants pockets and made his best attempt at a schoolmaster's glare, but he couldn't quite pull it off.

Annette put an arm around Jillian and escorted her to a spot in the open dayroom, a dozen feet to one side of the television. She stopped and turned toward Jillian. A serious expression dropped over her face.

"You have anything to say. This is where you come. This is the only spot where they can't hear you," Annette said.

"Who can't?" *Aliens, or maybe the voices in your head*, Jillian thought.

"The staff. There's one in the booth to control the doors, two on the floor, plus another who roves from unit to unit."

Jillian glanced around and confirmed Annette's account of staffing levels in the unit.

"Another thing—the cameras. There are three cameras in the dayroom. One over the television, one in the far corner tracks movement into the corridors, and one over my right shoulder."

Jillian looked up past Annette's shoulder and saw a large clear glass dome protecting a black camera lens. The lens swung around and locked onto the two of them. The inside circle of the lens rotated, focused in on Jillian, and she felt a spike of paranoia. Her face flushed slightly, and she turned away from the camera.

"Can they read lips?" Jillian asked.

"We don't think so. As far as we know, the guy in the control booth runs the cameras. If you walk up to the glass, you can see what looks like a video game joystick. It's how he controls the cameras."

"How do you know all about this place?"

"I've been here before. It don't take long to get a handle on the routine. Shift changes, breaks, and which staff you can get over on. Hell, half the time they talk to each other like we ain't even here. You can learn about their families, and who's havin' affairs with who. See the guy by the door?" Annette tipped her head toward a tall, thin black man, dressed in pale blue medical scrubs pushing a small metal cart.

Jillian nodded.

"He hands out the medication. He also has his hands on that guy's wife," Annette said and pointed to a short, balding Hispanic counselor near the control booth. "In exchange for me not letting his dirty little secret out in the open, our little drug connection hooks me up with Oxy and other goodies. Let me know what you want, and I'll hook you up too."

"Thanks, but I'm not into that," Jillian said.

"You will be. You spend any time in here, you'll do it so you can feel something. What meds do they have you on?"

"Nothing," Jillian said.

"They will, trust me. It makes us easier to control." Annette motioned for Jillian to follow her to a corridor. "What are you in for?"

"You make it sound like prison," Jillian said.

"Well, we are locked in and they go home at night. I get it if you don't wanna tell me why you're here jus' yet, that's cool. Me, they say I have anger issues. No anger about it. I stabbed my boyfriend 'cause he was bein' a prick. Anger issues my ass, he had it comin'."

They stopped in front of the first room on the left. A bare-walled room with sparse heavy-duty furnishings; a bureau, a narrow table, and a wood-framed bed lined each side of the space. The set on the right was vacant with bedsheets and a blanket folded neatly on the end of the bare mattress. The left side of the room showed recent occupancy with the bed linens balled up, bi-polar workbooks strewn on the table surface, and a small photograph of a family taped to the wall above the bureau.

"Is this your room?" Jillian asked.

"It's mine," a voice from in the hallway called out.

"Chill Dani, you have a new roommate," Annette said.

Dani was the solitary woman with the hidden face Jillian spotted on the sofa across the room when she spoke with Sheldon. Her long dark hair framed a face with deep-set brown eyes hidden within dark hollowed sockets. The woman anxiously scanned her room while absently rubbing the bandage on her left wrist.

"Don't touch my stuff," Dani said.

"I won't," Jillian said.

Dani pushed past Annette and approached the desktop where she straightened the workbooks in perfect alignment with the side of the desk. She repeated the task twice more before she was satisfied the placement was perfect. Then, Dani touched the photograph with a soft hand and made certain it remained undamaged.

Jillian leaned in for a closer look at the picture; Dani held a young girl, maybe three to four years old, on her lap and a man stood behind them. A jagged hole, roughly torn from the photo replaced half of the man's face. Dani and her daughter wore bright smiles for the camera. The photograph appeared recent. Jillian noticed small gold lettering on the lower right corner. Carson Arts Photography.

"Where did you take this?" Jillian asked and turned the photo over to see if there was an inscription on the back as she found on the fake photo of Mattson at the fundraiser.

"Don't touch my stuff," Dani said and slapped Jillian's hand away.

"Where was this taken?" Jillian said.

Dani tore the tape, pulled the photo from the wall, and clutched it to her chest. She glared at Jillian, but the fire retreated from within, and Dani hunched on the edge of her bed. She rocked back and forth slowly and sobbed, once more disappearing behind a shroud of dark hair.

"Don't worry. She gets weepy and shit all the time," Annette said.

Jillian knelt in front of Dani and said, "I'm sorry, I didn't mean to upset you. Would you let me see your picture?"

Dani held the photo tighter.

"I promise I won't hurt it. Is that your little girl? She's so pretty."

Dani nodded.

"I promise I'll give it back," Jillian said.

"You promise you won't take it? It's all I have," Dani asked from behind her hair.

"I promise."

Dani's face turned upward, tearstains lined her cheeks, and her hands trembled as she offered the photograph.

Jillian handled it gently and flattened the creases where Dani's grip crushed the photo. "What's your daughter's name?"

"Emma."

"How old is she?"

"She was supposed to be five this week," Dani said in a whisper. "I killed her. I really didn't mean to. You believe me, don't you?" Dani grabbed Jillian's hand.

Jillian sat next to Dani and looked up at Annette who rolled her eyes in response to the emotional outburst.

"Yeah—yeah, we've heard it before. You're the mother of the year," Annette said.

"What happened to Emma?" Jillian said.

"She was sick. Emma had juvenile diabetes."

"That's not your fault, Dani."

"There was a drug trial. They said it would fix her autoimmune system and prevent her insulin-producing cells from being destroyed. I agreed to it, and she died. I didn't mean it. I only tried to help her. You have to believe me."

"I believe you, Dani. I'm so sorry."

"I wanted it to work. I really did. My husband worked for the drug company, and I thought…"

"What company?" Jillian tensed and glanced at the family photograph once more. The missing face of Dani's husband was troubling, but what made Jillian's shoulders tense was the man's posture. There was a familiar feeling from the sliver of the man's profile. "Was it Dynalife Pharmaceutical?"

Dani nodded. "How did you know?"

The fragment of the man in the family portrait looked pleasant enough, and the scar down his cheek was hardly noticeable. He didn't look as menacing as he did chasing Jillian on the train platform.

Chapter Twenty-Four

"Your husband works for Dynalife?"

"Three years. Tommy worked there for three years, and when Emma died, he started asking questions, you know, to find out what happened. And they canned him."

Dani pulled her hand out from under Jillian's grip. The recognition of the man's face caused enough fear that Jillian clamped down on the woman's arm with a white-knuckled grasp. Dani's expression changed, and she slid to the far end of the mattress, away from Jillian. The photo dropped to the mattress between them.

"Who are you?" Dani said. Her voice trembled.

"I'm not gonna hurt you," Jillian said. "Where is your husband now, Dani?"

Her shoulders shrugged, Dani said, "He blamed me for what happened. Tommy never said that, but in my heart, I know he thinks it is my fault for pushing him to get Emma into the drug trial program. About a week ago, Tommy left me, right after he lost his job at Dynalife."

"What did Tommy do for the company?"

"He worked in a place called Black Label."

"Black Label?"

Dani nodded.

In countless hours of board meetings and endless organizational reviews, Jillian never came across any division or office within Dynalife named Black Label. She tried another angle. "Did he talk about his job at Black Label?"

"Only once. He never said much about his work. I knew it must be important, the way he carried on about trade secrets and stuff. One time, he got a little drunk and started saying, like how he had the power of life and death. He said he was like Saint Peter, deciding who gets into new drug trials and who got left out."

"Trials are supposed to be random."

Dani shrugged. "I don't know what happened. When our little girl got sick, and the doctors told us nothing worked, I begged Tommy to do something. I pleaded over and over for him to save his daughter. He finally gave in and got her into a trial program for a new miracle drug, or at least it was supposed to be."

"You remember what it was called? The drug, what was it?"

"Who are you? Tommy said people would try to get me for this." She looked wary and inched away. "I don't want to say no more."

Dani rolled back onto the bed and curled up into a tight little ball. Her small frame shuddered, and soft muffled cries came from the broken woman.

"She'll be like this for hours," Annette said from the doorway.

Jillian reached out a hand and stroked Dani's back. "I'm sorry, I didn't mean to upset you."

Dani recoiled from Jillian's touch as if pricked with a jagged thorn. The woman pulled closer to the wall and distance herself from the outside world.

In Dani's fragile state, she would shatter into pieces if Jillian pressed her for more. Frustrated by the abrupt end of the conversation, Jillian got to her feet and paced in the small room.

"Did she ever mention any of this stuff to you?" Jillian asked Annette.

"She's said some of that before, in group. We're not supposed to talk about what goes on in the group sessions. They are supposed to be a safe place where you can talk about shit."

"She ever talk about her husband?"

"Tommy?"

"Yeah," Jillian said.

"He came and visited her the day after she got here. I didn't hear exactly what she said, but he got loud. The staff warned him to calm down. He was angry, yelling about what happened to their kid."

"Did he blame her?" Jillian said as she hooked a thumb toward Dani.

"That's the funny thing—he didn't. In spite of everything she says, her husband didn't think she was responsible. He said he was going to bring them down," Annette said.

"Bring who down?"

"Everyone behind the drug that killed his daughter."

Chapter Twenty-Five

"What do you mean I can't make a phone call?" Jillian said.

"Lady, you're on orientation status. You don't have phone privileges yet," said the staff member in the control booth, his voice muffled in the static over the small rectangular speaker box.

"You don't understand. I need to call my attorney."

"It don't matter. No calls." The conversation ended with an abrupt click over the speaker.

Jillian banged her fist on the speaker grill. The dents and gouges in the malformed cover gave evidence others experienced similar frustration in this spot. Her outburst drew attention from few patients on the dayroom floor. Most seemed used to the emotional thunderclap, while some appeared too medicated to care.

On the far end of the room, Annette looked at Jillian and shook her head in mock disgust. She tilted her head in the direction of the television area and got up from her seat.

Jillian caught up with Annette, and they sat in two vacant chairs at the outside edge of the television area.

"What did I tell you?" Annette asked.

"What? I have to make a phone call," Jillian said over the din of an educational DVD about the perils of relationships and bipolar disorder.

"Shh," a nearby patient with long stringy grey hair said.

Annette pulled closer to Jillian. "I told you to come to me if you had an issue.

"I need them to let me use the phone."

"They won't let you. That's the rules," Annette said.

"What am I supposed to do?"

"Don't play by the rules."

Annette laid a folded magazine in Jillian's lap and stood from her chair.

"Let me have it back when you're done," Annette said as she left Jillian alone.

Jillian folded back the magazine cover, and a slick black cell phone hidden within the pages slid into her lap. She popped her head up and surveyed the room, certain one of the staff members would find her in possession of this contraband. Paranoia crested once more, and she tucked the phone back inside the magazine. None of the staff noticed her shove the phone back into hiding.

With both hands clutched tight around the magazine, Jillian fled from the television area and sought a place out of staff view affording her privacy, in a place where privacy is forbidden. She couldn't return to her room because Dani was there, and the dayroom space provided nowhere a patient could linger without staff supervision. Jillian scanned the room for possible locations. She must connect with her attorney, Ryan McGowen. She couldn't reach out to William Comstock because he was a self-centered prick, only interested in the money, and the company's bottom line. Jillian's outcome in the process didn't matter to him. Prison, in his view, was an acceptable sacrifice for the company's stock price. Jillian gave up her private life for Dynalife and always kept the bottom line in mind when she made critical decisions. The fact that she was now the bottom line left her unsettled.

Privacy came in the form of a plastic cup. From over her shoulder, a staff member appeared. She was engrossed in her search for somewhere to hide and missed the orderly's approach. The high-pitched squeak of his Nike's on the linoleum floor hadn't registered.

"Jillian, you need to give us a urine sample," the man said, handing her a urine collection bottle.

She palmed the plastic bottle from him, while she maintained a death grip on the magazine and its promise of freedom.

"Whenever you feel like it. We were supposed to collect a urine sample this morning, but you were kinda busy with intake." He pointed to a door marked with a restroom placard. He sensed Jillian's apprehension and said, "Don't worry, this ain't that kind of drug test, nobody's gotta watch or nothing."

The bottle's label bore her name, the date, and a doctor's name she didn't recognize. Before Jillian could respond, the staff member left delivering bottles to other patients. She waited a full minute as she composed herself and silently rehearsed what she would say to the attorney.

She covered the distance from the chair to the restroom in slow, measured steps to mask how panicked and anxious she felt under her skin. The door opened outward and there was no locking mechanism to secure her privacy. She supposed the staff needed to make certain a suicidal patient couldn't take care of things behind a locked barrier. Inside, two wall-to-ceiling partitions separated two toilets, with no door or hooks for tie off points from which despondent patients could hang themselves.

Jillian crept to the far stall and pulled the phone from the magazine. She set the magazine and the collection bottle on the rear of the toilet. The phone flickered to life when she hit the power button and then she realized she didn't know Ryan McGowen's phone number.

A diversion to directory assistance cost precious few seconds before Jillian heard a voice announcing, "McGowen and Price."

"Ryan McGowen, please," Jillian said.

"May I ask who is calling?"

"Jillian Cooper," she said, as her voice seemed to boom off the toilet stall wall.

"Oh, Miss Cooper. I'm sorry. Mr. McGowen is out of the office at the moment. May I leave him a message you called?"

"No. I must speak with him. Please transfer me to his cell phone."

"I'm sorry, but it's not allowed. If you give me your number, I can ask him to call."

"Please, help me. I need to talk to him about Dynalife and drug testing. It's critical I speak with him."

"Please hold," the voice said.

CHAPTER TWENTY-FIVE

"Don't put me on hold," Jillian said to the music playing in the background.

A full chorus of an elevator music version of Green Day's "American Idiot" played before the phone picked up again.

"Miss Cooper?" said Ryan McGowen.

"I need to tell you what I've found out..."

"We can speak at court in the morning."

"There is a Dynalife employee out for revenge over his daughter's death. He blames the company," Jillian said, the weight lifted as she finally got the words out.

"Who is with you right now?"

"No one. I'm alone." Jillian peeked at the unlocked restroom door to be sure.

After a pause from McGowen, "Do you have a name?"

"Tom. Tommy something." Jillian realized all she knew was the first name of Dani's husband. She'd neglected to find out more information. "His wife is a patient here, she told me about it."

"Tom? That's what you called me with? We'll speak when you're dropped off at the courtroom. Get some rest, Miss Cooper."

"Wait. He worked in a division, or section named Black Label," Jillian said.

Silence on the other end of the phone.

"Did you hear me?"

A second voice came on the line. "Where did you hear the name?"

"Mr. Comstock?" Jillian said.

"Where did you hear about Black Label?" Comstock asked again. Anger wrapped around each of his words, a thick layer of venom palpable over the phone line.

"Don't you realize what this means? If this Tom guy was out to hurt the company, then he killed Jonathon. Don't you get it? It could prove I didn't do what they're saying I—"

"You keep your mouth shut. You hear me? Not another word about this. I told you I would make sure you're taken care of if you go along."

"And if I don't—go along?"

"Jilly, don't make any foolish decisions. There are things far worse than going to prison for a couple of years. In fact, you might not survive long enough to see prison."

Chapter Twenty-Six

Comstock's threats tumbled through Jillian's mind; they broke into thousands of smaller bits, each with sharp jagged edges slicing her fragile grip on reality. Comstock knew. He didn't come out and say it, but he knew about Black Label. He didn't ask her what it was, he only asked where she heard the name. How could Dynalife operate an off-the-books drug development operation she knew absolutely nothing about? As the Vice President of Marketing, she monitored every facet of the firm's research and trial programs. She worked her ass off keeping up to date on the projects and programs to keep Dynalife at the top of the pharmaceutical pyramid. Pride, and her need to succeed, blinded her to the truth. If Dani was right, Comstock, Paulson, and the others ran shadowy Black Label drug trials. They counted on Jillian's focus to keep their work hidden.

An hour later, as Jillian lay on her bunk in her shared room, she cursed herself for allowing the corporation to gain such total control over her. She tossed and turned on the thin mattress, unable to sleep in the torrent of unresolved questions.

"Can't sleep?" a voice called out in the swampy darkness of the room.

Jillian noticed some movement in the opposite corner of the room. In the scant light, Dani's eyes glistened and gave away her perch on the far corner of her own bed.

"I can't sleep either," Dani said. "They tell me I should take a pill to help me sleep, but I don't want to. I need control over one thing in my life, just one thing. They tell me when to wake up, when to eat, when to take my meds.

Tommy was the same, you know? He told me what kind of job I could have, what friends I could hang out with, and where I could spend my money. My own money. The only thing I asked him for was help for our daughter and look what happened."

"It is not your fault, Dani. Emma was a very sick little girl."

"Tommy was right. I was a horrible mother. The drugs killed her, and I made him get Emma into the program."

Dani's eyes glistened once again, but Jillian's attention found a slick, wet area reflecting on the bed linens gathered around the woman.

Jillian reached for the switch on the small bedside lamp, flicked the dingy yellow light on, and saw blood pooled in Dani's lap. Flecks of red dotted her face where Dani used her teeth to rip the sutures from her wrists. A small, steady rivulet drained from the open wounds.

Jillian hopped from her bed. "What did you do, Dani?" Jillian grabbed a pair of clean socks from Dani's bureau and wrapped them around Dani's wrists.

"Leave me alone," Dani said as she tried to pull away from Jillian. "Don't touch me. I don't want to do this anymore, let me go."

Blood soaked through the white cotton socks readily, but the flow diminished with pressure applied to Dani's thin wrists.

"I need help in here!" Jillian called out.

The hallway remained dim, but a shadow bobbed outside the small square window in the door, joined by a second, then another.

"Help me," Jillian repeated.

The door inched open, and one of the patients peeked her face inside. Annette bulled past and shouldered aside the other woman.

"Jesus, Dani!"

"Go get someone," Jillian said.

Annette didn't move. She remained transfixed on the blood-covered bed linens.

"Go," Jillian said as she tightened her grasp on Dani's thin slick wrists.

Annette disappeared back into the hallway, swallowed up by a half-dozen patients who gawked at the open doorway.

140

Dani stopped resisting Jillian's pressure and relaxed her body against the wall, hands extended to Jillian.

"Back off," a male voice sounded from the hallway.

The patients parted from the doorway and Annette followed a thick-necked man into the room.

The staff member looked like he spent hours in the gym lifting weights; his arms bulged against the fabric of the light green medical scrubs the night shift favored. Tattooed clusters of tribal patterns and rings of barbed wire circled both massive forearms.

"Move away from her," the staff member said as he pushed Jillian off the bed to the floor. At the instant Jillian's hands left the makeshift pressure bandages, the blood seeped through.

The man peeled back one of the socks, heavy and dark with the blood absorbed into the fabric. The tough guy winced at the sight of the ragged open wound. He snatched a radio from his belt.

"This is Paul, in B Pod. I got a medical emergency up here."

Another voice sounded over the small radio speaker, "It ain't Annette is it? That phony bitch can hang there all night…"

"No, I got a bleeder. She's gonna need an ambulance."

"All right, I'll call it in," the radio voice responded.

Paul looked at Jillian, said, "Did you put these bandages on?"

Jillian nodded. She sat on the floor where she'd fallen after Paul shoved her aside.

"You did a good thing. Why did she do this? Did she say why?"

"I woke up and found her like this. She was upset about losing her daughter," Jillian said.

"Yeah, I heard about that," he said. "Listen, why don't you go and clean up while we take care of her. Sorry, I shoved you."

Jillian didn't understand until she followed Paul's gaze to her hands and clothes, covered with blood.

Annette guided Jillian out to the hallway and grabbed her roughly, pushing her to the wall.

"We need to move," Annette said.

Jillian shoved Annette's arm away. "What are you talking about?"

"We have less than ten minutes until the ambulance gets here. They'll open the control room door and leave it unlocked while they wheel Dani out. I watched what they did when I faked hanging myself." She shoved a fresh pair of navy blue sweats at Jillian. "In the bathroom and clean up. Hurry."

Jillian grabbed the clothes and hurried into the same bathroom where she used the cell phone. She was surprised at the amount of Dani's blood coating her arms and hands. She scrubbed and soaped her hands until they felt raw. She couldn't wash away Dani's sorrow. With the fresh clothes on, Jillian left the bathroom as the paramedics pushed a gurney from the control room toward the crowd now taking up most of the hallway space.

A second staff member in green medical scrubs accompanied the paramedics. He pointed to the room where Dani waited, and he remained at the door, blocking the exit route.

Jillian caught Annette's figure in the hallway among the crowd of patients. Annette signaled with her hand out like a stop sign. Wait.

"Out of the way," one of the paramedics said.

The staff member who blocked the exit started to move. He started down the hall, urging the onlookers back, and then said, "Everyone back to your rooms."

The patients were more interested in what happened in Dani's room, and each wanted to tell their version of the incident.

Like a goose-herd, the staff member spread his arms and ambled down the corridor. "Come on now...back to your own rooms. Let's go."

As soon as the staff member passed Annette, she hurried to the control room door and motioned for Jillian.

They shot through the door and down the corridor. Jillian reached out for the down button on the keypad next to the elevator. Annette snatched her hand away before she touched the button.

"No, don't. The elevator goes down to the main lobby, remember?"

Annette retained her grip on Jillian's hand and pulled her down the corridor. At the end, a door marked "Fire Exit" evidenced dust and grime from lack of use. A second smaller sign read, "Must Remain Unlocked

During Business Hours." Annette didn't break stride, kicking the thick metal push bar holding the door closed. The fire door flew back against its hinges and banged off the stairwell wall with a loud thud. Somewhere in the deep stairwell, an alarm sounded, a shrill electronic chord wafted up from below.

"Come on, we don't have much time," Annette said as she released Jillian's hand and bounded down the first set of stairs.

Jillian glanced down the corridor and considered going back; the thought of running again terrified her. The consequences of Comstock's threat that she wouldn't survive if she stayed locked up in this place, tipped the scale in favor of the terror of running headlong into the unknown.

Jillian caught up with Annette at the bottom of the stairwell where a thick metal door with a push bar marked an exterior door.

Annette opened the door a few inches and peeked outside. "Come on," she said.

The doorway opened onto a fenced asphalt courtyard, a fire refuge in the event of an evacuation of the facility. The open space held faint white lines from its former designation as a parking lot, a valuable commodity in the city, one not willingly abandoned without the government requirement of a fire escape. Two mercury vapor fixtures flooded the space with blue-tinted light blinding Annette and Jillian when they stepped outside.

Annette pushed Jillian to the decorative iron fence lining the side of the courtyard. The fence was absent rolls of sharp razor wire or protective barriers to prevent escape. The City Planning Department didn't approve the harsh curb appeal of prison-like fashion design measures.

Annette reached the six-foot fence first and pulled herself over the topmost rail with athletic ease. She dropped off on the other side and motioned for Jillian.

Jillian grasped the rail and pulled, her shoulders burned from the effort. She dropped back down, inside the compound.

"Come on, hurry," Annette said.

"I can't do it."

"You want to stay here, that's on you. I'm out." Annette ran down the alley and disappeared around a street corner.

Distant sirens grew louder, horns blared as fire trucks responded to the alarm at the mental health facility. The flicker of red lights reflected off storefront windows down the block. Annette was right; Jillian didn't have much time.

She grabbed the iron rail once more, hooked her elbow around the top rail, and pulled. Woozy from the exertion, her vision dimmed, and she thought she was about to fall back into the courtyard. The yelp of a fire engine siren jolted her, and a shot of adrenaline surged for a final pull over the top of the fence.

Jillian landed awkwardly and twisted her left ankle. She rose from the pavement and started to run from the facility, but the pain from her left ankle hobbled her gait. She felt the swelling in the loose-fitting, slip-on hospital-issued sneakers.

In the courtyard, the fire exit door flew open and a stream of patients flowed into the courtyard with their staff escorts. Some of the patients were giddy with the field trip, but from her vantage point down the alleyway, Jillian saw others held confusion and fear etched on their faces. The madness was temporary, and it wouldn't take long until the keepers figured out Jillian escaped. Forces aligned against her and it was time to take control.

Chapter Twenty-Seven

C arlos Umberto Sanchez-Milar snuck a smoke in the alleyway behind the shipping and receiving dock at Dynalife Pharmaceutical. He stood behind a dumpster because the company protocol prohibited employees from smoking inside the building and the tree-hugging city council passed ordinance after ordinance outlawing smoking in public places, sidewalks, even in your own goddamn car. It wouldn't be long, Carlos figured, until the city told him when he could take a crap.

He pulled one last draw from his illicit cigarette, tossed it to the pavement, and crushed it with the heel of his tasseled Italian leather loafer. Carlos started toward the loading dock door when a voice stopped him.

"I figured I'd find you here."

Carlos turned and recognized Jillian. His brow furrowed as he looked over her appearance.

"You've kinda let yourself go eh, Cooper?"

A night of wandering the streets after fleeing the psych ward left her eyes red and puffy. She felt hollow.

"Your wife know you're still smoking?"

"She thinks I'm a saint. Don't you be telling her no different. His face darkened, and he spoke in hushed tones. "We've heard all the crap. Sorry, you're going through that. If it helps, not many of us in the business operations side believe any of the nonsense."

"Thanks, Carlos," Jillian said.

"I didn't mean me." A crooked smile beamed across his face.

"I need your help," Jillian said.

"I figured you weren't here to bust my balls over my smoking."

Jillian shifted. "I need the R&D financials."

"What do you need the Research and Development books for? Wait—wait, I don't wanna know why. I can't simply turn over the ledgers without a court order. The company's new drug development data is in there, you know, the real proprietary shit."

"That's why I need it, Carlos. There's a hidden account in the R&D operation and it stinks."

"Gonna sell secrets? I wouldn't blame you if you wanted to. Be worth millions. The accounting system is automated and won't let me print out the R&D accounts without bells and whistles going off from here to Phoenix."

"I need the information. You've seen it, right? Was there a line item that didn't look right to you?"

"Like what?"

"I can't exactly say, but duplicate testing and development lines for the same drug compounds," Jillian said.

"No way. You can't hide any significant amount in the R&D budget. Testing and drug trials cost millions; it ain't exactly budget dust you're talking about. A second line of testing and trials would be cost-prohibitive."

"Please, I need to see it for myself. I know the budget's wrong there and it could help me prove I didn't have anything to do with…"

"Killing Jonathon Mattson," Carlos finished.

"And David Paulson," Jillian said.

"Yeah, that too."

Carlos fumbled with his cigarette pack and pulled one out with trembling fingers. He needed three attempts until his hand was controlled enough to operate his lighter. He inhaled a deep drag, and blue-grey smoke trailed upward.

"What are you hearing?"

He shook his head. "The nerd herd has our offices in the back side of the building. I couldn't tell you what color the sky is." He drew another hit off the cigarette and tossed it to the pavement, not bothering to crush it this time.

"What aren't you saying, Carlos?"

"I wonder if that's why Mr. Mattson wanted me to look at the R&D accounts?"

"When?"

"Mr. Mattson came by my office late Thursday, and he's never done that before. I've only met the guy once before back when—"

"What did he want?" Jillian said.

"He asked me about a spike in expenditures for warehouse operations in San Francisco."

"Is that unusual?" Jillian said.

"Considering we don't own a warehouse facility in the city, yeah I'd say it was unusual."

"How did Jonathon come across the warehouse expenditures? I mean it's not like he got involved in the day-to-day business."

"I don't know. But, it's his company, he gets to poke around wherever he wants."

"Did he say why he wanted the warehouse data?"

"He said he was gathering some cost-cutting options for a Board of Directors meeting next week and stumbled onto it. He did say I was not to mention his inquiry to David Paulson. You know David, he'd get his knickers in a twist if someone started snooping where they shouldn't."

"Jonathon wanted to know how the warehouse was funded."

Carlos nodded.

"How much are we talking about?"

"Seven-and-a-half million a year for the last four years," Carlos said.

"That's one hell of a storage locker. What did you find out?"

"I pulled our facility operations files and got as far as confirming Dynalife has no billing for any warehouse in the region. The closest thing we run is a distribution center in Los Angeles," he said.

"David acted really strange the last few days. I chalked it up to Mattson's suspicion and the company's vulnerability. Suppose Jonathon Mattson uncovered a problem. He wasn't supposed to find out and it got him killed."

Carlos nodded, pulled out his cigarette pack, and nervously fingered it before he shoved it back in his pocket without lighting up. "A seven-and-a-half million-dollar scam is pretty risky, and you'd have to know the company's financial structure in order to pull it off without getting caught."

"I need to see what Jonathon found, and the R&D accounts too. I know they are tied together somehow," Jillian said.

Carlos thought for a moment, looked hard at Jillian. "If Mr. Mattson was bringing down that kind of heat, you're gonna get me killed. Well shit. You bring nothing but sunshine into my life, you know that Jillian?" He looked at his wristwatch, and said, "Meet me back here after six. The nerd herd will be gone by then, and we can have the place to ourselves. I must be crazy to do this. Consorting with a felon, harboring a fugitive, and God knows how many other laws I'm breaking. For all I know, you want to get me alone and kill me too."

A sparkle shown in his eyes, and Jillian knew he was in.

"Thanks, Carlos. I promise I won't kill you. Besides, if I'm half the stone-cold killer they make me out to be, I should have done you in and sloughed your body in the dumpster by now. I guess I'm getting soft," Jillian said.

"Yeah, yeah, whatever. Be here after six, and I'll let you in," Carlos said as he turned toward the doorway. He stopped after a few steps, said, "I hope you know what you're doing."

"I hope you can find the money," Jillian said.

"Thanks for the shot of confidence there, Cooper," Carlos said, turning back to the door.

"That's all I've got. My life depends on it," she said, sounding more desperate than she planned.

"Mine too," Carlos said, disappearing inside the Dynalife building.

Chapter Twenty-Eight

J illian couldn't hide all day behind the Dynalife loading dock. An old line from a television crime drama about the guilty returning to the scene of the crime boomed in her mind. The police believed she murdered David Paulson in this building, and they knew she escaped from the mental health facility by now.

Staying on the street wasn't an option. Jillian needed cover and conceal-ment, a safe place she could wait out the time until the Dynalife building was empty.

She backtracked to the public library on Larkin Street and slipped inside. The place was busy, as Jillian hoped. The illusion of blending in turned to smoke fast, as she followed a buttoned-up nanny guiding her two blonde wards into the building. The nanny steered her charges away from the disheveled Jillian. A sneer of judgment and disappointment on the young woman's face was a reminder Jillian didn't fit in here. Jillian wasn't sure where she belonged anymore.

Jillian wandered through the stacks, avoiding others, until she found a quiet row, on one of the upper floors. The history section on the sixth floor was devoid of library users, everyone she knew seemed to be consumed by the present, or worried about the future. The past was, well—past.

She sat cross-legged, leaned back on the bookrack, and tipped her head, taking in the smell of old books around her. The collective wisdom in these moldy volumes seemed foreign and out of touch. Long dead scribes wrote of struggle and survival in the heady days of the 1850s gold rush. There weren't any volumes on these shelves lamenting over parenting errors or a misguided search for self. There was no time for such luxuries back then, there was only the day-to-day fight for existence.

Jillian leaned across the aisle and tipped a worn brown-backed book out of its place on the shelf. It plopped on the floor and fell open to a story about early settlers resorting to deception to hide gold from thieves. Deception struck a chord with Jillian. Nothing was as it seemed since she crawled out of the bed in what she believed was Mattson's apartment. The inspector said the place belonged to Renee Marquez, whoever the hell he was.

She stiffened. Who was Renee Marquez? She dropped the book in a bin at the end of the row and found an empty computer terminal on the fifth-floor Computer Learning Center. Two clusters of terminals spread out on long counters facing one another and only one terminal was occupied. A rail-thin man, wearing thick black-framed glasses with equally thick lenses, tapped on a keyboard and glanced at Jillian as she sat on the far end of the counter. The glance occurred without a break in keystroke and Jillian accepted the gesture as an "I won't bother you, you don't bother me" offer. They were two people uncomfortable with the outside world and shared an unspoken agreement—a détente.

Jillian brought up a browser window and keyed in the name, "Renee Marquez," in a search engine window. The results snapped back in seconds with over twenty-five thousand hits on the name.

"Of course there are," Jillian said.

The man in the black glasses sighed, glanced up until Jillian made eye contact, and held her gaze for a second, a warning of a breach in protocol. He returned to his monitor and tapped away.

She changed the search terms and included "Renee Marquez" and "Dynalife." A sharp tap on the enter key and the search returned with red letters proclaiming, "No Matches."

"Son-of-a-bitch."

The key tapping down from the other terminal stopped. Jillian didn't look up but felt the disapproval covering the distance between them.

Jillian typed in "Renee Marquez" and "drugs." The search narrowed down to five hundred hits, the entire first page of results was link after link to news articles and reports on the arrest and trial of a gang member on drug charges.

She clicked on one of the top links, and a Bay Area news service told of an elaborate heroin smuggling operation involving networks of suppliers, distributors, and anonymous middlemen, spanning the west coast. An Enrique Marquez was arrested following a yearlong federal undercover operation and indicted on a dozen counts of organized crime, drug trafficking, and arms dealing. Marquez used illegal migrant labor to move thousands of pounds of heroin over the border from Mexico to California.

Marquez was considered a high-ranking member of the Mexican Mafia, a ruthless, violent criminal gang spawned in the state prison system. His arrest cut off the gang's southern heroin supply.

Jillian clicked on another link, with the headline, "Prosecution's Case Falls Apart." The massive drug seizure forced the Mexican Mafia to find new suppliers for their products to meet the continuing demand in their market. But the case against the gang crumbled because witnesses disappeared before they testified. Informants recanted their stories, changed their recollection of events, and street rumors of a Mexican Mafia hitman brought the prosecution's case to its knees.

The body of a protected witness was a powerful message to those who considered turning on the gang. All but one witness disappeared and the feds ended up dropping interest in the matter. The state charges of Conspiracy to Commit Murder and Drug Possession resulted in a life prison term for Enrique Marquez. The lone witness died within weeks of his testimony, in what local authorities laughingly reported as a random drive-by shooting.

Jillian scrolled ahead to a photo of Marquez, taken at Pelican Bay State Prison. The gang kingpin, dressed in prison orange, bore a defiant expression, close-cropped hair, and square jaw.

Jillian's breath hitched at the sight of the Mafia boss. A familiar paranoia snaked up her spine. The man in Pelican Bay was an older version of Tommy. The scar-faced man had the same chin, skin tone, and most chillingly the same dead eyes. Tommy was the gang's hitman.

"Why the fuck are you after me?"

The bespectacled man stopped tapping on his keyboard and sighed. He gathered up his books, notes, and belongings and left, but not before he shot Jillian a look of judgment and disgust.

Jillian shrugged an apology to the man but was glad the place was hers. She glanced back to the screen, at the older version of her pursuer. Tommy could have snapped her neck on the train platform. Why hadn't he? Jillian stumbled onto this connection but found no clue about the mysterious Renee Marquez.

The last paragraph on the screen claimed authorities were unable to capture the Mexican Mafia enforcer before he disappeared and went underground. No description of the killer existed, but some sources reported the hitman was "disfigured" in some manner.

Jillian's mind recalled the scar on Tommy's face.

A connection between a prison gang and the Vice President of Marketing seemed improbable, yet Tommy's words, "I know what you did," more than hinted at the link between them. There was a connection, and Jillian didn't know how it was possible.

Jillian searched property records for the owner of apartment 6B of the Nob Hill building. Public tax records listed a corporate owner, one Jillian hadn't heard before. Given enough time, she could trace the corporate offices and uncover a name. But, it was coming up on four p.m., and Jillian wanted to arrive early at Dynalife to make certain she wasn't walking into a snare set by the police, or now the Mexican Mafia, apparently.

Chapter Twenty-Nine

At twenty past six, Carlos reemerged from the building into the alley. He ventured only a couple of steps from the lighted loading dock, peered into the purple darkness where the tall buildings blotted out the last remnants of sunset, the alleyway draped in layers of shadow.

From a recessed doorway, some fifty feet down the alley, Jillian watched Carlos under the bright lights inside the loading dock. He shifted his weight from one foot to the other, clearly uncomfortable, perhaps nervous, Jillian thought. She waited.

A subtle sound trickled from the loading dock behind Carlos, a low murmur of voices. Others were there with Carlos. Jillian pressed back into the concealment of the doorway and prepared to slip down the alley the moment Carlos turned away. She'd nearly fallen into a trap, lured here, and set up once again. The sounds of conversation in the loading dock persisted and Carlos turned to speak to someone hidden behind him.

Jillian noticed elongated shadows of two figures moving behind Carlos and coming in her direction. Carlos pointed into the darkness and spoke to the men with him. It looked as if he ordered the others into the alley to find her.

She moved out of the recessed doorway and with her back to the building, pressed inch by inch deeper into the swell of the shadows. Jillian froze as two men, in coveralls passed under a streetlight. The men carried insulated lunchboxes, and their coveralls bore Dynalife emblems emblazoned on the front.

"Good night, Jefe," one of the men said to Carlos.

"Night, guys," Carlos said in return.

Jillian felt her face flush in the dark. The men were dockworkers on their way home, not a conspiratorial posse out for the bounty on her head. Paranoia was a powerful bitch. Jillian waited until the men disappeared out of sight, down the far reaches of the alley before she moved.

Carlos didn't see Jillian until she crossed to the near side of the alley and into the light pooling on the asphalt apron of the loading dock.

"I was beginning to think you were going to stand me up, Cooper," Carlos said.

"I wouldn't want you to have flashbacks from your senior prom. I wasn't expecting anybody else around."

Carlos nodded, said, "I told you the accounting staff would be gone—and they are. But, the building has people working late. You should know that."

"Yeah, I guess you're right. I haven't been thinking too clearly lately."

"No shit. Come on, let's do this before I chicken out."

Jillian followed Carlos to the freight elevator, which in her years at the company, she'd never used. He punched the button for the third floor, and the car lurched upward, the whine of the hydraulic lift prevented awkward conversation. The car shuddered to a stop, the doors parted, and exposed a small passageway in the rear of the accounting offices.

"This way. We have the floor to ourselves," Carlos said.

Jillian scanned the warrens of waist-high cubicles designed to improve worker productivity, but the impersonal workspaces looked more like feeding stalls at a stockyard. Instead of troughs of hay and grain, computer terminals, invoices, and stacks of printouts fed this lot.

Carlos keyed open an office door, one of the few offices outlining the walls of the cubicle farm. A small bronze nameplate labeled his office, and Jillian felt a pang of embarrassment she hadn't bothered to meet with him here before this happened.

Along one wall, a cheap, brown laminate table held piles of printouts, files and folders, pushed to one side. In the center of the table, red and white boxes of Chinese takeout were set out with paper plates, plastic chopsticks, and a six-pack of Tsingtao beer.

The exotic aromas of sesame chicken, sweet and sour pork, and chow mien uncovered Jillian's suppressed hunger. She'd eaten nothing since the apple at the farmer's market.

"I thought you could use a little pick-me-up," Carlos said as he popped open the container and slipped generous portions onto the paper plates. He slid one of the plates toward a chair, motioned to Jillian, and said, "First, you eat, then we'll work."

The pair ate in silence and washed down the takeout with the cold beer. Jillian pushed her empty plate away and began peeling away the beer bottle label with a fingernail.

"Why did this happen?" she said, without a glance upward from the shredded label.

Carlos took a pull from his Tsingtao and shook his head. "You're not asking the right question, Cooper." He put his feet up on a corner of the table and tipped his bottle at Jillian. "You think this is about you. The authorities blamed you for Jonathon Mattson's murder and the company issued a reward for your capture."

"How is this not about me? Setting me up to rot in some prison cell for the rest of my life sounds personal to me."

"The question you need to ask is, what was Mr. Mattson into that someone didn't want out in the open? What was so important they needed to take him out?"

The shreds of paper from the label covered Jillian's lap. She held the empty bottle like a magic eight ball and hoped some answer would appear. "How am I supposed to know?"

Carlos removed his feet from the table, rolled his chair close to Jillian's, and grabbed her by the arms. Face-to-face, he looked at Jillian with an impish grin. "You already know. You told me to look at the Research and Development accounts, remember? And, I'll bet you another beer Mattson knew what was off-balance in R&D too."

Jillian swept the scraps of beer label into her hand and deposited them in a trash bin next to the table. She got up and paced the office for a moment. "That has to be the connection. Mattson and Paulson found out about an off account product testing and development program."

"And the people behind that program didn't want it exposed," Carlos said. "How can we prove it?"

Carlos spread his arms wide. "Follow the money, Cooper."

"This is gonna take a while. Why don't you grab some rest," Carlos said as he tapped commands on his computer keyboard shooting line after line of account code and transaction detail to one of the monitors on his desk. "There's a sofa right outside my door, in the waiting area. I've used it myself more than once."

"I don't think I could sleep right now. You sure there isn't anyone else on the floor right now?"

Carlos stopped working on the computer. "What'd you hear?"

"No. No, nothing like that. The gym is on this floor. I might have stashed some fresh clothes in my locker in case I needed to change after work, and I'd love a chance to clean up."

"I–I suppose it would be okay. Be careful. I don't know if anyone uses the gym this time of the evening."

"I need your building access card," Jillian said with her hand extended toward Carlos.

"Oh great. In addition to aiding and abetting a wanted felon, the security records are gonna show I like to prowl around the women's locker room at night. It can't get any better." He unclipped his access card from his belt and handed it to Jillian.

"I'm not a felon. You have to be convicted first," she said and snapped up the card.

Carlos turned back to the monitors, said, "Not yet you're not."

Jillian slipped out of his office and waded through the empty work cubicles and halfway across the expanse, a trickle of fear dripped into her mind. She stopped and listened intently, but heard nothing but her own heartbeat and the clacking of Carlos on his keyboard. She cracked open the door and peeked in the hallway. Once she was certain it was empty, with no telltale footsteps, she crept into the hallway and made her way through the silent corridors to the employee gym.

The lights inside the frosted glass door were on, but Jillian wasn't certain if they always remained lit at this hour, or not. She slid the access card Carlos gave her into the slot and the electronic lock popped open. A glimpse inside the gym door revealed lines of empty exercise equipment; top of the line recumbent bikes, stair steppers, and elliptical machines. Assorted weight training equipment also sat empty on an opposing wall, reflected in floor-to-ceiling mirrors.

The men and women's locker room doors were located on the far side of the gym, opposite the door where Jillian stood. With no signs of after-hours Dynalife employees, she slipped inside, and the door clicked shut behind her. Temporary relief settled around her in the silent gym and she strode to the women's locker room. Motion-activated lights flickered on when Jillian pushed the door. Three banks of lockers filled the room, one on each wall, and one in the center. Four shower stalls, with frosted glass fronts, lined the back wall.

Jillian's assigned locker was on the far left side, halfway down the bank of red enameled lockers. From where she stood, near the locker room entrance, she saw lengths of bright blue and red tape strung across her locker door. The words, "Police evidence, do not disturb under penalty of law," threatened fines or jail time if someone tampered with the length of tape.

The warning didn't slow Jillian. She jogged to her locker, spun the combination dial, pulled the locker door ripping the tape seal. Inside, an extra set of casual clothes hung as she left them, a blue small nylon satchel lay on the bottom with her workout gear, and a few cosmetic and makeup accessories lined the topmost shelf. Her things were as she'd left them. It was as if the police hadn't rifled through her locker.

She pushed the thought of DiManno searching through her things aside, although she thought it odd that he didn't leave a receipt along with a copy of the warrant as he had in her apartment. She grabbed a change of clothes, shampoo, a towel from a bin near the shower stalls, and started the shower. Jillian stripped off the institutional clothes she'd worn since her escape from the mental health facility and stepped into the steam. Hot water coursed over her skin, kneading the knotted muscles on her neck and shoulders. She rested her forehead against the shower wall and let the water scald her back, and hoped fear washed down the drain along with the filth and grime.

The motion-activated lights in the locker room clicked off. Jillian considered the sudden darkness as a signal she showered long enough and shut off the water. The dim light from the illuminated exit sign allowed her to see her towel, so she grabbed it and quickly wrapped it around her body. As she reached for the shower door, a sliver of light from the far end of the locker room split the near darkness. Someone entered the women's locker room with her. The motion-activated lights flicked on.

Jillian slipped open the frosted shower door an inch and couldn't see who entered, but she saw her clothes on the bench outside her shower. She put one foot outside the shower, snagged her clothes, and stepped back into the shower stall. Footsteps echoed from the far side of the locker room, and they were heavy steps, a man's stride.

Pressed against the shower wall, Jillian felt the approach before the shadow grew larger through the shower door. The chill of the tile against her back matched the sensation running up her spine. The man came closer with each step, and Jillian realized she'd trapped herself in the shower stall. The imposing shadowy person blocked the only way out.

A few feet from the shower door, the figure stopped, his shadow nearly filled the frosted glass door.

Jillian's breath grew shallow. The muscles in her legs cramped as she held herself rigid against the shower wall. She expected the shower door to fling open at any moment.

A metallic clank and the sound of metal on metal filled the locker room. The visitor banged against the bank of lockers and wasn't concerned about the noise. One of the lockers gave and sprang back on its hinges with a distinctive twang, and the banging stopped. A metal bar crashed to the tile floor, and Jillian heard the man rummage through a locker, hers no doubt. She'd closed it out of habit, not because there was anything of value inside.

Moments later, the shadow shrank from the shower door, and the footfalls reversed toward the locker room door. Jillian stayed shivering in the shower stall until the motion-activated lights flicked off once more.

She gave herself a quick, rough once over with the towel and threw on her own clean clothes, a navy blue polo shirt and jeans. The familiar clothing felt comforting against her skin. The motion-activated lights snapped on once again, and a sharp jolt of panic put a catch in her breath until she realized she triggered them.

The mental health facility sweatpants and t-shirt she'd worn when she arrived were destined for the trash bin. She padded over to her locker where her locker door hung open, bent where the metal pry bar forced against the frame. Nothing was taken, but Jillian spotted something new stuffed in a corner of the locker. She bent close and recognized a scarf, one she wore regularly, tucked under her gym bag. She didn't remember leaving the scarf in her gym locker. The pattern looked wrong. Mixed in with the grey and white geometric print was a red design.

Jillian unrolled the scarf and dropped it to the locker room floor when she realized the design was a large bloodstain. It was Mattson's blood. She was certain of it. The faint blood outline in the shape of the knife sent a shiver down her spine.

She used her towel to hide the scarf in the trash. Another link between her and Mattson's death. Someone wanted to make sure she went down for the murder and was making it easy for Inspector DiManno.

Jillian grabbed a pair of running shoes from her gym bag, put them on, and headed for the locker room door. She scooped up the metal pry bar left by the intruder and hefted the weight in her hand as she pushed through the door into the gym. She brandished the crowbar like a Louisville Slugger and found no one in the workout room, except for her reflection in one of the mirrors near the weight equipment.

The likeness of a slightly built, damp-haired, disgraced corporate executive, wielding a crowbar in the mirror wasn't as menacing as Jillian hoped. It looked desperate. It was a woman who clung to the last tattered remnants of a life, a life beyond redemption—mirrors don't lie.

Jillian turned away from the image, she didn't need another reminder of how broken she was.

Alone in the gym, Jillian's thoughts cycled. Who'd come into the women's locker room and hid a bloodstained scarf added to the unresolved cloud swirling around her.

How much more evidence do they have?

Jillian noticed the men's locker room door ajar. She pushed the door open with the pry bar and the motion-activated lights popped on. Two locker doors were pried open in a similarly brutal fashion. She approached the first locker and saw the nameplate above claimed the empty space belonged to Jonathon Mattson. She'd never seen Mattson in the gym during the years she worked at Dynalife, so the lack of as much as a stick of deodorant in the locker didn't surprise her.

Down the bank of lockers, Jillian figured the second ruptured door was David Paulson's locker space. Items of clothing and hair products lay on the floor along with a broken bottle of skin moisturizer.

On the opposite bank of lockers, Jillian noticed the names of other executives displayed proudly. The women's lockers bore no elaborate brass plaques claiming their spaces. Another vestige of the male-dominated corporate culture within the firm.

Jillian spied a clock on the wall and figured Carlos would give up on her if she didn't return soon. Toward the front of the bank of lockers, Jillian caught a whiff of cologne, harsh, and abrasive. If it was supposed to be alluring, it missed the mark. Wait—she'd come across this scent. It was exactly the same scent McGowen, the attorney, wore when he came to the PHF.

She leaned toward the lockers and followed the smell. It seemed to waft from the vents of one locker in particular. She glanced at the door, and the nameplate proclaimed, Ryan McGowen, her attorney. At least one of her senses hadn't failed her.

Jillian jammed the crowbar in the space between the locker door and the frame and pulled against the thin metal. The lock popped open, and the door sprung ajar, the odor of McGowen's cologne was strong inside. No exercise gear, clothing, or toiletries cluttered the shelves. The only items in the locker were on the center of the top shelf, a blue terrycloth bundle and a toppled, leaking bottle of cologne.

She tucked the crowbar under one arm and removed the wad from

McGowen's locker. The folded cloth package was a fine cotton face cloth and Jillian held it to her nose, wincing from the overpowering odor. She unfolded the fabric slowly, preventing the contents from slipping within its folds. She felt a hard object, perhaps two inches long and half that wide between the layers of material. Jillian opened the cloth and found a micro-cassette tape, the kind the company used to record board meetings and telephone conferences before they went digital. Only a few of the company's older execs used them, shunning new cloud-based technology.

The tape bore no markings and Jillian turned the cassette in her hand and noticed the label was gone with fragments of adhesive bits left behind.

Jillian quickly folded the cloth over the micro-tape, grabbed a fresh towel from a rack nearby, and rolled the cologne-drenched package inside, deadening the odor in a crude protective layer. She left the men's locker room and returned to her own ruined locker space, where she shoved the wadded towel in her handbag along with a makeup mirror and a few cosmetic items.

Jillian felt charged by the discovery of the tape. Whatever was recorded on it was important, she figured. Important enough that people died to keep it undiscovered. She needed a tape player, and she knew where one was in her old office.

On her way across the gym floor, Jillian noticed a faint outline through the frosted glass entry. Jillian edged closer. The shadow outside pulled on the handle but didn't open the door.

She slung the handbag over her shoulder and made sure the crowbar was at the ready. A few soft steps closer to the door, Jillian raised the metal bar over her head and readied to strike whoever entered. No more running away.

The shadow wavered behind the frosted glass but made no move on the door. It waited in the hallway.

Enough with reacting, Jillian decided it was her time to attack. She wasn't going to be a victim this time. The pressure caused by hiding, running, and waking up in foreign apartments and mental wards boiled to a white-hot rage. Her free hand gripped the door, and the crowbar cocked in the other.

Jillian drew in a breath, flung open the door, and charged into the hallway toward the shadow.

The metal bar sliced downward and swiped a fraction of an inch in front of her target's face. The sharply curved end of the crowbar slashed into the drywall and plaster wall surface, the tines ripping open a three-inch gash. Jillian grunted as she pulled the bar out of the wall and cocked it back for another strike.

Her target fell and crabbed backward away from her. The man's face came into focus. It was Carlos Umberto Sanchez-Milar.

Chapter Thirty

"What the hell are you doing here?" Jillian said as the crowbar quivered in her hands.

Carlos drew himself into a ball, hands, and arms coiled to protect his head. "Jesus, Cooper, it's me."

Jillian lowered the bar and pressed the rounded hooked end against his chest. "I know it's you," she said. "What. Are. You. Doing. Here?" Each word punctuated with a prod from the end of the crowbar.

"What's wrong with you? Have you lost your fricken mind?"

She pushed the crowbar under his chin, added a bit more pressure, and said, "Answer my question."

He scrambled back. "I got worried, and you were gone a long time."

"You came to find me? Why were you out here in the hall?"

"You took my access card, I couldn't open the gym," Carlos said.

She unpinned the crowbar from his throat and let him sit up. "You didn't come into the gym or the locker rooms?"

He looked confused and rubbed his hands over his face. "I told you. You have my access card, that's why I was out here waiting to get my head bashed in. So, no, I didn't come inside."

Jillian lowered the crowbar to her side and leaned back on the wall, considering his response. "If you didn't, then who was it?"

Carlos got to his feet, shrugged, and said, "I didn't see anyone leave until you came out and got all Warrior Princess on my ass."

"Sorry," Jillian said.

"What was that? I put my job on the line for you, sneak you in here, and face going to jail, and you say, 'sorry' like it is no big deal."

"I meant…"

"You make me punch through every accounting system firewall on a snipe hunt for phantom accounts until I find one. Then you try to take my head off and nearly make me shit myself and all you have to say…"

Jillian stiffened. "Wait. Back up. You found it?"

"Of course I found it. Don't sound so surprised. It was pretty clever, but you're not gonna like it," Carlos said.

"What do you mean?"

"Come on. It's best if I show you." They marched down the hallway to the accounting offices. Carlos deliberately kept his distance from the crowbar sticking out of Jillian's handbag. "Whoever did this knows the company accounting systems inside and out. If someone started to track the transaction back, they appeared to come from one individual."

Carlos held open the accounting office door for Jillian. She noticed an odd glimmer in his eyes.

Jillian stopped halfway through the threshold. "Who?"

"You, Cooper."

"That's not possible." She put a knuckle to her lip and tapped. "It does explain what Inspector DiManno said about grand theft and conspiracy to commit fraud. I didn't know what he was talking about. How much did I supposedly embezzle from Dynalife?"

"I'll show you what twenty-five million looks like."

"It's a chunk of change, but that's not enough to run a clinical trial program."

"Twenty-five million is what you have sitting in the account now. That doesn't include what churned through the account in the last couple of years. Double that—maybe triple the amount. Come," he said and opened his office door.

Mounds of printouts and accounting spreadsheets on the worktable replaced the Chinese food cartons and paper plates. The paper smelled of warm printer toner and covered the entire table surface. A dozen printouts bore bright red highlighted portions with lines connecting each highlighted section to the next. Carlos displayed several pages in a line, taped across one entire wall of his office.

Carlos looked quite proud of his discovery and gestured to the page he'd taped to the wall. "Mr. Mattson started asking about the R&D accounts, and about a discrepancy there. That's where I started poking around."

"I thought you couldn't pull those reports without bells and whistles going off somewhere."

"If you drill down to the specific product line details, the system requires multiple levels of authorization, and they know when anyone accesses the R&D expenses for a particular drug."

"They know?" Jillian said. She whirled around and expected a rush from the outer office.

"Would you chill for a second? God, you're making me as neurotic as you are."

"You said you needed authorization for this. They know you pulled the account information."

"You're not listening, Cooper. I said *if* I accessed the specific product line detail, the bells and whistles would go off. I thought I could pull the information we needed by looking elsewhere, and I was right." Carlos held a self-satisfied smirk and gestured to the spreadsheets taped to the wall.

"I don't understand. I know there is a secondary line of clinical trials. I saw the bottles. That must be what Jonathon suspected and he came to you for confirmation. The information is in the product line accounts."

Carlos shook his head like a disapproving schoolmaster. "I guess you're not a visual person. I'll walk you through and use small words."

Jillian flipped him off.

He faced the centermost spreadsheet made up of row upon row of numbers, with a hand-drawn red circle around one particular column. He tapped a column with a fingertip. "Does this look familiar? It should, it's you—or your Marketing Division, anyway."

"Not mine anymore," Jillian said.

"To a forensic accountant, this sheet shows twenty-five million of company assets transferred to Marketing, the transaction made under your authorization."

Jillian looked at the numbers. "I recognize the marketing account codes, but I didn't transfer twenty-five million..."

"Here's where they dropped the ball. Whoever set this up–set you up–thought this was as far as anyone would look because the next month shows twenty-five million gone. Again, with your authorization." Carlos pointed to an adjacent sheet. "You'd have to assume Cooper has the money."

"Is it all gone?"

"Oh yes, every dime. But I found where it went–literally where."

"You know what the money bought?"

"Most of it. Some made it into new accounts, funding purchase orders for lab equipment, microscopes, centrifuges, glass beakers, and machinery to encapsulate pharmaceuticals. I got it from purchase order details. But, I found a monthly ten-thousand-dollar lease payment for a facility here in the city, where this equipment got shipped."

"You found it?

Carlos grinned, handed Jillian a slip of paper, and said, "I did."

She snatched the note from his hand and read the address, an unfamiliar one somewhere south of Market. Jillian glanced up at the accountant's Cheshire grin.

"What are you holding back?" she asked.

"The company automated the facility operations records eighteen months ago and scanned in the existing paper documents." Carlos stepped to his desk and plucked a thin sheaf of paper. "This is the lease for the address in your hand."

Jillian held the lease document and scanned the first page. "The place has a clean room, air filtration system, a laboratory set up, and the utility connections required to operate," Jillian said.

"Turn to the last page," Carlos said.

She thumbed to the end of the document. There, on the bottom of the page, was the signature of the person who executed the lease and oversaw the facility.

"David Paulson was behind this? He ran the off-the-books clinical testing program? What was in it for him?"

Carlos fumbled with his cigarette package, considered lighting up inside his office, and changed his mind, tossing the pack on his desk. "Why does any company do clinical trials and testing? For the revenue, Cooper."

"Twenty-five million sounds like a lot of money—hell, it is a lot of money, but it's a drop in the bucket compared to the cost to research, develop, test, and market a new drug. Drug development runs into the billions with FDA approval and oversight during the process. Why would David go to this extreme when he couldn't possibly put Bosphizion on the market?"

"From the money trail, there are no expenses noted for research, phased clinical trials, or marketing, like you'd expect to see from a pharmaceutical product line. It was a big sucking black hole where the money disappeared, but nothing came out—on paper anyway."

"You're saying Dynalife didn't earn a return out of this elaborate scheme?" Jillian asked.

"Nothing shows up in revenue from any product from this off-the-books lab. My guess is he used some form of separate account, out of the company's oversight where the revenue ended up."

"Like an off-shore account?" Jillian said.

"A bit melodramatic, but yeah, something along those lines," Carlos said as he looked at his watch. "Listen, like I said, you can park on the sofa tonight if you want. You'll need to be out of here before the staff starts showing up around six-thirty or so."

The soft, warm sofa called a siren's song, tempting, alluring. It was welcoming, if not for the creep roaming in the locker room. The chill on the back of her neck cautioned against another run-in with the shadow man.

"Thanks, Carlos. I should move on. But, I have a favor to ask."

"Oh, wonderful. Well, I'm going to prison anyway for helping you. What?"

Jillian unfolded the towel-wrapped microcassette. "Can you find me a recorder to play this with? I kept one in my old office, but I don't think I should be wandering around the place."

"What's on the tape? Wait. I don't wanna know."

Carlos got up, strolled a few steps outside his office, and rummaged through a line of desks. Less than a minute later he came back with a slim handheld tape recorder. "We don't have much use for these anymore." He handed the device to Jillian.

She flipped the cassette recorder open and the tape popped in with a soft click. Her thumb hovered over the play button.

"I don't wanna hear nothing I might have to testify about." Carlos grabbed his jacket and turned to leave.

"Thank you, Carlos," Jillian said.

"I was gonna say, I'll visit you in prison, but then I figured helping you probably got me some time behind bars too. But, I'll parole out before you," Carlos said.

Jillian's mood darkened for a moment. She regretted getting Carlos involved in her nightmare. "Please be careful. The people involved in this, Mattson and Paulson, are—"

"Dead?"

She nodded. "I don't know who else is involved, but I don't trust McGowan. For that matter, I don't know if I'd trust anyone in the company."

"You could go to the police. You have proof of a conspiracy now."

"I can't, not yet, anyway. I needed them to believe I wasn't involved with this." She held an account ledger sheet. "The accounting makes it look like I was up to my neck in running an off-the-books drug facility. I want to poke around the lab."

"I don't think it's a good idea," Carlos said. "If people are dying for knowing about the place, don't get caught snooping around."

She nodded. "Thank you for believing."

"Everyone's got to believe in something, why not you?"

Carlos left Jillian alone in the office. She didn't move until she heard the elevator door close on the far side of the offices. Her thumb hit the play button, and a five-second gap of static began to crush her spirit. Then a voice sounded over the small speaker. It was tinny but recognizable. It was Jonathon Mattson.

"It wasn't supposed to be like this. You promised me, goddammit," Mattson said.

"You knew the people we were dealing with. You can't stop the Black Label shipments." It was David Paulson. She was listening to the conversation of two dead men.

"It's my goddamn company, I can do whatever I want," Jonathon countered.

A crash sounded on the tape. A glass object shattered in the background. "Don't you get it? It's not your company anymore. It belongs to them. The moment you took those prison drug contracts, they owned you. You didn't complain when their cash rolled in and you can't back away now."

"I built this company, and you and no bunch of thugs are gonna take it from me. Let them cancel the prison contracts. We don't need them. The real Black Label profit is from the other market."

"Cancel contracts? These people don't deal that way. They'll cancel you," David's voice responded.

"Shelly will only be able to save your ass for so long, Jonathon. Do you really think she'll bail you out of this deal?" The third voice said. It wasn't David or Jonathon.

Jonathon cleared his throat. "She's addicted to money, of course she will. Shelly knows where her priorities are. Speaking of which, she's waiting for us…"

"I can't let you do this," David said, his voice trailing off.

The tape continued to burn with faint background sounds for four minutes before it clicked off, the tape having run its full length.

Jillian leaned back on the sofa and tried to tie together the conversation, prison drug contracts, and Jonathon's murder. Finally, a thread that pointed at someone else. It didn't exonerate her completely, but combined with the accounting work Carlos provided, there was hope.

Jillian flicked off the recorder, shoved it in her purse, and gathered a few of the accounting records Carlos accumulated. A chime echoed from the elevator, the one Carlos used when he left. He wouldn't come back here and risk getting caught with her. She raked the documents together with her arms and stuffed them in her purse.

The elevator doors parted, and Jillian crouched behind a cubicle wall outside of the office, closed her purse, and the paper wrinkled threatening to give away her position. A flashlight beam swept the accounting office space. The main office floor was dark, but Jillian neglected to turn out the light in Carlos's office. A man entered the cubicle aisles, checking each cluster of desks and partitions. He was drawn to the office light. It wasn't until he was halfway through the warren of cubicles Jillian recognized the security uniform.

Jillian stayed to the outside edge of the cubicle farm, and as the security man moved in, she matched his pace in the opposite direction. She was ten feet from the hallway door as the man reached the office. Jillian readied and bolted into the hallway when he stepped into Carlos's office.

She retraced her route to the freight elevator and hit the call button. Jillian pressed the button again, urging the car to her level. A glance over her shoulder made certain the security man, or the creep from the locker room hadn't followed her. The freight elevator clunked to a stop, its heavy hydraulic system locking the platform in place. The doors rumbled open, unaccompanied by the telltale chime of the main elevator. In the quiet building, the mechanical noise would draw attention.

Jillian entered the elevator, pressed the button for the loading dock, and the doors rumbled closed. As the last sliver of a gap disappeared, Jillian caught the edge of a flashlight beam from down the hallway.

She jogged to the loading dock exit and made it out of the Dynalife building.

From the cover of the pitch-black alleyway, she caught the scuff of shoe leather on the rough pavement. The sound came from the end of the alleyway, in the direction of the Dynalife loading docks. Jillian turned and witnessed a shadow as it morphed into the figure of a man in a security uniform. Jillian hunched in the dark, she couldn't risk standing in the open. The man stood with a sense of alertness under the yellow-amber glow of the spotlight at the back of the dock. The security guard flicked on his flashlight and stabbed the beam out into the darkness.

Jillian's knees buckled. She toppled against the graffiti-laced alley wall and remained motionless, her eyes locked onto the man. All she heard was her own rapid breathing and the percussion of her heartbeat.

"Clear at the back dock. Nobody's here," he said into a microphone clipped to his uniform shirt.

Jillian couldn't hear any reply at this distance. After a pause, the man responded, "I don't care what you beat outta Carlos, I'm tellin' ya' she ain't here."

The old confident Jillian would have launched at the security man right there, demanding to know where Carlos was. But, the new broken version of herself turned away from confrontation and shifted to self-preservation. Not so much flight versus fight, as it was anger and calculated revenge. Carlos helped her and now he was getting worked over to give her up. The events made the acid boil in her stomach. The sesame chicken threatened to come up.

Jillian slipped down the alley until she rounded the corner onto Montgomery. She leaned against the dirty alley wall, and her mind spun with the content on the microcassette, the thug at the bus station, and a lease document with David Paulson's name on it. He and Mattson were responsible, and they were both dead. David lied to her to protect his own ass. The deception stung, but it may have saved her life, until now. The two men who worked together to crush her life paid for their betrayal. There were others involved in the Black Label operation. Mattson and Paulson were killed first because they were the easiest to find.

Carlos must have tripped an alarm accessing the Black Label account and his financial database. Carlos said someone with insider knowledge of the company's financial operations covered up the illicit drug facility. Jillian felt like a small fish, baited to the sparkle and movement of a deadly lure trolling in murky water.

Black Label. Jillian's thoughts clicked back to the train station and the parolee with the prescription bottle. She noticed the Dynalife Pharmaceutical label on the bottle, but the differences on the label weren't significant enough to register, at the time. The logo and lettering were black, not the usual blue and white label. It must be where Dani's husband got their daughter into a drug trial. There was more than a prison drug contract involved here; Black Label killed an innocent girl.

The recording held the keys to her freedom. Jonathon Mattson and David Paulson orchestrated the fraud and the cover-up of the illegal drug manufacturing operation. While she held scant proof, she was certain David was involved in Jonathon Mattson's death. The tone he held with his superior bordered on threatening. But tone wasn't enough to convince the police Mattson didn't die by her hand. Paulson could have cleared her, and now he was dead, too.

Jillian recalled the smug, self-assured way the company attorney told her to take the plea deal in court. Take the eleven years. He said it like it was nothing. Do some time, and there would be money in it for her. He wasn't the one going to prison, and he put in a lot of effort to make sure she disappeared fast and without a whimper. David deserved what he got. But, the question remained; who wanted her out of the way? Mattson and Paulson were dead, yet Tommy, the aggrieved father, and hitman was after her.

Anger welled within. Jillian found huge holes in the gauzy cloth of her memory, but the fact Comstock and the board wanted her muzzled set her on edge.

You think you can buy my silence. How much is it worth to you?

She flagged a taxi, and it slowed, the driver looking over the potential fare before it pulled to the curb.

Jillian hopped in the back seat and told the driver the address. He looked in the rearview mirror; his eyes showed concern, or curiosity, Jillian couldn't tell which.

The cabbie lurched away from the curb and started the meter. Again, his eyes flicked up to the mirror.

"You sure there ain't someplace else I can take you? It ain't a good area, you know? After dark and all."

Jillian nodded and said, "Thank you, I'll be fine. I'm meeting someone there."

"It ain't none of my business, but you want to wait in the cab until they show up? Off the meter, of course."

"Shouldn't be necessary, but thanks for the offer," she said.

The cab turned into a deep industrial part of town framed by shuttered manufacturing plants, rusted steel-framed buildings, and an occasional structure clinging to life in this desolate patch. Grime-coated windows partially obscured the signs of dead businesses. Iron bars and blacked-out security glass marked the survivors. Most of the streetlamps were dark, and the cab's tires crunched over the shattered glass remains of the bulbs as it cruised to the address Jillian provided.

The address was a large two-story warehouse with undecipherable graffiti scrawled across the front, like most in the area. This one bore no windows on the lower floor, and a single iron door marked the entrance. Jillian hadn't expected a flashing neon sign announcing an illegal drug lab, but she expected a lab with an elaborate front, not a dilapidated commercial building.

The cabbie pulled up, short of the building, and turned in his seat, facing Jillian. "Lady, it doesn't look like the place is open. You sure you got the right address?"

"This is it." Jillian opened the door.

The driver got out, and a worry line creased his forehead. "I don't think it's a good idea to leave you here."

"Thanks, but this is the place I'm looking for." After a pause, she added, "I'm meeting someone here."

The driver saw through her thin lie. "You sure?"

Jillian nodded.

"You get stood up, you call me, understood? I don't like the thought of you being out here. I told you this ain't a good area." He handed her a business card with his contact information.

Jillian removed a twenty-dollar bill from the purse she liberated from her work locker and handed it to him. "Thank you." She closed the passenger door and stood back, waiting for the cabbie to drive off.

Once he disappeared, Jillian approached the warehouse at an angle and saw the structure was designed to appear flimsy and dilapidated. But, the mottled color was paint on concrete block, made to appear like the thin metal siding cladding the skins of the other buildings. The second-floor windows were opaque and prohibited any view of the inner workings, even from the taller adjacent buildings. As she drew near to the building, Jillian spotted small black camera units, invisible from a distance, tucked under the roofline above her. Any closer and Jillian figured she'd find herself featured on someone's video screen.

Jillian backed off a few steps, glanced up at the second floor and the flat roof above. No claxon of alarm bells sounded, no sudden snap of floodlights descended down upon her, and no one rushed out from the front door.

Jillian retreated to the shadowed well of an abandoned auto parts store across the street. The door gave in under slight pressure, and Jillian slipped inside. The pungent odor of urine wafted from the far end of the dilapidated store. Shelves and empty display cases lay in haphazard piles on the chipped cement floor. Valuable material, like recyclable copper wiring or other scrap metals, disappeared from this space long ago. Rags and cardboard reeked of body odor, marking the old store as a squatter's nest.

Exhausted, Jillian didn't want to venture deeper into the space. She found a shadowed corner near a cracked window with a view to the Black Label building across the street. She hoped the window was filthy enough to shield her and keep her hidden.

Patience always eluded Jillian. She'd been the person who saw what she wanted, went out, and grabbed it. Patience was a polite term for purposeful procrastination, an excuse for being lazy and slow. She bounced on her toes, anxious and growing more intolerant by the minute. "Come on, come on, come on." Seconds felt like hours.

Patience...

The minute Carlos gave up the location of the Black Label facility, the balance of power swung in Jillian's favor for the first time. No one could deny the existence of this space, a brick and mortar symbol of greed. The building held the secrets proving she was innocent. Jonathon Mattson and David Paulson were killed because of the secrets hidden behind those walls. As important as the facility was to Dynalife, Comstock was certain to send someone to make sure the building was secure, and then they would come for her. Patience was a bitter pill.

Chapter Thirty-One

Amidnight-black form prowled toward Jillian's hideaway on the vacant industrial street. The approach silent and undetected, until the glass shards from the broken streetlamps sounded a shattered alarm.

Jillian hunched low behind the window's heavy frame and peered into the darkness. The broken glass crackled down the street, but all Jillian saw was black on black emptiness.

"They're coming," a rough whisper called from behind her.

Jillian whirled around, tumbled against the wall, searching for the source of the voice.

From behind a toppled auto parts display case, the voice said, "Get out of the window, or they'll see you."

Jillian slid down the wall and dropped to the cold cement. Her butt firmly planted on the floor near the window, she looked into the void, toward the unseen voice, then to the door and tensed her legs ready to bolt. She couldn't decide which way to go.

"She's gonna ruin everything, Jason," a female voice said from deep within the space. "She doesn't belong here."

"Hush up," Jason said as he popped up from the shadows. He sported stringy bleached hair sticking out in all directions, in an expensive cut trying to look casually hip. A dark designer t-shirt hung on his thin frame. He looked at Jillian, then over to his female companion and said, "We aren't supposed to be here either, Hailey. She's hiding, like us." Then to Jillian, "Please, lady, don't let them see you."

Jillian crept back from the window, away from the allure of the door, back into the protective shadows. Broken glass shattered under heavy pressure outside. A reflective surface gave away the stealthy approach of a vehicle without headlights. The apparition revealed itself as a black Cadillac Escalade when it passed under the light mounted at the Black Label lab. Momentary silence signaled the SUV's pause to deposit a figure in front of the facility. The Escalade continued the slow, dark stalk down the street, announced by shards of shattered light bulbs.

"Are they gone?" the young girl whispered.

Jillian turned and saw Hailey next to her standing on her toes to catch a glimpse of the street outside. The girl was barely five-foot-tall, with dark, blunt-cut hair and pale white skin accented by heavy mascara and eyeshadow. Jillian thought of it as a teenage girl's attempt at grown-up sophistication, but it tipped the scales more toward raccoon than high fashion.

"Across the street," Jillian told her and pointed to the location she last saw the Escalade's passenger.

Hailey saw them, and her eyes flashed. "They came back, Jason. You said they wouldn't."

Jason climbed out from under his hiding place behind the clutter, stood next to Jillian and Hailey while he tried to look out the window. "I don't see anyone Hailey. It's fine."

"It's not fine. Don't tell me it's fine," she snapped. "I want to go home." Tears welled in the young girl's eyes.

"Where's home?" Jillian said.

"Paisley, Oregon," Jason said.

"I don't think I know where that is," Jillian said.

"No one does," Hailey said. "It's between nothing and nothing on the way to nowhere. Paisley is one of those places, if you grow up there, you never leave. You grow old and die in the same spot. I don't want to do that. Least, I didn't think so."

"Your parents know where you are?"

Hailey shook her head.

"Hailey read some magazine about how San Francisco was *the* place to

177

make a fresh start, so we came here. Some start huh?" Jason said.

Hailey held her face in her hands and sobbed softly. "I'm sorry Jason."

"Me too, baby," he said as he put an arm around her. "It didn't turn out like we planned is all. We still have time to make it right."

"How long have you been here?" Jillian asked.

"In San Francisco? About three weeks," Jason said.

"How did you find this place?"

"A couple of dudes in Golden Gate Park said if we could find one of the empty stores out here we could make a go of it if we kept to ourselves. You know, don't bother anyone, stay out of the street during the day, and don't poach on another's turf. It was supposed to be okay," Jason said.

"What happened?" Jillian said.

"That man—that's what happened," Hailey said as she wiped tears with her sweatshirt sleeve.

"A few nights back, a car pulled up in front of that place in the middle of the night. It seemed really strange, so we found a safe place to watch and checked it out. Hailey and I met up with a few others who hang out in the building next door because sometimes things fall off the trucks, you know? Other times people give you food and stuff you can sell."

Jillian nodded.

"The guy in the car didn't want anyone around," Jason said.

"There was a body in the car," Hailey said. "So, we all split."

"As in a dead body?" Jillian asked.

"It was all wrapped in a blanket and all, but you could totally tell it was a body—a woman's body," Hailey said.

"How could you tell?"

"Because she dropped this," Hailey said with her hand extended toward Jillian.

Cupped in the palm of the girl's small hand was one of Jillian's missing Tanzanite earrings. The twin of the piece Inspector DiManno kept in an evidence bag.

"She wasn't dead," Jillian said.

"How do you know?"

CHAPTER THIRTY-ONE

"Because it was me."

Hailey tilted her head, confusion glazed across her face.

"The person you saw was me. The earring you found is one of mine, and it explains a lot," Jillian said with relief etched in her voice.

Hailey pulled back the earring, in fear Jillian threatened to take her found treasure.

"But we saw—it looked like the woman, was dead," Jason said.

"It was me. The earring, the unexplained gaps in what I can remember. I think I was drugged," Jillian said.

"Were you—you know—raped?" Hailey asked.

Jillian flashed on the condom wrapper in the Nob Hill apartment building where she'd come to. In spite of the evidence, she believed nothing happened, consensual, or otherwise. It was part of a pattern, a staged set of events, designed to plant a seed of paranoia. Nourished by the frustrating memory loss and Mattson's murder, the seedling flourished into a dense terror-ridden thicket of self-doubt, fear, and confusion.

"No, I don't think that was the point," Jillian said.

"Sounds like a date-rape kinda thing," Jason said.

"Whoever did this to me—they wanted me to be confused—to believe what they wanted me to believe. A man was murdered, and they left a trail right to my doorstep. And the reason for it is in that warehouse."

Hailey took a step back at the mention of murder.

"What's the warehouse got to do with it?" Jason said.

"An illegal pharmaceutical operation," Jillian said.

"A meth lab?' Jason said.

"No. Prescription drugs like antibiotics and antivirals." Jillian saw the confused looks on the two runaways and tried to explain. "Like the drugs you get from the doctor when you're sick. Except, what they make over there isn't inspected or tested and could be dangerous."

"Why are they doing it?" Hailey said.

"Money, and a lot of it."

Hailey nodded thoughtfully.

Outside, the improvised broken glass alarm sounded once more. The

SUV circled back to the warehouse and pulled to a stop. A tall man stepped out from behind the wheel, and the person who got out on the earlier pass joined him. Hushed tones of urgent conversation exchanged between them.

Jillian didn't have to hear the words to know what the two people were after. The winds of coincidence hadn't carried them to this place. They came for her.

She saw the tall man head to the Black Label facility's steel front door where he punched a code into the keypad attached to the frame of the door. The sequence unlocked the door, and it popped open, releasing a sliver of bright light from inside the compound. The glow washed over the man's face and Jillian caught a telling glimpse. It was the scar-faced man from the bus station, Dani's husband, Tommy.

His driver pulled the Escalade down the darkened roadway and disappeared behind one of the vacant, faceless buildings.

The door's self-close mechanism suspended the door ajar for a moment before it started closing. Jillian watched Tommy disappear inside the facility doorway.

"Stay here," Jillian said and shouldered her way out of the auto parts store and sprinted toward the warehouse door as it swung shut. Her feet kicked up chunks of chipped asphalt and broken glass as she headed to the narrowing gap of doorway light. She caught a toe on a raised lip of concrete walkway in front of the door and fell forward on her hands and knees against the rough surface.

The door continued on its slow track, narrowing the open space between the steel door and the frame. Jillian scrabbled closer, stretched out as far as she could, stabbed her hand out, and grabbed the edge of the heavy door. The inside edge of the door pressed into the fresh abrasions on her palm, flecked with bits of concrete from her tumble. Sharp fragments pressed deeper into her flesh as the door's weight pressed onward. Jillian pushed against the pain until her fingers gripped the rim of the door, and the back of her hand kept the door away from the frame.

Jillian hunched next to the entrance, shoved her free hand into the partially open door slit, and pulled the gap open. She slid inside, sprawled on the floor while the door closed and an electronic tone confirmed it locked behind her. A glance upward found no push bar, or doorknob on the inside of the door, only another keypad.

A spark of panic ignited in the inner reaches of her mind with the realization she sealed herself inside with Tommy.

Chapter Thirty-Two

Panic quickly traded for fear when Jillian heard Tommy's voice. A second set of doors separated the entrance lobby from the main area of the building. Thin swinging doors featured an inset Plexiglas window panel in the upper half of each door spilled light from the inner facility. Jillian rose up from the floor, peeked through the window, and saw row upon row of overturned boxes, thousands of pills and capsules spilled from them littering the warehouse floor.

White powdered footprints trailed through the rubble and tracks led off to the far end of the floor. Tommy cursed and grabbed boxes, tossing them to the floor. Shelves came down with the Black Label bottles rolling on the concrete surface. She parted the doors with her hand and slipped inside while his back was turned. Jillian snuck behind a large shipping crate to the left of the door.

"You'll never do this again." He kicked a spilled pile of unfilled gelatin pharmaceutical capsules.

Jillian risked a peek out from behind the crate. An unexpected woman's voice struck a familiar chord.

"You can't do this!" the woman said over a phone in Tommy's hand.

"It's done, get over it. The Cooper woman was supposed to die. She is next."

"You screwed it up. She's as good as gone anyway. Don't waste your time, she only knows what's in the marketing brochures."

Asshole. There was more truth there than she wanted to admit.

"She doesn't know everything about Black Label. We can contain this," the woman said.

"There is a paper trail proving she was responsible. She sold the products made here," Tommy said.

"She'll pay for what she did. Cooper will take the fall for Jonathon's murder," the voice said. "Isn't that enough?"

Jillian finally put the voice in context. It was Shelly Mattson talking to the scar-faced stalker.

"No, it's not enough. I tried playing the game your way. I want her gone. All of it gone—now."

"Do I need to remind you we have clients who put out cash and won't tolerate an interruption in access to our drugs," Shelly said.

"Fuck them!" Tommy said.

"These aren't the people you can piss on. You, of all people, should know."

"She has to pay for her part in this. The Cooper woman—"

"Can be bullheaded, and stubborn like a pit bull with a baby when she sets her mind to it. But, she's busy hiding from the police. If you're bent on taking the woman out, you need to do it soon and do it right this time. And soon, before she can screw everything up," Shelly said.

Bullheaded and stubborn, or focused, determined and driven. All in the eye of the beholder.

"Carlos told me she was here. He lied and I'll deal with him later. I'm done here. Black Label is done, you hear me?" Tommy said. He didn't wait for a response. He shoved the cell in his pocket and looked at the destruction.

At his movement, Jillian ducked, her weight shifted, and a mound of pharmaceutical capsules snapped beneath her feet. The fragile shells cracked and popped at the slightest touch. The sound betrayed her position and Jillian tensed, waiting for Tommy to crash upon her.

A knot swelled in her stomach at the sound of his footsteps. Every fiber in her body frozen, a wounded animal's instinct to play dead wouldn't help her now. Jillian cupped her hands over her ears and curled up, knees to chest against the shipping crate. She waited for the death blow, but the attack didn't occur. Tommy's footsteps continued, but they didn't advance in her direction. Instead, glass shattered and metal objects crashed on the other side of the shipping container. Jillian wiped a pile of pharmaceutical capsules away with the blade of her hand, giving her a place to move without popping the empty plastic pill shells. She got up and edged to one side of the crate as he pulled a shelving unit to the floor. Glass containers and small tubs of powdered substances rolled onto the floor.

Tommy dumped two gallons of acetone over the broken bottles of chemicals and documents spilled from the toppled shelf. He poured the chemical and formed a liquid trail through boxes of packaged drugs and into the lab equipment and encapsulating machinery.

He dumped the last of the acetone onto the shipping crate, inches from Jillian's head. Some of the compound seeped down the side of the crate. The sickening-sweet chemical burned Jillian's nose and made her eyes water. Tommy was so close she feared her thundering heartbeat would give her away. She held her breath and fought a cough reflex burning deep in the back of her throat.

Tommy toppled another shelving unit, glass and pharmaceutical-grade powder spilled to the floor. He worked his way to the front of the facility, eradicating the Black Label operation in his wake. Jillian popped out of hiding when she heard the electronic keypad sound as he keyed in the code.

He turned, and Jillian ducked, uncertain if he'd spotted her. Tommy flicked an old-fashioned metal lighter open, thumbed the wheel, and ignited a flame. He tossed the lighter underhand and stepped outside, without bothering to see where the device landed.

A low rumbling whoomp, sounded where the lighter hit. A blue flame spread from the center of the warehouse, following the path Tommy left to the front of the building.

Flames separated Jillian from the front door. Through the waves of heat generated by the chemical fire, Jillian watched as outside air rushed in, fed the flames, and doubled the size of the wall of fire. Jillian shielded her face from the heat and felt the skin on her hands burn.

The exit door slammed shut behind Tommy, and the electronic lock secured the bolt in the doorframe. Flames and bitter chemical-laden smoke cut off any access to the door. Behind her, a wall of flames licked at the wooden support beams in the old structure. Jillian backed away from the heat and tried another course, only to discover the fire circled around her in every direction, sealing her inside.

A dense black smoke pillow lofted above the floor, with tendrils snaking and gathering on the inside peaks of the pitched roof. The chemical fog burned with each breath. The lining of her throat and lungs ached from the effort. The smoke-filled half of the space in less than a minute and Jillian looked up to the rafters and followed the trail of the pitch-black smoke. In the center of the roof, fifteen feet directly above her head, a two-foot diameter stainless steel vent stack poked down through the mist.

The lease documents. She recalled the contracts that detailed the specs for the facility included a high-powered air filtration system with exhaust vents and fume hoods for work with caustic chemicals. Behind a flame barrier, the switch for the fan system was enclosed within an electrical box. Jillian couldn't reach the control mechanism to activate the exhaust because of the intense heat. She picked up a broken length of shelving and dropped it when the hot metal singed her hands. Gritting her teeth, Jillian grabbed the hot metal shelf piece and jabbed at the switch box.

On the second attempt, Jillian broke open the box. Another jab found the switch. She pushed up at an angle and hoped she didn't slip. The electrical switch flipped on, and the exhaust system activated, pulling the smoke up through the central vent. The flames also responded and built intensity. With the smoke moving out, Jillian found she breathed with a bit less pain, but she remained isolated, away from the only locked exit door.

Above her, the smoke changed direction and exposed a narrow metal catwalk that ran the perimeter above the rafters. The walkway provided access to the windows in the upper reaches of the pitched roof. Jillian scanned the walkway for a ladder or landing leading to the catwalk. Against the far back wall, she spotted an old ladder, one looking like it belonged on a fire escape of a century-old city apartment building, bare metal rungs with a cage wrapping its entire length. Between the ladder and Jillian, a bright blue and white flame curtain blocked the path.

Near the front of the building, a bottle of chemicals succumbed to the heat and exploded, followed by another. The explosion accelerated the flames and the liquid fire pooled outward toward Jillian.

Jillian grabbed a handful of pills from the floor, shoved them into her pocket, tucked three pharmaceutical bottles into another, and pulled a shipping manifest from the side of a container. If she was going to die, she wanted it to have meaning.

She made a dash to the far wall and assessed the distance to the ladder, through the flames. Jillian found a white lab coat, ripped the sleeves off, pulled them over her hands like mittens, and wrapped the remnants of the coat around her face. She backed up, took a running start, and leaped through the flames. The cuffs on her pant legs ignited, small flames turned the fabric into molten slag, melting to the skin on her ankles. She patted down the flames and scurried up the ladder. Below her, Jillian saw the entire floor rolled and boiled in flame. The catwalk was her only option for survival.

From outside, the opaque windows seemed like typical commercial-grade glass for the structure. Up close, Jillian found them reinforced with wire mesh and secured into the building with heavy lag bolts. She stood opposite the nearest window, grabbed the rafters above her, and swung her legs at the window. The glass bent but didn't break with the first kick. Jillian swung back on the rafters and brought up her legs once more. She kicked at the glass, and it shattered, but the wire mesh held it in place.

The exhaust fan stuttered and stopped. The fire shorted out the electrical lines feeding the equipment and the lights inside. Without the exhaust fan, the smoke rose to the rafters and obscured the window a few feet away from her.

Breathing became heavy, and after a coughing fit, Jillian grabbed the rafters with her arms and kicked at the window. She wasn't sure how much longer she could fight, how much air remained in the smoke-filled warehouse, or if the window would yield. One last kick was all she had left in her. Jillian swung out and pushed her feet against the glass. The last reserve of breath in her lungs exploded out with the effort. The windowpane gave way, and her momentum carried her halfway through the opening.

Precious thick oxygen filled her chest, and she couldn't suck in enough. Jillian coughed, and she felt like she was drowning in a pool of fresh air. Drifting on the edge of consciousness, she didn't react after a strong hand gripped her burned ankle. She was aware of the pain, but the neurons in her brain misfired and prevented a physical response. Whoever it was, grabbed both legs and pulled her out of the broken window frame and onto the roof.

Jillian felt the heat from below and tasted the soot in her mouth. Bright flames alternated with darkness, red and black, red and black, a man pulled her toward what must be hell. She tried to fight off the unseen hands, but her body wasn't strong enough to resist. Brighter now, harsh red and darker black, Jillian floated downward into a circle of light. At the bottom of a well, she saw the faint outline of a hand cupped over her face. She turned her head away. With her eyes closed, she knew Tommy returned to finish her, to suffocate her.

The strong hand gripped her face and held a hand over her mouth and nose. A voice came through, "Relax and take a deep breath." A soothing voice, not Tommy's acidic tone.

Her breathing grew less labored, and Jillian's eyes flicked open. The red flashes continued, but Jillian saw they were not the fires of hell, but rather, lights from a half dozen fire trucks.

"That's it, keep breathing," a soot-covered fireman said from above her. His pale green eyes showed a calm, confident presence putting her at ease.

Behind the fireman, the two teenage runaways, stood huddled together.

"These two ran for a payphone and called 911. I'm glad they called when they did, or we might not have gotten here in time."

Jillian nodded beneath the oxygen mask. She parted her lips to speak and coughed. The fireman put a hand gently on her shoulder and patted.

"Don't try to talk, that will come later. Just breathe," he said.

"We got worried when you didn't come out. Then the smoke started coming out the top of the roof," the boy said.

The exhaust fan, Jillian figured. It sent the smoke signal warning them.

The girl said, "The man looked mad when he left. And we saw the fire, I thought for sure you were..."

"So did I," Jillian choked.

"I'm glad you weren't," another voice said from behind the kids. Inspector DiManno stepped between them and edged up to Jillian. "We have to stop meeting like this, Cooper."

Chapter Thirty-Three

Groups of squatters slithered from their dens, drawn out by the evening's entertainment. A rare street gathering provided a momentary diversion from the isolation and hustling needed to patch together an existence in this community of castoffs. Most viewed the spectacle like kids at a fireworks show, with "oohs" and "ahs" at each burst of flame, or fiery explosion. A few hardened predators used the opportunity, looted unguarded property, and lifted vials of morphine sulfate from an unlocked paramedic vehicle.

In the center ring of the spectacle, DiManno took a knee next to the gurney where the paramedics tended to Jillian. Ash and soot painted her exposed skin. DiManno noticed the melted fabric on her legs.

"How's she doing?" he asked the attending paramedic.

"Not bad—considering. She's one lucky lady. This could've ended differently. She has second-degree burns on her right lower leg, some minor, first-degree burns on her hands, face, and ears along with the smoke inhalation."

DiManno watched as the paramedic cut Jillian's pant leg with a pair of scissors, then cleaned and dressed the bubbled patch of skin near her ankle. Strands of melted material stuck to her flesh in spots and the paramedic carefully cut around the wounds.

"Miss Cooper, you haven't been entirely forthcoming with me. I'm beginning to think you had your reasons. Why the hell were you in there?" DiManno said, pointing at the smoldering warehouse.

Jillian boosted herself up on the gurney and induced a fit of ragged coughs.

The paramedic wanted her back down, but she brushed his hand aside and reached into her right pants pocket. She held the contents for DiManno. Jillian dumped a handful of pills and capsules into his palm. Then she retrieved a partially melted Dynalife Black Label bottle and a soot-stained packing label from her left pocket and handed it to the Inspector.

"I don't understand," he said as he looked at the items in his hands. "You telling me this was a Dynalife facility?"

Jillian nodded, whispered, "The man who killed Mattson and Paulson, he set this fire. Why are *you* here?"

DiManno paused a moment before he responded. "Shelly Mattson. She called and told me I'd find you here."

Paramedics lifted the gurney, releasing its wheels to the asphalt. They loaded Jillian into the ambulance before she could absorb what the police detective said. The jostling of the gurney sent a fissure of pain from her burned leg. The doors closed and Jillian focused on the Inspector "As far as Mrs. Mattson knew, I wasn't inside. I overheard her talking to the man who torched the place. Why would she tell you differently?"

The ambulance ride and exam in the emergency room went on for the better part of two hours. Her wounds dressed, and lungs pumped with fresh oxygen, Jillian signed herself out against the attending physician's advice. Armed with a bundle of fresh gauze pads and burn ointment, she tossed off the thin backless hospital smock and pulled on her smoke-stained pants, only to find them cut from cuff to hip. She tore them off, shoved them back in the plastic bag with the rest of her personal effects, and wrapped her torso in a thin cotton blanket from the bed.

She poked her head out from behind the curtain and snagged an orderly restocking the adjacent bed. She explained her situation and a few minutes later exited her bed dressed in green hospital scrubs.

Inspector DiManno was parked in a chair outside the nurse's station while the doctors and nursing staff attended to Jillian's injuries. Jillian thought he looked weary, and in spite of the circumstances, she was relieved to see him.

He rose from his spot. "The doctor told me you should really stay, at least overnight."

"I'll be fine."

"You missed your court appearance. The judge issued a bench warrant for failure to appear."

"I'm confused and tired as hell. I don't know what's going on. I know I've told you before and you don't give a rat's ass. Do what you have to do, but I'm going to fight this thing and get my life back." Jillian squinted and scowled at the police Inspector, who towered over her by a foot and a half.

"You hungry?" DiManno said.

Jillian pinched her forehead. "What?"

"Are you hungry? It's a simple question."

"You're taking me to jail, why do you care if I'm hungry?"

"I'm not in any rush. I'm hungry and thought you might be," he said.

"You said the judge issued a warrant for my arrest."

"Okay, if it makes you feel better—you're under arrest." DiManno made the sign of the cross with his hand in front of her. "Now, don't misunderstand. If you try to run again, I won't run after you. I'll shoot you. Got it?"

Jillian cocked her head. "Yes and yes."

"Yes what?" he said.

"Yes, I know you'll shoot me—and yes—I'm hungry."

"Then it's settled. I know a place that serves breakfast all day, where we can talk over blueberry pancakes."

"I didn't take you for a foodie. I thought cops ate cheeseburgers and doughnuts."

"Only when we're not swilling bad coffee and bourbon," DiManno said as he gathered his jacket from the chair.

As they entered the emergency room lounge area, Jillian felt a nagging sensation, deep in the lizard-brain part of her, telling her, screaming at her, to run. Trust no one. Run and make a new life somewhere.

DiManno sensed the tension growing within her and stopped, looked at her, and said, "I'm giving you a chance to make this right. Something's eating at me about Mattson's death. Every trail comes back to you. I've never worked a case with such compelling evidence."

"I thought you said—"

191

"Never a case with as much damning evidence. Too damn perfect, if you ask me. I started digging some. I don't think you did it," DiManno said.

Her eyes welled up at the slightest indication someone else believed her, believed in her. "Thank you."

"Don't thank me. Me thinking it doesn't count for squat. Prove it to me."

"How?"

"That's where the pancakes come in. I do some of my best thinking over blueberry pancakes. We need to figure this out."

He said we, Jillian thought. She allowed her mind to dial back a few notches on the anxiety scale and accompanied the police Inspector to what he claimed were the best blueberry pancakes in the city.

Chapter Thirty-Four

J illian devoured the pancakes. She couldn't decide if they were the
best she'd ever tasted, or if she was simply ravenous beyond hunger.
DiManno flipped another pancake onto her plate, her fourth, and the
hot blueberries oozed from the golden-brown surface. The inspector carried
his spatula back to his small apartment kitchen, and Jillian made sure he
wasn't looking as she dabbed up a spot of blueberry with a fingertip. She
licked off the sweet, warm berry juice.

"Glad you like them," DiManno said as he came to the table with his own
plate.

Jillian blushed when she glanced up. She finished licking her finger, then
said, "They're not bad, I guess."

DiManno sat at the table, poured some warm blueberry syrup over his
short stack, and dug in.

Jillian finished her meal and sipped her coffee while DiManno silently
ate his pancakes. She noticed he was precise and deliberate in everything,
including the way he prepared the pancakes from scratch, set the table for
them, and cut each bite into perfect one-inch squares.

"Is this how you interrogate murder suspects? Force-feed them?" she said.

DiManno's eyes flipped up and in between bites, he said, "Didn't look
forced to me. I've seen a pack of feral dogs do less damage." He forked the
last of his pancake, swirled it around in a vein of syrup, and tossed it in his
mouth.

"Know what my secret is?" he said.

"Waterboarding, rubber hoses, or electrodes attached to my testicles, if I were a man?"

"Lemon."

"Lemon, what…"

"A hint of lemon zest in the pancake batter. It accentuates the blueberry flavor," DiManno said.

Jillian smirked, and sat back in her chair, arms crossed. "You're a strange man."

"I prefer complex," he said as he gathered the dishes from the table and returned them to the kitchen.

"I didn't kill Jonathon Mattson," Jillian said. "I don't care how much evidence you say there is. I didn't do it."

"I know," he said, his voice carried over the running water and rattle of dishes in the kitchen.

"I'm telling you the truth!"

He shut off the water in the kitchen, came back to the table, wiping his hands with a dishtowel. "Do you ever listen? I said I know. I know you didn't murder Mattson."

"You said there was evidence—evidence pointed at me."

"Yes, there is, and it's too perfect. Remember I told you I'd never seen as much evidence against one person in my entire career. It got me to thinking. And again, I do my best thinking over a good meal. I think I know what happened, but I need you to fill in some gaps for me."

"You believe me? What changed your mind?"

"When Jonathon Mattson was murdered, where were you?"

Jillian stood up from her chair and stepped away from the table and put some distance between DiManno and her. *This is a trick. He's trying to trick you. Run!*

DiManno made no move to come after her. Instead, he sipped his coffee and said in a matter-of-fact tone, "You can't remember, can you?"

Jillian shook her head.

"Feel like you went through a bout of amnesia? No memory of what happened, right?"

"No."

"And why do you think that is? Ever have blackouts like this before?"

"Never. I can't explain what happened," Jillian said.

"I can." DiManno took a swig from his coffee mug. "You were drugged."

Jillian sat back down at the table with DiManno. "It makes sense with what happened in my apartment when I was attacked. I remember the attack–then nothing. Like before—I woke up in what I thought was Mattson's apartment."

"When you were admitted to the psych ward, they drew blood samples," he said.

"Smart."

"I asked the crime lab to take a run at it. There was a two-drug combo working on you."

"Two? The pills…"

"I'm not sure why someone would go to the effort of making you lose your memory."

"You believe me? I didn't do this. The drugs, Mattson, all of it."

DiManno held his palms outward. "Whoa, slow down, one step at a time. The lab work proved you were drugged. There are little things pointing to someone doing this to you."

"Like what?"

"Your blood work came back positive for GHB and a drug called Versed."

Jillian leaned forward, a shiver of recognition shot through her.

DiManno read the reaction. "You know what Versed is?"

"Dynalife distributes a generic version, Midazolam. They sell amnesiac drugs to hospitals and outpatient surgery centers. Versed is a pretty common drug. It's used so the patient doesn't remember unpleasant events during a procedure. It's usually injected into the patient's bloodstream. I was dosed with Versed?"

"Looks like it. The lab ran it through a mass spectrograph and pinpointed the chemical makeup of Versed and Rohypnol."

"The memory loss, the headaches, dizziness—Versed and GHB side effects. Are you certain?" Jillian said. She rubbed a fingertip over her inner arm looking for an injection site.

"Uh, huh," DiManno said. "Versed isn't exactly high on the drugs-of-abuse list, so, it got me to thinking. Why would someone go to the trouble to push you out of the way, when, quite honestly it would have been easier to kill you?"

"I was worth more to them alive."

"It's the 'them' part of this equation I haven't filled in yet."

"William Comstock and Shelly Mattson," Jillian said, a bit louder than she intended.

"According to that bimbo reporter, Shelly was pretty damn quick to leak David Paulson as the victim in the garage." DiManno slumped back in his chair and rubbed his temples. "You know what this means, right?"

"If Shelly Mattson leaked the identity of the body to the reporter, then she's trying to get your attention off of someone else."

"Are you absolutely certain you saw this Tommy guy? I mean, the Versed could be messing with your mind, and all. We can't go knocking on Shelly Mattson's door in the middle of the night without rock-solid evidence," DiManno said.

"I know what I saw. He was at the warehouse and torched the place," Jillian said.

"Tommy killed Mattson and Paulson! He and Shelly were in it together." Jillian stood, she rummaged through her burn-scarred purse and snatched the microcassette recorder. She rewound the tape to the beginning and hit play. "God, I'm glad I managed to take this out of the fire."

She replayed the conversation between Jonathon and David for Inspector DiManno. He listened and glanced at Jillian when Mattson mentioned canceling drug contracts and again when Black Label was mentioned.

Jillian stopped the tape and pushed the recorder across to the inspector. "I guess you'll need this."

He sighed and tapped the recorder with a tentative finger. "I'm afraid to ask how you got this, so I won't. That's Jonathon Mattson and David Paulson on the tape? You're certain?"

She nodded.

"The Black Label they were talking about—it's the warehouse from tonight?"

"Black Label was a separate hidden division of Dynalife, distributing pharmaceuticals hidden from the company's financials."

"Okay, I gotta ask. What's the big deal about a drug company running a local warehouse?"

"It's a big deal when the warehouse isn't listed in the company's books. It means they're hiding an off-the-books operation for drugs manufactured without oversight or testing. It's a dangerous proposition and people are dying because of Black Label. With these guys, it's always about the money. Black Label generates unlimited, untraceable income," Jillian said.

"Enough to get people killed over? I don't know. What did they mean when Mattson mentioned thugs taking over the company?"

Jillian shrugged. "The guy who's been following me has to be the thug they were talking about."

DiManno rested his elbows on the table and pushed his coffee cup away with a forearm. "Something doesn't fit. Mattson wanted to shut down the Black Label operation, according to the tape, right?"

"I guess so."

"Then some thug comes and torches the place."

"Yeah," Jillian said. Her eyes lit in recognition. "Why were they scared about shutting down the operation?"

"Shelly Mattson knew about the lab and was willing to see it taken down. Why else would she call me and tell me you were there?"

"Someone's taking out anyone and everything with a Black Label connection. It won't stop until everyone is gone. It's not over until they scorch the earth."

DiManno smiled across the table.

"What," Jillian wiped her lips in case a big blob of blueberry goo smeared on them.

"I told you so."

"What?"

"The pancakes worked. There's someone pressuring Dynalife to keep Black Label up and running. Then, another force destroys it. There's a war going on and Shelly Mattson is in the middle of everything. I'm gonna have to get clearance from the brass to approach her on this one. The family is connected. They donate a ton of cash to charitable foundations, and local political campaigns, the Chief and the Mayor included. I could step into a shit storm by looking at her," DiManno said.

"Then you stay away from her. With you charging in, she'll shut down tight and won't say a word not scripted by her handlers. Shelly is a piece of work. Maneuvering corporate takeovers, making deals, and attending her high-brow social gatherings; she set the direction for the company and told Jonathon Mattson what to think."

"All I can do is watch and follow. She'll slip up, and then I'll have the proof I need to make the city bosses listen. If I have her tied to this mess, then they can't stop me from questioning her."

"That settles it. You won't approach her with it. I will."

"Oh, no you're not. Are you out of your flippin' mind? There is no way I can let you near that woman. No way," DiManno said.

"You don't know her. She's not about to slip up. She's way too slick to make a silly mistake. She has a reason for everything she does, and she told you I was at the lab. She doesn't do anything by chance."

"Give me some credit. I've been at this a few years. If Shelly Mattson has something to hide…"

"You won't even get close to her. I can draw her out; I know how to get under her skin so she has to respond," Jillian said. She stood from the table and looked into the living area of DiManno's apartment.

"I can't have you threatening Mrs. Mattson."

"Threaten? Who said anything about threatening her? She doesn't care about personal attacks. Her reputation, on the other hand, she'd kill to protect. Can I use your phone?"

Chapter Thirty-Five

"This is a shitty idea." DiManno sat behind the wheel of his personal car, an older model Toyota Camry featuring faded, cracked dashboard vinyl and threadbare, once gray, seat covers. He'd parked the car in a wide-open parking lot in Golden Gate Park. During the daylight hours, the lot overflowed with visitors to the lush picnic grounds, the Japanese Tea Gardens, and the Steinhart Aquarium. In the darkness, the place seemed otherworldly; cold, desolate, and void of life.

Jillian sat in the passenger seat, watching the entrance of the De Young Museum, framed by posters featuring an exhibit of abstract art that looked like coffee stains on a tablecloth. Spotlights washed the steps of the museum in a jaundiced yellow light ebbing into the parking lot. "You didn't have to come," she said.

"Yes, I did. You're in my custody, remember? Doesn't change the fact meeting this woman out here in the middle of the night is a stupid idea."

"It is the only way to get to Shelly."

DiManno turned in his seat to face Jillian. "There is no reasoning with you about this, is there? The woman is poison. She's proved she is out for you and you think you can *talk* to her?"

"Leave me here if you don't want to do it," Jillian said. She started to open the car door, and DiManno grabbed her arm.

"Stop. We'll do it your way, this once. If it blows up, so help me, Shelly Mattson will be the least of your problems," DiManno said, followed by, "God you're bull-headed."

"You won't have to wait much longer," Jillian said, pointing to the parking lot entrance to the west. Headlights swept an arc through the lot as a single vehicle crept in from the access road.

A silver Mercedes-Benz pulled to the curb in front of the museum, the exact spot Jillian arranged for the meeting. The headlights blinked out, and the interior dome light flicked on when the driver's door opened. The dim glow revealed the single occupant, as agreed.

"So far, so good. She came alone," Jillian said.

"Last chance. We can leave now. God, I hate this woman," DiManno replied.

Across the parking lot, the light flicked out in the Mercedes, and a compact silhouette approached with a deliberate pace, the bearing of a woman who didn't care for clandestine meetings in the middle of the night.

The rear door of DiManno's Camry opened, and the woman slid in.

"Miss Cooper, Inspector. Is this nighttime intrigue really necessary?" Action News reporter Pia Lopez asked.

Jillian turned in the passenger seat and nodded toward a file folder in Pia's hand. "Did you bring it?"

The reporter held the folder in her lap. "You promised me an exclusive."

"Doesn't get much more exclusive than this," Jillian said, gesturing to the empty parking lot.

"I mean him," Pia said, not happy about DiManno's presence. "You never said there would be police involvement."

"If it makes you feel any better, I'm not thrilled to see you either," DiManno said.

"Pretend he's not here. Were you able to find the purchase orders?"

"I don't see the significance…"

"You will. Were you able to track down the pharmaceutical purchases?"

DiManno groaned, "Oh, now wait a minute. You can't have her playing fetch for evidence…"

"Fetch? I'll show you fetch, you incompetent son-of-a-bitch. Why couldn't you find this? I'm sick and tired of doing your work, the City's work."

"Anything you touched is inadmissible in court. You've tainted everything. The evidence will get tossed," DiManno punctuated his displeasure with a fist on the steering wheel.

"I don't care about the evidence," Jillian snapped.

"What?" DiManno said.

"What?" Pia echoed.

"I want my life back, and your precious evidence won't give it to me. The people who screwed me are going to suffer, and I want them to know it was me who did it to them," Jillian said.

"You can't run off on a vigilante mission. I need evidence to nail Mattson's killer. I won't allow you to get in the way," DiManno said.

"Won't allow me? *Allow* me?" Jillian said.

From the back seat, Pia said, "Wait, you mean she didn't kill Mattson? I thought the district attorney filed charges against her?"

"No, I won't allow you," DiManno said, ignoring Pia.

"They stole my life, not yours. Shelly Mattson is up to her ass in the Black Label business. She won't talk to you, but she'll have to listen to Pia and me."

"Shelly Mattson? What does she have to do with–are you saying she killed her husband? What's Black Label?" Pia asked while she fished a cell phone from her purse. "I need to call this in. My editor will save some space with my byline, for the eleven o'clock broadcast, if I can send this in."

Jillian reached over the seat and plucked the cell phone from the reporter's hand. As Pia started to protest, Jillian said, "I promised you an exclusive, and you'll have one, but you have to do this on my terms."

Pia thought for a moment, slunk back into the seat, and regarded Jillian and DiManno. "Before I agree to go along with any of this, you two need to answer some questions."

"Fine," Jillian said.

"To a point," DiManno followed. "I'm not going to tell you anything that will jeopardize my case."

"I will hold publication until you agree unless I dig up the same information from another source, then I'm free to report." the reporter said.

"Agreed," Jillian said and returned the cell phone to Pia.

"You can't agree for me, Cooper," DiManno said.

"I think she can," Pia said, putting the cell phone back into her purse.

"Besides, she's the story here, not you."

"I want Mattson's killer, and I can't risk a glorified cable news weather girl turning my case to shit for a headline. You have priors."

"That was then, this is now," Pia said. "I found out about that witness on my own. Besides, last time, we didn't have an agreement."

"The last time, you put my witness on television, he told a different story, and a rapist got off."

"It's not my fault he changed up his story when he got to court," Pia said.

"The way I see it, you're responsible for letting a sexual predator loose."

"All the more reason for us to be on the same page." Pia shifted in her seat. "Look, we both need this. You need the conviction, and I need the story. It sounds like I can help you with Shelly Mattson and I need your help on the story. I want a serious story, a real story; I'm more than a flashy cable news bimbo. I need to prove it."

DiManno relaxed, silent for a moment. "I didn't call you a bimbo," he said quietly.

"You didn't have to. I've heard it enough."

Jillian waited until the tension waned in the suddenly small Toyota sedan. "Pia has to approach Shelly. The only thing Shelly Mattson cares about is Shelly Mattson. The moment Pia starts asking questions about her precious reputation, Shelly won't be able to resist."

"I don't like it," DiManno said.

"I can do it," Pia replied. "How do I approach her?"

"Find out why she tipped the police off to the Black Label facility and me."

Pia listened; her mind moved behind quiet eyes. "That's why you asked me who tipped me off on Paulson's murder this morning?"

Jillian nodded.

"Son-of-a-bitch! Shelly Mattson's the one who gave the station the reward information for your capture," Pia said.

Jillian smiled. "That's how we get to Shelly."

"What? The reward money?" Pia asked.

"Yep. Tell her you're prepared to collect the bounty, but you want more money to keep her little secret about Black Label," Jillian said.

"Blackmail?" Pia said.

"No way," DiManno jumped in. "You can't commit another crime to prove your innocence."

"Then tell her you want the reward, and in exchange, you'll give her your source."

"What source?" Pia said.

"Me," Jillian said.

"No, no, no," DiManno said.

"She won't expect you to turn me over. It will put her off guard," Jillian argued.

"It might work," Pia said.

DiManno felt vastly outnumbered and overpowered by two small women. He slunk back into the worn fabric of the driver's seat and wished he were anywhere else. He pinched the bridge of his nose and said, "If we do this, we do this my way."

"We'll get her. I promise. You won't regret this," Jillian said.

"I already do," DiManno said.

Chapter Thirty-Six

The city exhaled in the hours leading to daybreak, a short pause before the fishing boats chugged out from the piers, a short respite ahead of the commuters clogging the narrow arteries into the business districts. Sounds of the bustling sidewalks and the calls from hawkers in front of tacky tourist traps receded in the gloom hours ago, but the city vibrated with the certainty of their return.

The cable car roundtable at Market Street attracted thousands daily for the trek North through Nob Hill toward Fisherman's Warf. In the predawn darkness, the cable car transfer point was empty, except for Jillian and Pia Lopez. The two women stood, close together, in the center of the roundtable tracks.

Jillian checked her watch. "She's late."

"Oh, she'll be here. You could hear it in her voice. I told her I knew about Black Label—I thought she was gonna swallow her tongue."

"A crack in the dam." Jillian shifted her feet and nodded in the distance, where a pair of headlights turned onto Market and headed in their direction. The car pulled to the curb, and the headlights shut off. "I guess we're about to find out."

"Well, let's do this," Pia said and strode toward the car.

Twenty feet away, Shelly Mattson's face appeared through the windshield, grim and pale, the entitled façade shattered. Jillian thought she seemed pathetic, in a way, like one of those silent movie queens, who clung to past glories, ignorant her time had passed.

"Looks like you struck a nerve," Jillian said to Pia. "Remember, we need to make her talk about her husband and Black Label."

"I got it," Pia said as she reached into her purse and flicked on a small digital recorder.

As the two drew close, Shelly refused to make eye contact with Jillian and addressed Pia. "Get in. Make the whore wait on the sidewalk."

Pia stepped around to the passenger side and slipped in. Jillian retreated to the sidewalk, using a storefront as shelter from the cold breeze kicking up from the bay. Through the window, Jillian saw Pia's head bobbing with emphasis as she spoke with Shelly Mattson. The matronly Mrs. Mattson listened without any outward reaction, the practiced stoic poise reforming.

Directly opposite Jillian's position, Inspector DiManno huddled against a line of newspaper racks. Jillian wouldn't have noticed him in the deep shadow if she hadn't known he was there. Her attention returned to the car as Pia opened the passenger door.

"She wants to speak with you," Pia said.

Jillian left her sheltered cove on the sidewalk and approached the car. Pia stepped aside, and Jillian parked in the front seat. Pia opened the rear door, climbed in, and closed the door.

Shelly glanced up in the rearview mirror at Pia's reflection and spoke without looking at Jillian. "You ruined everything, Miss Cooper. Why couldn't you leave it alone?"

Jillian started, "I didn't—"

"Don't play innocent with me. You destroyed Jonathon, the Mattson name, and the company my husband built."

Jillian changed direction, pressed closer, and asked, "Why did you put up a reward and tell the police I killed your husband?"

"I had no choice."

"Why?" Jillian said.

Finally, Shelly faced Jillian, her eyes seared with anger. "Because of you. Because of what you did to Jonathon and my family."

"I didn't kill him," Jillian pleaded.

"Oh, spare me the theatrics, Miss Cooper. There are far worse things in the universe than death. You didn't *murder* Jonathon. But you used him and threatened to bring down his reputation, and *that* was far worse than killing him."

From the back seat, "You know who killed your husband?" Pia asked.

Shelly's eyes flashed up into the rearview. "Miss Lopez, you will leave us now. My business with you has come to an end."

Pia stalled in her exit from the rear seat, and the matron's eyes bore down, the point made, no conversation would occur if the reporter remained in the car. Pia opened the door, slid from the seat, dropping her purse on the floorboard as she stepped out. She hurriedly scooped up her belongings, tossed them into her purse, and closed the car door. The door locks clicked, shutting the reporter outside.

Jillian broke the silence first. "I didn't use Jonathon. I have no idea what you mean."

Shelly leaned toward Jillian. A strong bourbon odor wafted from her. "I have no illusions about my husband's many failings, his taste for younger women like you among them."

"Jonathon and I never—"

"Your necklace was in my garden. *My* garden, Miss Cooper. You dropped it after your illicit rendezvous with Jonathon. I could care less, but in my own home, flaunting it in my face. For that, I can never forgive you."

"But, I didn't."

"You ruined my husband the second you betrayed him with your under-handed plea to the board last Friday. Jonathon tore you apart at the board meeting because he needed to protect the company. You wanted to give away our newest products to relief organizations in some misguided altruistic dream. A dream, even you have to admit was about good press and Dynalife's goodwill in the marketplace."

"It was the right thing to do. And yes, I admit the company stood to gain from a public relations standpoint..."

"Black Label was already selling our product to these organizations. We *sold* them, and we made a profit. Jonathon and I didn't want to start Black Label, but David managed to make it work for us. He actually made the damn thing work."

"Why start a secondary line with Black Label?"

"We had no choice." Shelly's hands started to shake, and she grew quiet. "Did you know I have a son?"

Jillian shook her head.

"His name is Tomas, from a previous marriage. A previous life, really. Tomas was a rebellious teen when Jonathon and I met. The boy never accepted Jonathon as a stepfather and was incorrigible, staying out all night getting high. He spent a great majority of his teens and twenties in juvenile treatment facilities, and finally, prison."

"I'm sorry, but what does Tomas have to do with Black Label?" Jillian prodded.

"Four years ago, Tomas was sent to prison a second time for heroin. The District Attorney over in San Joaquin County made a push to prosecute him for possession for sale. The charge would have sent my son away for ten years. Jonathon and I got him an attorney and worked out a plea deal for simple possession. Two years and he'd be out in twelve months if he stayed out of trouble.

"A few months in, Tomas got into debt with some bad people. He bought heroin and couldn't pay for it. He begged me for the money, and I refused. 'I'm not going to support your drug habit,' I told him. The prisoners found out who his family was and threatened to kill Tomas unless we helped them."

"Helped them how?" Jillian said.

Shelly didn't look at Jillian as she said, "Black Label was created to smuggle drugs into prison."

The interior of the car grew cold, and Shelly turned the ignition to bring the heater back to life. Jillian hadn't noticed the slight mist of condensation on the windows until the defroster chewed away at the edges of the pale film.

"Jonathon wouldn't go along with a drug-smuggling scheme," Jillian said.

"He resisted at first. None of us wanted to do it, for God's sake. We had to. I needed to make certain Tomas wasn't harmed. The thugs in prison were good to their word. They left him alone; in fact, they treated him well, brought him magazines, CDs, and things he couldn't get inside."

"What made Jonathon give in?"

"He received a visit from two of my son's new 'friends' who got out on parole. They were unpleasant thugs, shaved heads, and long-sleeved shirts with only the top button closed over white t-shirts. They had gaudy tattoos on their necks, and dark sunglasses so you couldn't see their eyes. One of them pulled a pistol from his waistband and put it to Jonathon's head. The other gangster told Jonathon they would kill the whole family if he didn't go along."

"Why didn't you go to the police—tell them you were being blackmailed?"

"That's where David came in. Jonathon went to him for advice on what course of action we should take. Jonathon was leaning toward getting the police involved, but David talked him out of it and came up with the Black Label plan," Shelly said.

"If Black Label was up and running, why was Jonathon killed?" Jillian said.

Shelly regained a bit of composure and turned to Jillian. "Your altruistic proposal to give drugs to the sick and needy gave Jonathon images of Angelina Jolie at a UNICEF conference. Publicly, Jonathon was forced to discredit your proposal, but the poor sap felt sorry for you. He wanted to shut down the Black Label program and apologize to you.

"David and I tried to talk some sense into Jonathon, but you know him, once he starts a crusade, there is no stopping that man. That is what you started—a damned crusade. He wanted to throw everything away and turn Dynalife into a damned non-profit charitable organization." Shelly cleared her throat. "It would never be allowed."

"David killed him?" Jillian said. The taped conversation between Jonathon and David sprung to mind.

The widow shook her head. "David had no choice. David knew he was next in line if the Black Label operation failed."

"Who killed him?" Jillian was close to getting an answer promising to unlock her nightmare. She felt it. The truth was there, and Shelly held it from her. "Please, I need to know."

"David and Black Label got us into business with some unsavory elements in and outside of the prisons. Jonathon's message got back to these people late Friday afternoon after you planted the seeds of charity in his mind. He told them we were going to pull the plug on Black Label. Once he told them, there was no retreat." Shelly put her head down. She looked weary, grey, and sullen. "Two hours later, he was killed, and David was next. So, who killed him, you ask? You did. Now get out of my car."

Jillian saw the flicker of hope extinguished. She needed to keep her talking. "Who told you Jonathon and I were involved?"

Shelly clenched her jaw. "Involved? How quaint. Why don't you call it what it was? You were fucking my husband."

"Who told you?"

"What does it matter now? I knew it. Your tawdry jewelry was in my garden. I figured you should pay for what you did to Jonathon, and to me."

"Who told you?"

"I didn't need anyone to tell me. David let it slip, but I knew Jonathon was seeing someone," Shelly said.

"David told you? When? Before or after Jonathon died?"

Shelly shook off the question and grew more agitated. "Get out," and she pushed weakly at Jillian, edging her closer to the passenger door. When Jillian resisted, Shelly slapped and punched wildly in her direction.

Jillian braced one arm against the door and grabbed one of Shelly's flailing arms with her free hand. "When did David tell you?" she said a bit more forcefully than she intended. Her voice rattled inside the car.

A rapping on the window next to Shelly's face startled her, and she stopped the frustrated lunges directed at Jillian. Pia knocked on the window a second time.

"Hey, what's going on?" Pia said.

With Shelly distracted, Jillian grasped both of the woman's thin bony wrists and held them. Rather than asking again, Jillian told Shelly, "David told you there was an affair after he killed your husband, didn't he?"

Broken, Shelly nodded slightly and gave up her struggle against Jillian.

Jillian released Shelly's wrists and said, "There was no affair between Jonathon and me–ever. David made it up. He wanted you to believe there was a relationship."

209

"No—the necklace and the photos. He found your little necklace. I know what I saw. Why would David want to hurt me and lie?"

"He wanted you to blame Jonathon's murder on me," Jillian said.

"It seemed a just reward for your influence over my husband."

"Why not go to the police and tell them it was David?"

"If the people behind Black Label found out the police were looking hard at David, they'd come for me and my son next."

Chapter Thirty-Seven

"Then why did you tell the police I was at the Black Label lab?" Jillian asked.

"The facility was compromised. Tomas would never let it run again. He found out what we were doing there—"

"The lab was a throwaway—an offering to keep Tomas out of danger while he was in prison?"

"Something along those lines. We knew we'd have to keep it in play long enough to keep my son's friends off balance. David's plans for another lab to expand the sales of Black Label drugs to relief organizations were coming together. We'd outgrown the lab you found and we secured another—one my son didn't know about.

"You let him believe he'd ended the Black Label business, but you never intended stopping the operation."

"You have no idea who these people are. They'd come after Tomas—come after all of us," Shelly said.

Shelly watched her husband die because of rampant greed. Yet she wasn't willing to cut loose the black market lab operation that killed him. The widow claimed it was to protect her and Tomas from violent gang retribution. Jillian felt the mother's anger, fear, and grief competing for control over the woman's soul. The emotions seemed foreign to the self-serving person Jillian knew. Shelly acted as if she experienced these feelings for the first time, raw, unfocused, and unfiltered.

"Leave my family alone, Miss Cooper. If you let this go, I will tell the authorities you were not Jonathon's killer. David isn't around to dispute the matter." A swagger of the familiar coldness seeped through the uncontrolled emotional window dressing.

"You'll tell the police about David and Black Label?" Jillian said.

"No, of course not. I'm not one to speak ill of the dead. I'll tell them it was someone else—someone I've never cast eyes on before. You're not in any position to dictate terms to me. Leave this alone, and I will make certain the police don't look to you for Jonathon's death."

"If I don't?"

"Then you will die in prison. It's really simple, Miss Cooper. The ultimate choice is yours. Either way, I will not allow you to harm my family any longer. You wouldn't know about family. I paid your sister, Hannah, is it, a tidy sum for getting you locked up in the psych ward. She said she'd have done it for free. You know nothing about what a family would do to protect one another. Now out of my car and out of my life."

The revelation of Hannah taking a payoff to paint Jillian as a danger to others didn't surprise her. It reinforced the door was irretrievably shut on their relationship. Jillian unlocked her door, pushed it open, and looked back at Shelly. The earlier display of emotion was real, but Jillian recognized the protective instincts she saw were not for Tomas alone. Shelly was out to save her own ass. "How do I let you know what I decide to do," Jillian said. Trusting Shelly to keep her part of any bargain didn't leave Jillian with warm and fuzzy feelings.

Shelly glanced out her driver's side window. "Tell your reporter friend to call me. She seems to know how to find me. Two hours, Miss Cooper. I will call the police in two hours. I'll tell them I saw a man kill Jonathon, or I tell them you confessed to me. Your move, Miss Cooper."

Jillian slid from the front seat and stood at the curb, the door ajar. "How can I trust you?"

"Trust? Trust I will crush you if you pursue this any farther." Shelly stomped on the gas pedal and the sedan shot forward from the curb, the momentum slammed the open car door closed as it pulled away.

Jillian managed a step back before the door pinched shut.

"Jesus, you managed to hit a nerve," Pia said.

"She told me—"

"David killed Jonathon, I know," Pia said with a smirk plastered on her face.

"How did you—?" Jillian said as she noticed a thin white cord under the reporter's hair to a cell phone in her hand.

Pia held the cell up. "When I dropped my purse, I left another cell phone on the floor and called this one."

"You heard—"

"Every word," Pia said.

"Who carries two cell phones? That's sneaky."

"I prefer 'resourceful.' But, I do tend to lose a few cell phones along the way."

Inspector DiManno dodged light traffic as he crossed Market and joined up with Jillian and Pia. He also sported an earpiece snaking to a cell phone.

Pia noticed Jillian's interest in the inspector's phone. "I called him after Mrs. Mattson kicked me out of the car. I conference called him into the open cell in her car," Pia said and beamed with her ingenuity.

"Were you going to let me in on this little stunt?" Jillian asked.

DiManno put up his hands, the cell phone plugged into his ear. "I didn't know she was gonna pull this. This was illegal as hell." To Pia, "Is this how you get your sources? Eavesdropping?"

"Don't get your boxers in a bunch," Pia said. "Besides, I needed to be certain Jillian wasn't involved in Mattson's death. Now I know she wasn't."

"Gee, thanks," Jillian said.

"We can't use any of the admissions Shelly Mattson made in court. It doesn't matter if she implicated David, you got the information illegally," DiManno said.

"But, I'm off the hook for Jonathon's murder," Jillian said.

"Not as far as the D.A. and the S.F.P.D. are concerned. The D.A. charged you with his murder and then you failed to appear in court. Nothing Shelly said changes what people believe. She'll deny she spoke to you and we can't prove she did."

"Unless she says otherwise," Jillian said.

"What?" DiManno said.

"In two hours, Shelly is supposed to call the authorities, right?"

"Yeah, so?" DiManno said.

"If she believes I'm leaving her alone, then she said she will tell the police some unknown man killed her husband."

"She won't call," DiManno said.

"She's protecting more than her son, much more. She'll call, and when she does, it opens the door."

"I don't know," DiManno said. "If, and I mean if, she calls, what's to stop her from trying to nail your ass?"

"She's afraid. She truly wants me to stay away from Dynalife and her family. We need to find out why. I'm close to exposing her dirty secret," Jillian said.

"More than David Paulson murdering her husband?" Pia added.

"There's more going on here. She was quick to drop this on David, who can't defend himself against her allegations. And who killed David? Whoever wants Black Label up and running blamed Jonathon and David for the shutdown. There's more here that I can't put my finger on," Jillian said.

"Like what?" DiManno asked.

"I don't know, yet. Someone threatened Jonathon, probably the same people who wanted him to keep their prison drug conduit open. Then, Shelly's son goes in and destroys the lab. Everything comes down to Dynalife's Black Label operation," Jillian said. "It's where we'll find our answer."

"A little thin," DiManno said.

"It's there; our proof will be hidden in the purchase orders for the prison pharmaceutical contracts. The answer is there," Jillian said.

"And we only have two hours," Pia said.

"After the clock runs out, Jillian, I'm afraid there's little I can do to keep you out of jail. I can't protect you forever," DiManno said.

"Then we better make the time count," Jillian said and followed with, "and I know where we need to start."

"Where?" Pia asked.

"Shelly Mattson's son and his prison friends," Jillian answered, a steely glint in her eye.

Chapter Thirty-Eight

T he trio agreed on a small utilitarian space at the Channel Five studios, because Shelly expected a phone call from the reporter, and the caller ID would show the news station as the authentic source of the call. Secondarily, the room provided computer stations with Internet access and a bank of phones. Inspector DiManno wasn't eager to enter the bastion of the liberal media, let alone using the station's archives, or what he considered, "the tools of the devil."

They divided the work they needed to complete before the two-hour deadline. DiManno used a terminal to log into his S.F.P.D. information system to find the details of Tomas's criminal history. The man should be in the system, if, as Shelly claimed, he did time in state prison. Pia dove into legal records with the station's LexisNexis account. Shelly's prior marriage and, most importantly, documents from the divorce proceedings promised an unvarnished account of the failed relationship. Jillian worked deeper through the financials she'd received from Carlos. The printouts held the key, and she tried to follow the money trail from Dynalife to David Paulson and Black Label on through to the prison pharmacy contracts.

Of the three, Pia was the first to get a hit.

"Working backward, I found the marriage license for Shelly and Jonathon, five years ago. It lists this as the third marriage for Mrs. Mattson. She changed her last name from Estrella at that time."

"Three prior marriages? Any chance the other husbands are dead too? A regular black widow, this one," Jillian said.

Pia scrolled her mouse and pointed at the screen. "I found the Dissolution of Marriage filing. Her second husband was Raul Estrella. The document claims they were married for ten years and lists extreme cruelty as the reason for the divorce," Pia said.

"Who was he? Another tech millionaire?" Jillian asked.

Pia turned in her chair. "Raul Estrella, *the* Raul Estrella?"

Jillian shrugged.

"Raul Estrella was huge in Latino circles in the Bay Area during the '70s and '80s. He was a financier and real estate mogul, who bought up huge sections of the Silicon Valley before it became the center of the tech universe. Estrella offered home mortgages to Latino families at a time all the big banks considered them too much of a risk." Pia tapped the key on a second terminal, bringing up Estrella's biographical information. "Raul Estrella was born April 23, 1957. Does it match with the date in the divorce decree?"

Jillian scrolled down on the screen until she found the details of the divorce. "Yes. That's a match. The dissolution of marriage looks like it was final on September 27, 2000. No children or custody settlements are mentioned."

"Tomas must have come from her first hook up," Jillian said.

"From all the accounts and stories I've heard, Raul Estrella doesn't seem the type to cause Shelly to file for a divorce on the grounds of extreme cruelty. His bio is full of commendations, awards, and recognition for his humanitarian work, including a number of women's shelters in the East Bay. I guess people change," Pia said.

Jillian chuckled slightly. "You met Shelly Mattson, right? She'd bring out the worst in a saint. But in this case," Jillian said as she tapped the screen, "it was Raul Estrella who filed citing extreme cruelty."

"That fits. Wonder what she did?" Pia said.

"I guess we'll never know. There's not a lot of detail in the filings. But I'd bet she made his life hell."

Pia tapped a few keys and waited for the search to finish. "Here it is. Shelly filed for a legal name change a few months before she married Estrella. Her name at that time was Renee Marquez."

"Renee Marquez! That's who owned the apartment I woke up in when this all started."

DiManno looked over at the two women. "With the last name of Marquez, I got a hit off the Department of Corrections inmate locator. Tomas Marquez served time at San Quentin and then at California State Prison—Sacramento. He bounced in and out on a couple of parole violations, but last hit the streets three years ago and failed to report to his parole agent. He's been a parolee-at-large, with a warrant out for his arrest since then. I guess that's a dead-end," DiManno said as he accessed a secondary law enforcement data system, CALPAROLE, and pulled up Tomas Marquez's fact sheet. "Not exactly a handsome devil," he said as he printed a copy of the wanted person's notice from the computer.

He handed a copy of the printout to Jillian.

Jillian's face locked onto the photo. She froze for a moment. He looked different with his shaved head in the prison photo, but the eyes and telltale scar gave him away. Tomas Carlos Marquez was the doorman at the Nob Hill apartment where her nightmare journey began. He was the man who accosted her at the BART platform and followed her to the photography studio. The face belonged to "Tommy," the suicidal woman's husband, who failed to save his daughter from the ravages of an unforgiving disease.

"That's him! That's the man who followed me. He was the phony doorman, and he torched the Black Label lab because it killed his daughter."

"Says here he's an associate of the Mexican Mafia prison gang, involved in gang activity in the prison, weapon possession, extortion, and drug trafficking. Spent most of his time locked up in Administrative Segregation for one infraction or another," DiManno said.

"Not exactly the picture mommy painted," Jillian said.

"This sounds like Tomas wasn't the poor victim. More like he was behind the pressure tactics," Pia added. "You think Shelly believes her son was pressured into the drug connection with Black Label, or is that her way of coping?"

Jillian considered the relative ease with which Shelly revealed Tomas and his drug-involved past. "She isn't protecting him. She's covering her own ass. Shelly gave him up too quickly. Tomas is nothing to her."

"You think she's distancing herself from him and the potential embarrassment a family member involved in gang activity would bring on the company?" Pia asked as her journalistic instincts peaked.

DiManno rolled his chair forward so they faced one another. "That's pretty cold to throw your kid under the bus like she did."

"Oh, Shelly didn't abandon him; she used him to take the heat off of herself. She knew we would find his gang connection and figured we'd chase down that angle. Why else would she tell me about him going to prison? Now she can pursue the Black Label operation without his interference," Jillian said.

"And she was right," DiManno said. "We found the Mexican Mafia connection and Sonny seems to be a player in that little social group. Mrs. Mattson will claim she and her dearly departed husband were blackmailed into starting Black Label." DiManno shifted in his chair and handed the wanted person's bulletin to Pia. "She might convince a jury to believe her bullshit. Who will get sympathy in that scenario, a prison gang member, or a recently widowed socialite?"

Jillian nodded. "Tomas can't be happy Mommy sold him out. Whatever she's hiding is worth the risk of getting the Mexican Mafia pissed off. Or…"

"She sold him out to us and told the gang Tomas wanted to pull the plug on Black Label," DiManno said. "He's got both sides after him."

"And Shelly Mattson sits back, watches the fireworks, and keeps cashing checks from the Black Label operation," Pia said.

"How much time do we have?" Jillian asked.

Pia glanced at a clock on the wall. "Less than thirty minutes." She passed the wanted person's bulletin to Jillian.

"Do you have any contacts in the Mexican Mafia?" Jillian asked.

Jillian's knowledge of prison gangs was on par with her familiarity with the doorbell ringing protocol of Jehovah's Witnesses. When DiManno said he'd have difficulty finding a Mexican Mafia connection in Northern California, she learned the gang operated out of Southern California, and various gang factions carved up the state into their home turf, primarily split along opposing North and South factions.

"The guys in the Gang Task Force of the Investigations Bureau monitored the activity of Hispanic gangs since 1982. There are dozens of street gangs, each with a claim on a particular neighborhood and the street crime associated with that kind of activity. The Mexican Mafia and the Nuestra Familia are the two major Hispanic gangs spawned from within the prison system. The N.F. and their supporters in the Norteno street gangs dominate this area and active Mexican Mafia members keep a low profile."

"How would Shelly know what gang she was dealing with? I mean, she specifically called out the Mexican Mafia," Jillian said.

"Tomas did his time at prisons dominated by Southern factions aligned with the EME. They have a history of inserting their influence into government operations at high levels, including manipulating state contracts. This Black Label pharmaceutical contract scam fits perfectly with their M.O., and I believe her on this one."

Pia interrupted, "It's nearly time for contact with her. How are we going to play this?"

Jillian and Inspector DiManno looked at one another, and the Inspector spoke first. "We tell her Jillian will go along with her. She won't interfere with the Black Label operations and..."

"I'll disappear. But, I'll need a token of trust from her," Jillian said.

"I like where you're going," DiManno replied. "Ask her for some money to help you reestablish somewhere. Say, what, fifty-thousand?"

"She has to say yes, but I know she will never part with one red cent," Jillian said.

"You want to blackmail the blackmailer?" Pia said. "From the little I know of Mrs. Mattson, she'll never dirty her hands with a transaction like that."

"Exactly. Tomas will make the delivery. That's the way I see it. Or that weasel of an attorney, McGowen," Jillian said.

"That's pretty dicey," Pia said.

"I think Jillian's on to something here. Jonathon Mattson was killed because he threatened to pull the plug on Black Label. No matter what Jillian says, Shelly knows Jillian poses a threat to Shelly's enterprise, and she's a loose end. If we tell Shelly Jillian will go along, for a price, we set the time and place for the delivery, she can't resist and we'll be waiting. I'd bet Shelly killed her own husband. She wants this tied up and can't leave a threat like Jillian out there. A payoff to make this go away will flush her out," DiManno said.

"With Jillian as bait," Pia added.

"This is the only way I can end this," Jillian said.

"Mrs. Mattson said she would call off the police if you agreed. We'll if she keeps to her word on that point. I don't trust that woman and we'll have to take Tomas down if he's with her," DiManno said.

"Time to call," Jillian said.

Pia picked up a desktop phone receiver and dialed the number she'd used the last time she contacted the widow Mattson.

"Put it on speaker," DiManno said.

Pia stabbed a finger at the speaker button, and the sound of the phone ringing filled the small room. After two rings, a male voice answered, "Yes?" He offered no greeting, or identification of a place of business, only the one impatient word.

"Shelly Mattson, please. Tell her it's Pia Lopez. She's expecting my call."

A click emanated from the other end of the line and sounded as if the call disconnected. Pia reached for the phone to redial when Shelly Mattson's voice came through the speaker.

"What's her answer?" Shelly said.

"She's in. Miss Cooper agreed to your proposal, with a condition," Pia said.

"I don't do conditions. She either agrees or goes to jail for the rest of her life."

"We both know she needs to disappear. To do what you ask, she needs a little stake to make a new start."

A brief pause from Shelly. She hadn't anticipated this turn.

"Mrs. Mattson?" Pia said.

"I won't give her a dime. I'll see she rots in a prison cell, if she even makes it to one."

Pia looked at DiManno and then to Jillian. "What about me?"

"What do you mean?" Shelly said.

DiManno motioned for Pia to stop, but she ignored him.

"What if I chose to write Jillian's story about you, your son, and Black Label? How much is that worth to you?"

The heat in Shelly's voice came over the speaker. "You pretentious little bitch! You have no idea what you're getting into. I could have you—"

"Killed? Like your husband?"

DiManno scribbled a note and slid it over to Pia. It read "Thin Ice!" Pia nodded and scribbled a return message on the note. "Money? Where?"

"This is extortion. I know people at your television station—"

"I'm sure you do, and I'm equally sure they don't know about your dubious connection to prison gang drug smuggling. It would make a great lead story for the evening news."

DiManno jotted instructions on the back of a transcript of yesterday's News at Noon broadcast and drew a deep breath before he slid it to Pia. He looked at Jillian and whispered, "We need to keep this tight. If Shelly or Tomas don't show for the drop, we have nothing."

"And I'm left hanging for Jonathon's murder," Jillian added.

He nodded. "She's insulated herself enough where nothing traces directly to her. To Jonathon, David Paulson, and Tomas, for sure, but she's left clean."

"Then it's time to get her dirty," Jillian said. She pulled the note DiManno prepared for the drop and tore it up. She quickly scrawled up another version and handed it to Pia.

The reporter read the note and looked back at Jillian with an expression that said, "Are you sure?" Jillian nodded.

"What did you do?" DiManno said.

Pia's voice held firm. "You are to meet me at Grace Cathedral at ten this morning. You give me two hundred and fifty thousand, and I give you Jillian Cooper. If you don't pay, your story goes on at noon."

Shelly started to rant, and Pia cut her off. "There is no negotiation."

Jillian reached over and disconnected the call on the receiver.

"I wish you hadn't done that," DiManno said. "I have a place in mind where I control the access points. I could've nabbed whoever made the drop before they came within fifty yards of you."

"I don't like the idea of you giving yourself over to her," Pia added.

"One of the first things I remembered, after waking up in that apartment, was the view of Grace Cathedral. It seemed right to go there, where my nightmare began. My life hasn't been the same since, and I know it never will. People I trusted used me, drugged me, made me believe I was insane, and nearly convinced me going to prison was my only out. This will end today. I will take back control of my life, or Shelly will silence me. There is no middle ground."

"That's risky," DiManno said.

"Getting out of bed in the morning is risky," Jillian said.

Chapter Thirty-Nine

"I have eyes on you and Pia," DiManno's voice carried over the wireless earpiece tucked in Jillian's right ear. DiManno insisted she wear the police-issued surveillance gear, and in spite of her protest, she admitted knowing DiManno watched from nearby made her feel a bit secure.

"Where are you?" she asked. Jillian looked across the imposing grey stone Cathedral tower looming over the steps where she and Pia waited for Shelly.

"The park, directly across from you," DiManno said.

Jillian looked in the direction of the patch of green that passed for a park in this part of the city. Hordes of schoolchildren invaded the small enclosure and passed the time running from conscripted parents who escorted them on their field trip to the historic Cathedral. In the center of the swarming madness, Jillian noted DiManno perched on a section of white stone wall along one side of the park. If she hadn't known who he was, she would've taken him for one of the parents who ran herd over the children.

DiManno pulled off a blue baseball cap and wiped his brow with the back of his hand. "I can watch the approach from here. If it's Shelly, or Tomas I will see them before they reach the bottom of the steps. If they send someone we don't know…"

"We'll wait for them to politely introduce themselves. They'll be the ones with the guns or knives," Jillian said.

"Watch for someone who isn't with a tour group, who looks like they don't belong there. This is no joke, Jillian. Shelly hasn't gotten her hands dirty on this yet. It would be like her to send in someone to clean up for her."

"I get it. We'll look for people who didn't come to the Cathedral for the right reasons. This is as personal as it gets to Shelly. I think she'll show." She paused. "Thanks for watching over us."

A moment later, Jillian's earpiece sounded. "Shelly's Mercedes is at the west corner of the block coming your way. Can't see who's driving from here. Time for you and Pia to get your game-face on," DiManno said.

Jillian stepped forward on the topmost step of the Cathedral entrance, visible to Shelly's approach. Jillian stood erect, straight and sure, contrasted by Pia, who shuffled from foot to foot, anxious and wary. The Mercedes was the same car Shelly drove last night, and Jillian picked it out of the approaching surge of traffic.

"I see the car. Can't tell who's in it. The windows are more tinted than I remember," Jillian said.

The Mercedes turned right and passed in front of the Cathedral steps where Jillian and Pia waited. The car slowed down but didn't stop before it disappeared around the next block. Shrouded behind the tinted glass, two people occupied the Mercedes' front seat. The driver cast the smaller outline within the car.

"She didn't stop," Pia said.

"Shelly's not buying it," Jillian said.

"Stay in place. The drive-by was to make sure you were there. If she's comfortable you're alone, she'll pass by again. Don't get in the car. Make her get out," DiManno's voice sounded through the earpiece.

Exactly five minutes later, the Mercedes circled the block once more, pulled to the curb in front of the steps, and left the motor running.

"You're on," Jillian said to Pia.

The reporter straightened her shoulders and tried to reflect the confidence she played into the camera every day. Jillian remained on the top step, as planned, while Pia trotted down to the curb and approached the car. The driver's window rolled down halfway, Shelly's profile shown through the open space. The stress from her charade collected a heavy toll. Pale, red-blotched skin and dark puffy bags under her eyes aged Shelly at least a full decade.

The reporter leaned to the window, after a moment of conversation both

Pia and Shelly turned and faced Jillian. In spite of the distance, Jillian picked up the hatred in Shelly's eyes.

"Last chance Jillian," DiManno said, "You can walk away right now."

"I have nowhere to go," Jillian said.

From the open passenger door, a figure in a dark hooded sweatshirt emerged. Head tilted down, the man cut a path behind the car, popped the trunk, and retrieved a brown paper grocery bag. He tossed the bundle on the sidewalk at Pia's feet.

"There's the payoff," DiManno said. "Is it Tomas? Can you see if it's him?"

Jillian hadn't noticed the Inspector change positions, and he was on the near wall, close to the sidewalk, directly opposite the Cathedral.

Pia reached the sidewalk and picked up the rolled brown paper bag. Jillian waited for her cue. If the money was in the bag, Pia was to walk away, through the park past DiManno. If the handoff went sideways, Pia was to walk in the other direction around the corner opposite the Cathedral.

Pia didn't do either.

The reporter stepped to the rear of the vehicle where a hushed conversation ensued. The hooded man's hand snaked out and slapped Pia's face. She recoiled from the blow and cowered for another. The second strike didn't come.

DiManno grabbed the back of the hooded sweatshirt with both hands, pulled the assailant off his feet backward, and sent him crashing to the pavement, flat on his back. The inspector moved over the sprawled figure and deftly applied a wristlock, forcing the man over onto his stomach, with his hands behind his back, quickly cuffing him.

Shelly gunned the engine and shifted the car into gear. The tires chirped as she steered the Mercedes into traffic. Tour buses clogged the intersection and blocked Shelly's path of escape. Bright white backup lamps flicked on, and the Mercedes accelerated backward through opposing traffic. Cars humped onto the sidewalks to avoid the chrome-plated battering ram.

Jillian jumped down from the steps, dodged a red Mazda sedan swerving into oncoming traffic to avoid Shelly's reverse-charging Mercedes. Horns bleated above the screech of tires and rendering of sheet metal as Shelly bounced her sedan between cars occupied by stunned drivers. Jillian ran in a direct line at the Mercedes and narrowed the gap between them. As the car bogged down in the confused traffic, Jillian approached from the front of the Mercedes, the back of Shelly's head visible through the tinted windshield.

Shelly cranked the steering wheel hard to the left, sending the rear of the car into the broadside of a city MTA bus. The impact wedged the rear of the Mercedes under the heavy bus chassis. Shelly slammed the shifter into drive, and smoke spun up from the rear wheels as they clawed for traction. The bus driver and frightened passengers spilled from the public transit vehicle's exit doors. The tire smoke convinced some the bus was on fire.

Jillian was six feet from the driver's window before Shelly looked around. There was a stark recognition of fear in the older woman's eyes, not the usual self-aggrandizing arrogance. Fear.

The Mercedes lurched slightly when the last of the bus passengers stepped onto the street. The empty bus shifted on its frame, unlocking the rear end of the Mercedes. Shelly stomped on the accelerator once more and the vehicle shot forward, across the traffic lanes, nose end pointed at the grassy park teeming with school children.

Jillian launched at the open window and misjudged the speed of the car. Instead of landing in the driver's window, she hit the frame separating the front and back doors with her shoulder. Sharp pain dazzled her vision and sent her right arm into a spastic twitch. She clamped onto the window frame with her weakened right arm, her feet dragging behind on the asphalt.

The Mercedes headed for the sidewalk and Jillian saw clusters of children with their adult escorts in the path ahead. The children stood frozen; unsure which way to run and Shelly made no effort to steer clear. With her right arm locked around the window frame, Jillian drew her left hand through the window and grasped the steering wheel. She gave the wheel a sharp tug downward, which sent the Mercedes into an abrupt left turn away from the helpless people.

Shelly struggled with Jillian's arm and didn't sense the sudden change in direction. Her foot was pinned to the gas pedal and the luxury sedan collided with the back end of a yellow and black school bus. The impact stripped the hood and front bumper off the Mercedes and pinned the broken car under the bus. The sheer weight of the bus, with its metal sides and heavy diesel engine components, kept it immobile against the impact. Crumple zones engineered into the front of the Mercedes performed as designed and folded upon one another like a sheet metal accordion. The instant stop tore Jillian from the side of the car and sent her rolling to the pavement under the bus. Instinct made her wrap her arms around her head before the impact with the cold pavement.

In the aftermath, only a rhythmic *tick, tick* of coolant and engine fluids against broken, overheated motor parts broke the silence. Small rivers of green, brown, and red viscous liquids blended into a dead pool beneath the crumpled hulk of the Mercedes. White powder from the airbag propellant floated from the passenger compartment, a fine coating of the burnt residue clung to Shelly's face, burning her eyes. In the fractions of seconds before the impact, Shelly attempted to cover her face with her hands. The steering wheel pinned her arms back over her chest in an awkward praying mantis position. A rivulet of blood trickled from the bridge of her nose and lips, where the wheel kissed her.

Inspector DiManno ran to the bus, propelling a handcuffed Ryan Mc-Gowen in front of him. DiManno held the links between the cuffs and raised them hard behind the attorney's back, moving the man forward on the balls of his feet.

"Cooper? Cooper, where are you?" The Inspector kicked away a piece of the Mercedes front end impaled into the bus engine cowling.

Jillian rolled into view, smudged with grease from the bus undercarriage. The smile plastered on her face seemed out of place amidst the wreckage and visible road rash on Jillian's shoulder and hands.

"What were you thinking?" DiManno said.

"I wasn't," she said. Jillian gingerly wormed her way from under the school bus, her left arm hung limply at her side. "I'm done running away. Time for the others to do the running."

DiManno smiled and shook his head. "There's a lot of room between running away and running into. Find a middle ground, would you?"

"Hey, I'm new at this, cut me some slack."

Chapter Forty

"Do you have any idea of the shit-storm you created?" District Attorney Eli Mercer said the moment he opened the door into the small examination room where Jillian and DiManno waited. Red-faced and breathing hard, Mercer pulled at his starched collar. An imposing man, in the courtroom, at a smidge over six feet tall, his persona filled the small exam room. Mercer wasn't an underling in the District Attorney's Office, he was the elected-anointed one, and Mercer was not a happy man.

Jillian sat on the edge of a padded exam table, her top half covered by two paper gowns, one opening in the front, the other in back. They weren't thick enough to cover the beginnings of a dark blue bruise on the front side of her shoulder, where she'd collided with the car frame. Red abrasions on both arms from the collision with the pavement ran from elbow to wrist. She gathered the gowns together in front and reclaimed some semblance of modesty stolen from her over the course of the last few days.

Mercer glanced in her direction but focused his furor on DiManno. The Inspector leaned back on a small Formica counter, the dark bags under his eyes and slumped shoulders painted him as a spent and exhausted man.

"You carted a murder suspect, a charged criminal defendant, out in public and made a spectacle of yourselves. I don't like messes, Inspector. Did you lose your mind?"

"He was helping me prove..." Jillian began.

"Was I talking to you?" Mercer said, flicking his glance to Jillian. "The next word I want to hear out of your mouth is guilty when the court asks

230

for your plea."

"Cooper didn't do it," DiManno said.

"Are you forgetting a key point, Inspector? You are the one who presented the case for a murder charge against her. Now you go off on some crusade against one of the most powerful families in the city…"

"That's what this is about to you? A power connection, a money connection?" DiManno stepped away from the counter toward the District Attorney. "How much did you take from Mattson in your last re-election campaign?"

"My campaign financing has nothing to do with your dereliction and poor judgment," Mercer said.

"I'd say it has everything to do with funding your political aspirations from drug money," DiManno said.

"Don't be absurd. Pharmaceutical companies fund major campaigns all over the nation," Mercer said.

"Not with the money from trafficking heroin and methamphetamine. That's what Mattson was into, and you were willing to look the other way. How will that play in the next election?"

Mercer's demeanor changed. Politicians anticipate the opposition, and any hint of dirty money changed the game altogether. A rumor of drug money would send his benefactors and donors slithering away, drying up his campaign war chest.

Jillian noticed the delay as Mercer mulled over the dirty money problem. "What if you were the one to bring down a major criminal drug ring? The way I see it, you only have two options; take them down, or go down with them."

Mercer's face reddened, a vein in the center of his forehead throbbed. "You're in no position to threaten me. Even if you were to confirm Jonathon and Shelly Mattson operated a drug trafficking organization, that doesn't get you off the hook for Jonathon's murder. Do you have evidence, can either of you prove, someone else murdered him?"

Jillian looked from Mercer to DiManno.

"Give me twenty-four hours," DiManno replied.

"You have until five this evening."

DiManno looked at his watch. "That's only six hours."

"Get me proof, or give me your resignation," Mercer said. "And keep her," the District Attorney pointed a finger at Jillian, "in custody." Mercer pivoted on his heel, left the hospital exam room, and nearly bowled over a young doctor in the doorway.

"I'm sorry I put you in this position," Jillian said.

"You didn't put me anywhere. This is on me."

"We will see it through," Jillian said.

The doctor looked confused and checked his clipboard. "Jillian Cooper? How are you feeling? Do we need to give you a prescription to help you cut the pain?"

"I'll let you know in six hours." Jillian grabbed her tattered blouse and pants from the back of the chair, took DiManno by the wrist, and fast-walked into the hospital corridor; her paper gowns flapped in her wake.

"You should stay here and let them take a look at you," DiManno said.

An excited Jillian said, "The doctor said, 'cut the pain.' I know what Black Label was doing."

"We know that already. Pushing heroin and other junk into prison for the gang."

"Did the lab results come back for the pharmaceutical supplies I pulled out of the lab before Tomas burned it?

"Yeah. Meth and heroin," DiManno said as he followed Jillian toward the hospital exit door. "I told you."

"What else?"

"Chemical compounds, I guess. What are you getting at?"

Jillian stopped outside the hospital doorway. "You have those reports? Shelly told me Dynalife was already selling products to non-profits. It was Black Label. They sold diluted pharmaceuticals—counterfeit drugs. The same drugs that killed Tomas's daughter."

Chapter Forty-One

Shelly Mattson steamed in the confines of the police interrogation room. The space was stark, utilitarian, and served its purpose as a place to interrogate suspects of every stripe. She was better than the common petty criminals who ended up here. They had no idea what real power was about. Shelly refused to sit on the plastic laminate chair, where, God only knew the amount of filth and contagious diseases festering on the dingy surfaces. The woman stood a safe distance from the grime-stained table and tapped a foot to an impatient internal melody. Her designer jacket ruined by blood spatter from her broken nose and the black rings around her eyes were only chic if attending a Halloween costume party. None of it bothered Shelly. She'd re-invented herself before, it was only money and plastic surgery, and she enjoyed plenty of both. She inhaled and pressed the wrinkles from her jacket, her practiced persona at the ready.

DiManno entered the room and gestured Shelly to a chair, but she remained standing, both arms clamped tight around her waist. She ignored the Inspector's request and looked down her newly crooked nose at the public servant.

"You'll be parking cars in Oakland before the end of the week, so say what you have to say," she said.

"You'll be strip-searched and deloused in ten minutes if you don't sit your ass down," DiManno said.

Jillian entered the room, lowered into a chair next to DiManno, and placed a folder on the table in front of her.

"What is *she* doing here?" Shelly said.

"Miss Cooper has some information which may determine how long you stay in prison. Now sit down!"

DiManno's voice reverberated in the small room, and Shelly reacted as if he'd slapped her. Meek, with a hard edge, she perched on the front edge of the chair opposite DiManno, her spine erect and hands folded demurely in her lap.

The police Inspector recited the Miranda rights from a laminated card and Shelly gestured with a backhanded wave. She tried to look bored with the process. "I've seen enough *C.S.I.* television to know my rights."

DiManno opened a file and laid it on the table. It contained photographs taken outside Grace Cathedral depicting the vehicular carnage caused by Shelly's desperate escape attempt. "What were you thinking? You placed the lives of these kids in danger?" DiManno said.

"Me?" Shelly said. "It was her." She pointed at Jillian. "If it weren't for her and that reporter, I wouldn't have been there. Extorting me. Blackmailing *me.*"

"Why did you show up without the money? The only thing in the paper bag was a phone book."

Shelly squirmed a bit before she spoke. "She was blackmailing me. She'd never leave me alone. If I paid that whore off, she'd come around looking for more. That was not going to happen. Everything I worked for—"

"What were you afraid I was going to find?" Jillian spoke, and DiManno put his hand on her arm.

Jillian shoved his hand away. "Did I threaten Shelly Mattson?"

"Oh, Please. I'm not afraid of you," Shelly said.

"Maybe, Shelly Estrella is afraid, or is it Renee Marquez?"

Shelly narrowed her eyes and glowered at Jillian, a twitch started in her tight jaw.

"Who else knew about Black Label?" Jillian said once more.

Shelly settled back, a false calm fell over her. "Other than David and Jonathon? Only Ryan McGowen and William—"

"William Comstock?" Jillian said.

"Yes. I never trusted that man. David told me he needed someone to make

234

certain the Board never got wind of the operation. He should've found someone else."

A nagging feeling gnawed at Jillian's confidence. "Why kill Jonathon, if you had the Board in your pocket?"

"Respect."

Dumbfounded, Jillian searched for a connection between respect and Jonathon Mattson's murder.

Shelly saw the confusion on Jillian's face and said, "One of Black Label's major buyers, the biggest, by far, is the Mexican Mafia. They killed Jonathon because he threatened to shut down their drug pipeline into the prisons. Threats like that are disrespectful. A message needed to be sent."

"You knew Dynalife smuggled drugs into prison?" Jillian said.

Shelly chuckled, regarding Jillian as an ignorant child. "It's not really smuggling if you have the contracts to do it. Of course Jonathon knew. That was the whole point of the joint venture with the EME. Jonathon expanded Black Label to other markets—international sales without the gang's permission. A highly profitable private market, which wouldn't draw too much attention."

Jillian sat forward and pulled a sheaf of papers from the folder in front of her. "These contracts with prison pharmacies, you're saying they are a front for illegal drugs?"

"Not all of them, but Black Label is the mechanism the Mexican Mafia needed to move their product into the prisons. The gang supplied the phony prescription, the product, and Jonathon gave them the means to do it. Black Label packaged the drugs and shipped them to the pharmacy inside, mixed in with our regular prison pharmaceutical orders."

"Something doesn't line up for me," Jillian said. "If Jonathon wanted to provide pharmaceuticals to worldwide relief organizations, so what? Why would my proposal threaten the Mexican Mafia? Black Label could have—"

Shelly cut Jillian off in mid-thought. "Because he was selling Black Label products to relief groups already. If Dynalife began distributing to them too, it would cause someone to investigate what Black Label sold."

"Investigate what? The pharmaceuticals can't be different—a drug is a drug, right?" DiManno pulled the lab reports prepared on the drugs Jillian pulled from the Black Label lab.

Shelly fell silent.

"What did you do?" Jillian pressed

Shelly fumbled with her hands. "Black Label made the company profitable. Jonathon cut a corner here and there and substituted some of the compounds in our formulary. I had nothing to do with this—it was Jonathon, all Jonathon. I was only his wife—powerless to stop him."

"Shelly, what did you do? What would the FDA find if it looked into Black Label?"

Shelly met Jillian's glare with one of her own. "They were going to die anyway. We aren't talking about innocent people here. More like War Lords and Third World nothings. They were fortunate to get what we offered."

Jillian glanced at a thick bundle of paper DiManno dropped on the table. "These reports say the Black Label drugs were less than twenty-five percent of the dose for anti-virals, and only half strength for a cancer treatment drug," Jillian said.

"David came up with the plan, and it took off. Dynalife's Black Label sold the watered-down drugs overseas and to free clinics, below market price. They were grateful to have it. Did you know Jonathon was going to receive a humanitarian award from an African AIDS organization for getting the drugs to the region?"

DiManno shifted in his chair. "What happened? Why did Black Label fall apart?"

Shelly chuckled. "Who said Black Label was falling apart?"

"Your son burned the facility, Jonathon and David are dead, and you smuggled heroin into state prisons. That doesn't sound like a Better Business Bureau endorsement for success."

"Don't you see? Tomas did what he had to do. He severed the connection between Black Label and the Mexican Mafia. Once he told them we were done with them, we figured the gang would go elsewhere. They can't ask for what we don't have."

"They didn't go away, did they?" DiManno said.

"No," Shelly replied. "They didn't. They told David and Jonathon we didn't call the shots any longer. The Mexican Mafia wanted all of Dynalife's operation, not simply a split of Black Label profit." To Jillian, she said, "Dynalife was Jonathon's creation, his legacy. He wasn't going to allow a bunch of thugs to take it away from him."

"They killed him," Jillian said.

Shelly nodded.

"Now you're saying it wasn't David Paulson? Where's your son?" DiManno said.

"You have to understand something. Tomas didn't have it easy, with the drugs and going in and out of jail. Jonathon made it clear to him he had no place for that kind of lifestyle. Even after he went to prison, Jonathon didn't allow me to visit him. My husband called it tough love. Things changed for Tomas, he met a woman, got married and they had a beautiful little girl."

"Emma," Jillian said.

Shelly looked surprised Jillian knew about her grandchild. "Tomas looked like he really changed and I begged Jonathon to help him. He gave Tomas a job at the Black Label plant, away from any possible public embarrassment."

"If Tomas was in trouble over a prison drug debt, why put him in a place where he would be in with the same element?" DiManno said.

"We did what they wanted and set up Black Label to ship their product into the prisons. By then, David set up the prison pharmaceutical contacts, and everything was in place."

"Then, Emma got sick, didn't she?" Jillian said.

Shelly nodded; a faint mist welled in her eyes. "Juvenile Diabetes. Tomas and his wife didn't have insurance, and the treatment was in the tens of thousands. They did the best they could and sold everything they owned for the medications she needed. Tomas asked Jonathon for help, and my husband refused. What kind of man would deny a child a chance at life?

"Tomas couldn't afford the medication, and the girl's condition worsened. He kept working at Black Label and poured every dime he earned into his daughter's care. Not long after, he found the Black Label facility held bottles of the same drug, destined for a clinic in Sudan. Jonathon didn't know

Tomas stole the Black Label drug. Tomas told his wife he got Emma into a clinical trial and gave her the drugs to battle her disease. My granddaughter died three weeks later."

"The drug was diluted," Jillian said.

"Less than half the dose she needed. Tomas had no idea."

"After the loss of his only child, Tomas lost his mind. He went against the Mexican Mafia and destroyed their pipeline. Once he found out the drugs were diluted, he set out to destroy everything and everyone responsible for the girl's death. All of us."

The door opened behind DiManno, a uniformed officer entered and handed a note to the Inspector. The officer remained standing as if he anticipated an answer. DiManno read the message and then handed it off to Jillian.

"Seems McGowen wants to talk, but he wants to talk to you first," DiManno said to Jillian.

"I've got nothing to say to him," she said.

DiManno looked back to Shelly and said, "You realize Ryan McGowen is going to throw you under the bus, right? He'll take a plea deal and testify against you."

"Ryan is a sweet man and would never do such a thing. Besides, isn't there attorney-client privilege?" Shelly said.

Jillian jumped to her feet, and DiManno stepped between them.

"Sweet? That bastard was willing to let me go to prison, and the two of you put thousands of people at risk because you changed drug formulas to make a quick buck."

"It was a business decision between Jonathon and David," Shelly said, distancing herself from the responsibility for Black Label.

"Where can we find Tomas?" DiManno asked.

"I wouldn't tell you if I knew," Shelly said.

DiManno turned to the uniformed officer. "Can you take Mrs. Mattson down to booking while we go chat with Paulson?"

"My pleasure," the officer said.

"Booking? I'm not leaving? I told you I'm not involved in this. I have an event that I really must attend this evening," Shelly said.

"The only event you'll be attending in the foreseeable future is chow line in the prison mess hall in Chowchilla," DiManno said.

"I'm innocent. It was all Jonathon and David," Shelly said as the officer grabbed her arm. "Unhand me!"

The officer escorted Mrs. Shelly Mattson from the room into the hallway which quickly filled with wails of protest from the fallen society matron.

"She really believes she didn't do anything wrong, doesn't she?" Jillian said.

"If she gets a good lawyer, they may be able to hoodwink a jury to think the same thing. That's another reason we need to make McGowen roll over on her."

"We?" Jillian said

"He wants to talk to you. Let's go see what that's about."

"Why me? All I really want to do is strangle him," Jillian said.

"Don't you want to know why you were pulled into this mess?"

"Greed. I already know that."

"How about for the satisfaction of seeing him squirm?" he said.

Jillian looked at DiManno, and her eyes glimmered in response. "There has to be more to the story. Ryan McGowen wouldn't give up his stake in a billion-dollar pharmaceutical firm for a quick buck from this dirty business."

"I've seen people carry out unimaginable acts of cruelty and violence for a few dollars. He's no different. McGowen believed he wouldn't get caught and now he sees his world unraveling," DiManno said.

"Don't misunderstand me. I'm not upset this creep is going to get what he deserves; it's I'm afraid. I'm afraid of what I might find."

DiManno wrinkled his forehead. "Afraid of what? We've established you didn't kill Jonathon, you discovered the Black Label operation, what is there to be afraid of now? Don't you want closure?"

"How do I know I didn't get Jonathon killed because I pressed for the drug shipment for the relief organizations? There are big gaps in my memory I will never recover. David and Jonathon manipulated me, and I will always wonder what role I played in distributing watered-down Black Label drugs to unsuspecting people. I will never get closure."

"Then make it right," DiManno said.

"Right? How is it even possible? People—children—died."

"It might not be possible. But, if there is a chance to backtrack what Mattson and Paulson did and correct it, or dismantle the operation that made Black Label possible, wouldn't that be worth the risk?" DiManno said.

They paused outside an interrogation room door and through the small square security glass, Jillian saw Ryan McGowen handcuffed to a thick eyebolt in the center of the table. He looked far from the image of the successful corporate attorney; his red-rimmed eyes made him look like a junkie, and his clothes were rumpled with grime, grease, and street dander marking him a broken man.

DiManno placed his hand on the knob and paused. "I'm simply a cop. I can give the District Attorney's Office what they need for a prosecutable case. But, I can't do the things you can do to undo the damage they caused. So, what will it be?"

Jillian considered the police Inspector's position and realized the police, courts, jail, and prison were hamstrung when it came to corporate greed. There was always another Jonathon, or another Paulson, and dozens of corporate giants like Dynalife who screwed with unwitting desperate people. Real change came from within, and whether it felt like some measure of atonement or not, Jillian knew her path.

"Then into the looking glass," she said as she pushed DiManno's hand off the doorknob and opened it for herself.

Chapter Forty-Two

Ryan's eyes followed Jillian as she entered the interrogation room. He paid no attention to the police Inspector, and the attorney's glare revealed contempt, anger, and hate; traits once well hidden in the man who tried to send her off to prison. Even shackled to the table, his smug confidence thickened the air within the small space.

Jillian stood with arms crossed in front of the table. "You wanted to talk to me?"

"You have no idea what you've done, do you?" McGowen said.

"Other than stop you from selling watered-down drugs? Why don't you enlighten me," Jillian said.

McGowen chuckled, and his handcuffs rattled. "You are so naïve, Cooper. Black Label—Jonathon, David, and I, sold hope. You know what hope is worth out there in the free market? I'll tell you. Hope brought in one-point-two billion dollars last year. People lined up for a chance to buy a drug offering a glimmer of a cure. Black Label outsold Dynalife's mainstream products three-fold."

"The people who bought the diluted drugs didn't know they were useless," Jillian said.

"They bought hope, and they got their money's worth—every dime. They were dead anyway. So, there is one less goat farmer in Somalia, or fewer villagers in some God-forsaken rainforest, who cares? You know how anti-viral drugs work. On the surface, the lower dosage looked like it put the disease in check, while the virus simmered and gained strength in the body only to resurface hard and fast."

"How can you sit here and defend this? You killed, God knows how many people. Living, breathing people."

"It is business, Cooper. You used to understand the rules. The more *people* who succumbed to AIDS, or whatever plague du jour popped up, the panic and demand for our drugs skyrocketed. You act as if we caused the disease. The *people* in those backwater, third-world nations, created the conditions for these diseases to flourish. It's like a damn Petri dish. There is some merit to the notion that only the strong shall survive."

"What right did you have to play God and decide who lives and dies?"

"We didn't make them sick. We gave them hope and a bit of relief while nature took its course."

"For a price."

"We are in business to make a profit. What's wrong with that?"

"What about the drug smuggling into the prisons? Is that part of your profit margin too?"

"If I had it to do over again, I would convince them to ignore the threats and extortion from the Mexican Mafia. If they killed Mattson's bastard stepson, Tomas, it would've been the end of it. We already ran the Black Label product line into the prison pharmacies and locked up a long-term contract for their HIV/AIDS drugs. I tried to talk them out of working with those thugs. I tried. We had a good thing going. The deal with the Mexican Mafia put everything at risk and it ended up getting Jonathon and David killed. The Mexican Mafia wasn't going to let him shut down the Black Label operation."

"That's where you draw the line? Selling worthless drugs to unsuspecting people is okay with you, but smuggling smack into prison is a deal-breaker?" she said.

Inspector DiManno slid the microcassette recorder across the table. "Care to hazard a guess what's on this tape?"

McGowen shrugged. "If it's Shelly Mattson, I wouldn't believe a word she says. She's always been about protecting her own ass, even at the expense of her own kid."

DiManno flicked the play button with a quick jab.

McGowen winced when Jonathon's voice came through the small speaker.

"I built this company, and you and no bunch of thugs are gonna take it from me. Let them cancel the prison contracts. We don't need them. The real Black Label profit is from the other markets."

"Cancel contracts? These people don't deal that way, They'll cancel you." David's voice responded.

"Shelly will only be able to save your ass for so long, Jonathon. Do you really think she'll bail you out of this deal?" McGowen's voice said before DiManno clicked off the recorder.

DiManno repeated, "You and no bunch of thugs. What did Jonathon mean?"

McGowen tensed, his neck muscles knotted from a tight jaw. "It would be interesting to find out how you happened to come into possession of the recording. It smells like a violation of attorney-client privilege."

"I think you forgot communication to commit or cover up a crime is an exception to the attorney-client privilege rule."

"I found this in your gym locker at Dynalife?" Jillian asked.

"Among other things. How did you know about the locker?"

"I was there and I followed a trail of reeking cologne to your locker."

"Mattson kept the tape. I should have flushed it the moment I found it. You know I planted that bloody scarf in your locker. It should have been enough to make sure you went away and stopped everyone from looking into Black Label. You wore it at last Friday's meeting with Mattson. Everyone would have remembered that."

"Jonathon made it sound like you forced him into bed with the Mexican Mafia on this little deal," DiManno said.

"It was like he grew a conscience. After your pitch to the Board, Jonathon started getting cold feet. He called us to meet him at his place and told us he'd given your drug giveaway proposal some thought. He wanted to shut down the Black Label operation and turn Dynalife into some noble non-profit enterprise. Can you believe that? Even if I went along with dumping the billion-dollar golden egg we created, the Mexican Mafia was not going to sit by and let him cripple their prison drug supply line," McGowen said.

"You told the Mafia he wanted out, didn't you?" DiManno said, breaking his silence.

McGowen flicked his eyes in the direction of the policeman, and then directed them back to Jillian. "You killed them. You realize that, don't you? If it weren't for your altruistic notions, Jonathon and David would be alive. There was no talking him down from the ledge. We argued, and it got heated. Shelly overheard us and came in with Tomas. Jonathon told her what he wanted to do with Black Label. She and that little bastard of hers wouldn't hear of it."

"Shelly didn't want to cut ties with the Mexican Mafia because she needed to protect her son," Jillian said.

McGowen shifted uncomfortably for the first time since Jillian entered the interrogation room. "You honestly don't know, do you?"

"Know what?" Jillian said.

"Shelly Mattson—she was born Renee Marquez."

"Yeah, so?" Jillian said.

She's the daughter of a Mexican Mafia shot-caller doing life up at Pelican Bay."

"Did Jonathon know?" Jillian said.

"Not at first. Shelly, or rather, Renee, was ordered to cozy up to Jonathon and position herself to gain influence over him and Dynalife's resources. I guess it's not the first time the gang ordered her to develop a relationship with an influential man. It worked better than anyone predicted; she married Jonathon, and he placed her on the board of directors. She funneled money to the gang through the company without Jonathon catching on. Over fifty million siphoned off to the Mexican Mafia. If I agree to testify against these guys, you've got to make it worth my while. And you need to keep me someplace safe."

"When Tomas got in trouble in prison—that's when Jonathon found out about her gang connection, right?" Jillian said.

"Tomas was never in trouble. He was a shot-caller on the yard and a hitman for the gang on the street. The gang deferred to him because he was Renee's child. She manipulated Jonathon into accepting the drug distribution arrangement with the gang, and he went along with it, believing he did it to save her son," McGowen said.

"When did Mattson find out the truth?" Jillian asked.

"After the gang's distribution network and the Black Label facility were set up, Jonathon figured out the operation wasn't right, and he approached me. By that time Shelly put David Paulson in charge of running the network and put Tomas in a low-level job inside the plant. He was supposed to monitor production for the gang. Mattson figured it out pretty quick and he pressed his wife about an addict working in a drug lab."

"But Tomas didn't steal drugs for himself, did he?" Jillian said.

"The thing was, the Mexican Mafia didn't drive the Black Label production. The operation was primarily for the third-world and prison drug contracts. The deal with the gang came later. Tomas put the pieces together that Black Label was doing much more than the prison drug smuggling deal. He found out about our shipments of off-label pharmaceuticals to relief groups. I thought he'd be pissed, but instead, he stole drugs from the Black Label production line and gave them to his daughter. The poor fool didn't know they were diluted. He said he'd never be able to continue her treatment. He didn't understand why Emma didn't respond to the drugs the same way she did in the hospital. David told him he shouldn't have taken the drugs off the line because they weren't as strong. The little girl died, and Tomas had a target for his anger–Jonathon and everyone connected to Black Label.

"He moved fast. Tomas dove at Jonathon, grabbed a letter opener, and stabbed him in the neck. He pointed the letter opener at David and told him he was next. Shelly stepped in between and gave us a chance to clear out of there. Next thing I knew, she and David cooked up the plan to hang Jonathon's murder on you."

Jillian felt the spring tension in her core ratchet down a small notch. Finally, a slight promise of redemption, but her life was forever transformed. She looked at McGowen and wondered if trust in another person was possible anymore. The betrayal from the topmost level of the company cut deep, more than she ever imagined.

"Why blame me? You wanted me to take a plea bargain and go to prison."

"Why not? It seemed fitting. You convinced Jonathon to turn his back on everything we built. Besides, if you were in prison, Tomas couldn't reach you. He wants you too, Jillian. In a way, you owe me for saving you from him."

"Saving me? You call drugging me, ruining my life, and setting me up for prison time, saving me? You bastard!" Jillian whipped out her right hand and slapped McGowen's cheek. A red handprint marked his face, and he rubbed the spot the best he could with the back of his cuffed hand.

"David slipping the Versed and rufie in your cocktail late Friday night was the easy part. You were licking your wounds from the board meeting. Jonathon was already dead, and you wanted a shoulder to cry on."

"You guys make a habit of carrying amnesiac drugs around with you?" DiManno asked.

"All it needed was a phone call. We keep Versed in the Dynalife distribution catalog. It was in your drink within fifteen minutes," McGowen said.

"Versed is a controlled item. There is a record of the person who removed it from inventory," Jillian said.

"True, but no one would think to look. If they did, it shows you signed for it. You can't remember if you did, or not, can you?"

"Who was it? My replacement, Ashley?" Jillian asked.

"I think I've told you enough. I need my deal in writing, then we'll talk some more. I'm not going to do *his* job." McGowen tilted his head in DiManno's direction.

"You only cared about keeping the third world and prison pipeline open. Why is that? You afraid of them, or Shelly?" Jillian said.

McGowen regarded her for a moment as a flicker of emotion shot across his face. "You need to forget whatever you think you know about the prison connection. That is my insurance policy–and yours. As long as the Mexican Mafia's pipeline remained open, there was no quarrel with us."

"What about Tomas? He's still out there," DiManno said.

"Tomas was a loyal Mafia enforcer. The shot-callers didn't want Jonathon taken out; they wanted him controlled. And he was under control until you planted the seeds of guilt in his feeble mind. Now, Tomas is on the outs with the gang hierarchy because he put the operation a risk. Tomas wants me dead too. Now I'm in police custody, and he can't touch me. You on the other hand—he's already shown how easily he can find you." The smugness returned.

"Where is Tomas?" DiManno said.

McGowen shrugged. "Don't know—don't care."

"Is Miss Cooper in danger?" DiManno said.

"Tomas knows Cooper's name was all over the Black Label paperwork, supply orders, and contracts."

"Tomas followed me and tried to kill me. I didn't give him the drugs his daughter got!" she said.

"He was following you to take down the rest of the people behind Black Label. Tomas had access to documents at the facility and he saw your name on the leases and contracts. He holds you responsible for his daughter's death, as much as he did Jonathon, David, and me. Hell, he's probably pissed he didn't finish you off in your apartment. Mommy convinced him to let you live so she could watch you die in prison."

"We can get you protection," DiManno said to Jillian.

"I'm done hiding and running." She turned to McGowen and said, "I'm not done with you."

Chapter Forty-Three

T he remaining members of the Dynalife Board of Directors called an emergency meeting to resurrect the smoldering remnants of the pharmaceutical giant. The value of the stock shares, which had fallen by half since Jonathon Mattson's death, now plummeted. Stockholder confidence in the Board was in the toilet, and the ongoing viability of the company was in serious doubt. Board members lamented over the potential legal exposure to Dynalife caused by the bombshell report from Pia Lopez which laid out the Black Label diluted drug operation. None of the members openly admitted knowledge of Black Label but eyed one another with suspicious contempt.

Dynalife needed more than a new image; it needed an infusion of ethical direction and a public service campaign directed by an industry White Knight, the pharmaceutical equivalent to Steve Jobs. But, board members couldn't get anyone with the credentials to take their calls.

"What do we do about Jillian Cooper?" Ralph Stevenson asked. Stevenson was the member with the most seniority on the Board.

"She has us by the proverbial short-hairs. A member of this Board, kidnapped, drugged, and tormented Miss Cooper. There is no getting around the fact she owns us, should she pursue civil remedies," William Comstock responded.

"Have we approached her with a settlement?" a third member said.

Stevenson shook his head and said, "No settlement has been proposed. She hasn't said a word since the arrests of Ryan McGowen and Shelly Mattson. That's been–what–six weeks?" He cleared his throat and continued, "I

248

prepared a proposal addressing Miss Cooper's potential litigation and serve our own immediate needs."

"I thought we went through this. You're not suggesting we appoint Cooper as CEO," Comstock said.

"That's exactly what I propose. Who better to guide the company from the darkness than the one person who uncovered the greed and corruption? Think of the public relations angle we can play on this. Our very own avenging angel. Besides, she can't bring the company to its knees if she's at the helm," Stevenson said.

A few heads nodded around the table.

"How do you know she'll do it?" a voice of concern asked.

"The last time Miss Cooper appeared before this Board, she took a hit for her high-minded plan to donate AIDS drugs to world health and refugee relief organizations," Stevenson said.

"We'll go broke," Comstock said.

"We are broke," Stevenson chided. "No respectable pharmaceutical clearinghouse, hospital, or clinic will touch Dynalife products. We can sit around and deny it all we want, but it will not change the outcome. Or, we can adapt to the market and put our products in play where we can. Miss Cooper can lead the charge and market the Hell out of it."

A muffled voice from an intercom speaker near Stevenson sounded. "Excuse me, Sir. You wanted me to notify you when Miss Cooper arrived."

"Thank you, Adele, please send her in," Stevenson said.

"What's she doing here? You–asked her to come?" Comstock said.

"I did. And I wasn't certain she'd accept my invitation," Stevenson said.

"I don't like this," the protesting Board member continued. "It is blackmail. Do what she wants, or..."

The dark wood conference room door swung open, and the conversation ceased. Everyone watched as Jillian approached the conference table, a note of newfound confidence in her stride. She wore a pale grey suit, her hair pulled back and a slight touch of makeup to cover a few lingering bruises. Most people who suffered through half of what she'd experienced would've appeared drawn and exhausted, but Jillian looked formidable and strengthened from her ordeal. She paused at the table, stood, and made eye contact with each of the anxious faces. A few members looked away uncomfortable with her presence.

Stevenson stood. "Thank you for coming, Miss Cooper, would you please join us?" he said and gestured to an empty chair at the table.

"No, I'll stand, thanks," Jillian said.

"Have it your way," Stevenson said. "Did you consider the proposal?"

"I have," she said.

"Did you come to a decision?"

"I've come to a crossroads. Part of me wants to see Dynalife burn for the rampant greed that fostered a soulless program like Black Label. How many lives were lost to make a buck with diluted and counterfeit drugs? This company lost its moral compass when we ignored the excess, abuse, and shortcuts as long as they helped the bottom line. But, I also recognize Dynalife is in a position to fill a critical void in the worldwide availability of essential drugs."

"Dynalife can regain a viable position in the market, with the right marketing approach," Stevenson said.

"I don't sleep much, which let me mull over all the decisions, actions, and maneuvers that got us to this place. Then it occurred to me, Ryan McGowen said one thing that was frighteningly accurate. We sold hope. Marketing and advertising campaigns got us to this dark place, and I hold myself to blame as much as anyone. Look at what we put out there–drugs to lower this, raise that, stiffen something else, or lose whatever you don't want. Dynalife sold hope as much as Black Label, and a new marketing approach alone won't fix what's broken."

"What approach will allow Dynalife to recover?"

"Not recovery—redemption."

"I'm not sure I follow."

"Dynalife has a unique production capability. We need to devote a portion of that to maintaining supplies of essential drugs needed in developing nations."

"Here we go…," Comstock said.

CHAPTER FORTY-THREE

"You want us to give away our products?" another member asked.

"Redirect production capability to relief organizations at cost. We need to do more than sell wrinkle creams, stiffy-pills, and vanity medications," Jillian said.

"Redirect? How much of our production line are you talking about?" Stevenson said.

"All of it," she said.

"Are you out of your mind?" a voice said from the far end of the table before Jillian cut his protest short.

"What choice do you really have?" Jillian said.

Stevenson hushed the room and leaned back in his chair. "Nobody will buy from a company caught diluting drugs. If the FDA doesn't sanction us to death, the civil claims will drive what's left of our net worth through the floor. I take it you have a solution?"

"I've spoken to the investigator the FDA assigned to work on the Black Label matter. They are poised to suspend Dynalife's licenses to possess and process pharmaceuticals. However, with certain assurances, the FDA would be willing to issue a provisional license," she said.

"Assurances?" Stevenson said.

"Dynalife will agree to cease production of medical-grade pharmaceuticals in the United States for five years. The FDA will permit humanitarian assistance in the form of production and distribution of drugs listed in the World Health Organization essential drug formulary. Formulation, production, and distribution of drugs within Dynalife facilities will be monitored by on-site FDA inspection teams and sales restricted to developing nations designated by the W.H.O."

Murmurs sounded around the table, hushed by Comstock. "And, after five years? Then what happens? This is unacceptable, Miss Cooper."

"How long did you want to serve in prison, William?"

"This is blackmail," another member responded.

"I thought you and the boys would react in this way. We have a small opportunity to reset the course of this company. We need to begin now." Jillian removed a file folder from her purse and placed it on the table. "This is a stockholder proxy authorizing me to dismiss the existing members of the Board of Directors. A majority vote of the stockholders found a lack of confidence in the present Board configuration. A newly appointed Board will assume their duties shortly. Thank you, gentlemen. You are dismissed."

Inspector DiManno waited at the door as the board members filed out.

"Comstock. William Comstock, would you come with me, please? I have some questions for you."

The handcuffs forecasted there were more than questions in store for the ex-board chairman. DiManno winked at Jillian as two uniformed officers led Comstock away.

Chapter Forty-Four

Exhausted and drained after another fourteen-hour day, Jillian trudged up the hallway to her apartment door. A laptop computer case slung over a shoulder, and a briefcase stuffed with FDA production monitoring reports foreshadowed the late-night session waiting for her.

In the two months since the dismissal of the entire Board, Jillian poured endless hours into purging the last remnants of Black Label from Dynalife. The illegal operation infested the infrastructure of the company; material procurement, shipping, packaging, and inventory control, infected with phantom accounts and computer script to support Black Label. Carlos, the Financial Officer, stayed on board and helped her tease apart the Black Label accounting files. In exchange for possible leniency, Ryan McGowen gave up Shelly Mattson's connections and the board members who knew about the Black Label drug scam. A multi-count indictment came down on Board Chairman, William Comstock. Dynalife was on the slow road to redemption.

Jillian fumbled the keys from a pocket of her briefcase, and they spilled to the wooden floor with a loud clank.

Behind her, Mrs. Tillman peeked through the crack in her open door; a small brass chain separated her from Jillian.

"Miss Cooper, another late night? Getting into your old habits, I see," the old woman said with more than a note of disapproval in her graveled voice.

Too worn to argue, Jillian picked up her keys and slid the key in her deadbolt lock. "How are you, Mrs. Tillman?"

"I'd be much better without the commotion from your comings and goings."

"I'll try to be more considerate," Jillian said. The deadbolt lock was unlocked. She must've unlocked it while Mrs. Tillman called out, or she forgot to lock it in the first place. Jillian opened her door, closed it behind her, and leaned back on the inside of the door. The full weight of exhaustion caught up with her, and she nearly melted into the door. She heard the neighbor's door shut followed by the clunk of the deadbolt.

Comings and goings? I leave in the morning and come back at night, alone. Over and over again. Nothing ever changes...

Jillian kicked off her shoes, dropped her laptop and work files on her sofa, turned, and stumbled on an overturned edge of the carpet runner. She stopped mid-step when edginess tingled across the back of her shoulders. At the edge of her vision, she caught the slight sensation of movement. Jillian whirled around and faced an empty living room.

In the months following the attack in her apartment, Jillian often felt watched, with an unshakable sense she wasn't alone. The first time she experienced the feeling, Jillian wondered if she made the right decision returning to the apartment. Her first night, and every night that followed, Jillian developed a routine bordering on obsessive-compulsive. Armed with a kitchen knife, she prowled the far reaches of the apartment, opened closets, threw back the shower curtain, and looked behind the doors. The most sinister thing Jillian found was the occasional dust bunny. Nonetheless, the nightly vigils continued. The ragged memories of what happened to her, David Paulson and McGowen with their manipulations nearly drove her insane. Some nights, with knife in hand, she wondered if they succeeded.

On this night, the apartment felt different, the rumpled corner of the carpet and the unlocked deadbolt heightened her uneasiness. Jillian padded to the kitchen counter to arm herself with her butcher's knife. The knife was not where she'd left it after last night's search. The butcher's knife and the entire wooden block holding the cutlery set were nowhere in view.

Jillian stood in the center of her kitchen, unsteady and off-balance. A voice from behind startled her.

"Looking for these?" Tomas rested in a dining room chair, the block of knives, on the table next to him. Jillian focused on the blue steel revolver in the man's hand.

Jillian backed away, trapped in her small galley kitchen.

"Sit," Tomas said. The revolver punctuated his command and pointed her to the chair opposite him.

Jillian complied and parked on the edge of the dining room chair. The knives were out of reach, and the gun's barrel warned against a dash to the door.

Tomas looked around the apartment. "You painted since I was here last."

Jillian stiffened.

"Ryan McGowen is dead. I thought you should know," Tomas said, his voice low and solemn.

"What?" Jillian said.

"Bad things happen in jail. McGowen thought he was going to testify against the Mexican Mafia to save his own skin."

"He was in protective custody," Jillian said.

"So were the Mexican Mafia dropouts who killed him. A sharpened toothbrush does a lot of damage."

"Why are you telling me this? Why did you come here?"

Tomas rested the gun on the table. "I've been watching you, waiting for you to make a mistake. McGowen, Paulson, and my step-father killed my daughter."

"Emma," Jillian said.

He nodded. "After Jonathon died, David made me believe you were responsible for the Black Label operation and Emma's death. You were supposed to die."

"I wasn't involved," she said.

"David came up with the idea to put Jonathon's death on your hands. He drugged you and gave me your jewelry. I planted it so Mommy Dearest would find all the incentive she needed to go after you. Then you were supposed to die as a guilt-stricken whore. Because you were involved in Black Label, you went on my list of those to hold accountable."

"But, I wasn't involved in Black Label," she said.

"You were part of that company. When Emma died, I wanted everyone involved punished. I confronted Jonathon about the bad drugs. He told me my little girl died because she came from bad stock. She wasn't *his* granddaughter."

"McGowen told me Jonathon wanted to shut down Black Label…"

"Too late! He killed my Emma. I killed him; he deserved what he got—David too. I finished that sniveling piece of garbage in the parking garage." Tomas collected himself and pushed an object across the table to Jillian.

It was a small, framed photo of his daughter Emma.

"Where did you find this?" he asked.

"From her mother. I met her at—"

"I know where you met her. I visited her in the hospital, and she said you were nice to her. Why did you keep a picture of my daughter on your desk?"

"I needed it. Emma is an example of what happens when operations like Black Label are dreamed up for a quick buck. I don't ever want to forget what that looks like. Emma reminds me every day counts. Dynalife and other faceless corporations put profit margins and their bottom lines over kids like her. I can't let that happen again."

"I came here to find out if you were serious about ending the Black Label legacy, or if you were simply covering your ass. Some people in the company seem to think you're for real. I'm not easily convinced. I came here once before and thought I'd taken care of it—of you. Funny, how the diluted drugs that killed my daughter couldn't kill you. I came back again because I needed to make certain this time. I came here tonight to send you to join Jonathon and David in Hell." The muscles in his hands tensed around the grip of the revolver.

Jillian was silent for a moment before she gently held the photo of Emma and propped it up so the girl faced her father. "What would she want you to do?"

"She would want me to make sure little girls like her don't die at the hands of people like you."

The black muzzle of the handgun twitched. Jillian waited for the flash and searing pain, but nothing came. Instead, Tomas put the gun on the table and pushed it toward her.

A rustling sound arose from the front of her apartment.

"Hands where I can see them," Inspector DiManno said. He short side-stepped around the table, keeping his service weapon aimed squarely at Tomas. "Miss Cooper, are you all right?"

She nodded in response, eyes wide at the sight of three police officers in black tactical uniforms, Kevlar helmets with automatic weapons who fanned out behind DiManno.

"Please get up and move away from the table, Miss Cooper," DiManno instructed.

Jillian did as told. As she backed away, she said, "How did you know he was here?"

"He called, and he left the phone on," DiManno said.

"Why would he do that?"

"Because this was going to end one of two ways," Tomas said. "You were going to die, or I was. Either way, it was going to end tonight. Did you get all that, Inspector?" Tomas turned to Jillian. "I've been watching you, and I couldn't decide if you were like Jonathon and David. The photo of Emma tells me you might not be like them."

One of the black-clad officers approached Tomas from behind and put him in handcuffs. Tomas didn't resist as the officer pulled him to his feet. A second officer quickly searched Tomas and removed a cell phone from his shirt pocket. The bright backlit screen on the phone showed an open connection.

"Don't let Emma down, Miss Cooper," Tomas said as the officer led him from the room.

DiManno glanced at the phone and the display showed his number. DiManno touched the small button on his Bluetooth headset, disconnecting the call. "If Tomas hadn't given his daughter the counterfeit drugs, would we have ever found out about Black Label?" DiManno said.

"It was bound to unravel one way or another. Producing bad drugs, smuggling heroin and meth into prison–Black Label was destined to fail. In a way, Emma's death saved hundreds of others," Jillian said.

DiManno picked up the girl's photo, looked at it, and handed it to Jillian. "She saved you tonight."

"Maybe. Was he telling the truth about Ryan McGowen? Is he–dead?"

"Happened this afternoon, a gang hit, like Tomas said."

"I can't believe it. McGowen was a bastard, but he didn't deserve that."

"I don't know I'd agree, but it's over now, Jillian. We couldn't have put this case together without your help. You're what my old man would've called a 'gutsy broad.'"

Jillian smiled. "I'm going to need all the guts I can muster if I'm going to keep my promise to Emma. She deserves nothing less."

Acknowledgements

Writing a book is a solitary affair—breathing life into the pages takes a collective effort. Jillian's Black Label story began at the Book Passage Mystery Writers Conference in Corte Madera, California. The first pages of the book were crafted in between and after conference sessions. I highly recommend this outstanding conference to anyone thinking about putting pen to paper. Thanks to Kathryn Petrocelli, Elaine Petrocelli, and Bill Petrocelli for creating a supportive environment where book dreams come to life.

Mario Dimanno's generous bid at The Sacramento Library Foundation's auction earned a character name in *Black Label*. Thank you for your contribution to children's literacy and I hope you enjoy the detective's journey.

My heartfelt thanks to Janis Herbert, Jessica Windham, and Megan Yaws for reading early versions, and to Karen Crain-Hedger for her review and early edits. Thanks to Tina Ferguson, the heart and soul of Face In a Book, a place so much more than a local book store.

I owe unending gratitude to my book family in the Mystery Writers of America, International Thriller Writers, and Sisters in Crime - Capitol Crimes chapter for their support and motivation. Eileen Rendahl, Holly West, Claire Booth, Danny Gardner, Allison Davis, Rae Franklin James, K. J. Howe, Hank Phillippi Ryan, Karen Dionne, Jennifer Hillier, Gabriel Valjan, and Andrew Grant offered a kind word or a push when it was needed most. They didn't know how much it meant at the time.

I appreciate Jessica Windham and Michael L'Etoile letting their dad off his leash from time to time. I try not to embarrass them and their encouragement means the world.

Thanks to #NotMyCat for hundreds of extra keystrokes in this manuscript as she walked across the keyboard. Emma and Bryn the Corgis helped mull over plot points during thousands of hours of walks.

I am forever grateful to Shawn Reilly Simmons for believing in me and *Black Label*. I'm so lucky to have Shawn in my corner. Many thanks to Shawn, Verena Rose, and Harriette Sackler—the Dames of Detection behind Level Best Books.

Most of all, to Ann-Marie L'Etoile who has been by my side for over four decades. Thank you for letting me wander off on this creative journey and for kicking me in the ass when needed. I love you.

About the Author

James L'Etoile uses his twenty-nine years behind bars as an influence in his novels, short stories, and screenplays. He is a former associate warden in a maximum-security prison, a hostage negotiator, facility captain, and director of California's state parole system. He is a nationally recognized expert witness on prison and jail operations. He has been nominated for the Silver Falchion for Best Procedural Mystery, and The Bill Crider Award for short fiction. His published novels include: *At What Cost, Bury the Past,* and *Little River - The Other Side of Paradise.*

https://jamesletoile.com

https://twitter.com/jamesletoile

https://www.facebook.com/AuthorJamesLetoile

CPSIA information can be obtained
at www.ICGtesting.com
Printed in the USA
FSHW011949010721
82876FS